BLEEDING FROM COUNTLESS WOUNDS

By

Ronald Jensen

Burlington, VT

Onion River Press
191 Bank Street
Burlington, VT 05401

Cover design by Annie Clark

ISBN: 978-1-949066-78-4 paperback

ISBN: 978-1-949066-79-1 eBook

Library of Congress Control Number: 2021906148

Berlin, Germany, April 1945, the Russians are only weeks away from the final assault on the city. Trying to survive in the dying remnants of a bombed out city, Reinhardt Stachel, a homicide detective with the German police, is investigating the murder of Sophie Holzer, the wife of one of Goebbels's ministers. She was found in the middle of the night with a parcel of food, probably purchased from the black market and five thousand U.S. dollars.

Stachel has no suspects and cannot explain why Sophie Holzer was buying food from the black market. Though the public is on strict rations, Nazi officials have plenty of food. And why was she carrying five thousand U.S. dollars? Sophie's husband, August Holzer, is angry at Stachel's line of questioning. Stachel feels he is hiding something.

Goebbels wants the case solved quickly. He fears a civilian uprising and wants an arrest so he can show the public that the Nazis are still in control. Goebbels doesn't care if he finds the real killer or not. Arrest someone quickly or else.

Germany is in ruins. The German people will become the slaves of the Allies. Stachel has nothing more to live for. He figures he will be arrested anyway, either by the Nazis or the Allies after the war ends. So, he ignores Goebbels and works to find the real killer, if only to prove to the Allies that there are still Germans who care about the law.

Then a high ranking Nazi official is murdered.

The Russians are at the door. The clock is ticking. Stachel knows that this might be the last murder he ever solves.

But how do you find a killer in a city of killers?

For fans of David Downing's John Russell series and the Netflix show "Babylon Berlin."

"In his first novel of crime fiction, Ronald Jensen has captured the very essence of Berlin in the final days of the Nazi era. With the Russians closing in and only days away, Hauptsturmführer Stachel, a professional German policeman entirely opposed to the Nazi party, must solve a series of brutal murders before the city falls. One of the victims is the wife of a Nazi party official which brings Stachel directly into the Nazi spotlight. Despite food and fuel shortages, daily allied bombings and a completely demoralized civilian population, Stachel struggles to solve these crimes to preserve the last fragment of German police professionalism as well as his own sense of right and wrong in a decaying society. You don't be disappointed at the final outcome!"

Colonel Andrew F. Love, United States Air Force, Retired

"Ronald Jensen's morally conflicted character has to investigate a murder as the city of Berlin crumbles around him. Should he do his job as a policeman or try and save his life? That is one of the questions in this compelling mystery that takes place in April 1945."

Tracy Nelson (author of the novel Dark Question)

Also by Ronald Jensen

Transients and Other Stories (forthcoming)

"...the German people 'are agitated passionately, even pathologically ... their souls bleeding from countless wounds.'"

From "Wehrmacht Priests," by Lauren Faulkner Rossi, page 208

"Beneath the hail of bombs, in the mayhem of destruction of towns and cities as the Reich collapsed... a semblance of 'normality' in the mounting chaos was sustained as bureaucracy strained every sinew to continue functioning...But where Germany had not yet fallen under occupied rule, there was no descent into anarchy. Civil administration continued...Military as well as civilian courts continued to hand out ever more severe sentences. Wages and salaries were still being paid in April 1945. Grants awarded by a leading academic body in Berlin were made down to the last weeks of the war...Limited forms of entertainment still somehow functioned...to sustain morale and distract attention...A last concert by the Berlin Philharmonic took place on 12 April...Some cinemas remained open...Even football matches were still being played...Truncated newspapers still appeared."

From "The End," by Ian Kershaw, pages 5-6

Chapter One

The call came at two thirty in the morning. Hauptsturmführer Stachel was sitting in a chair, staring at the one window in this flat that looked onto Marienstrasse, wishing he could fall asleep, waiting for the bombs to fall. The blackout screen had been pulled aside. He didn't care if anyone saw and reported him.

Already he could hear the rumbling from the west. Every day, around three, the British came and dropped their bombs on Berlin. Now the air raid sirens went off. Stachel knew he should retreat to the cellar of the building, huddle with the rest of the tenants, and pray that there would not be a direct hit. But he didn't care anymore. He would trust in God, or luck, or both. What did it matter when his city, his country, was lost? He prayed for one night when the air raids didn't come, when he could get a full night of uninterrupted sleep. For months now, he had moved through the day like a wraith disconnected from the world.

From the sound of the anti-aircraft guns, he could tell that their target that night was Hitler's Chancellery to the south. Good, maybe they would finally kill the bastard who had brought Germany to ruin. It was like this every night. Only the location was different.

He tried to count the bomb explosions, but it was all a muddle. After ten minutes he gave up and waiting, eyes on the small windup clock at his bedside, counting down the minutes until the British left.

The entrails of smoke drifted over the city like a shadow fleeing a crime scene, blocking his view. Opening the window, Stachel stretched his arms out and frantically waved, trying to push the smoke back into its grave. He could now see out his window, staring across the street at the gaping hole where the front wall of the second floor had collapsed into the street below.

The phone was still ringing. He walked across the room and answered the phone. It was the sergeant from the Alex. A body found in the Mitte district, at the Gendarmenmarkt. His first thought was to hang up and try and get back to sleep. Why bother, what's one more death among all the dying? But he had to go. It was his job. And after the death of his wife, killed two months ago in an American bombing raid, it was all he had left.

How did the sergeant know where he was? He was squatting in an abandoned apartment and had told no one. But they always knew, somehow, they always knew.

Now he was walking south on Frederickstrasse. He would have preferred to drive, but the luxury of an automobile, except for those at the top of the Nazi hierarchy, were long gone. What little petrol was left all went to the military. He kept telling himself that he needed the exercise. Even with the food shortages, he had lost none of his girth.

He pulled up his collar against the chill, peering through a small slit, walking carefully through the debris, the jagged pieces of concrete with rebar sticking out, the soot from burned out fires. It started to rain when he was about halfway to the Gendarmenmarkt; a cold drizzle that soaked into his overcoat and skin and made him feel like a pale corpse risen from the dead. He swore at himself for forgetting his hat. He had gotten use to propping it over the picture of Hitler behind his desk in his office, so he was constantly forgetting to reach back and grab it when he went out. He quickened his pace because of the rain, hoping that whoever was already at the crime scene had protected the area so it wouldn't be compromised.

As the raindrops dripped down over his eyes, plastering his hair against his forehead, he felt his mustache and thought of the irony that it had turned grey while his hair was still jet black. He badly needed a haircut. It was starting to drape over his ears and stick out like little bristles. But his barber had disappeared a few months back and he hadn't had time to find another.

He was still thinking about the article in *Das Reich*, the weekly Nazi newspaper, that he had read last night. Written by Hans-Ulrich Arntz, people were already calling it the hedgehog article because it compared Berlin to a hedgehog, with its prickly spines radiating out in all directions, ready to defend the city.

The Russians were closing in. Less than two hours by car to the eastern front. Thought running out of men, the military continued to fight at the Seelow Heights.

Arntz was a fool! He talked on and on about the *Volkssurrm*, a group of young boys and old men organized for the defense of the city, as though they were a powerful force that would push back the Russians. They would all be slaughtered. And no escape. The Nazi's wouldn't allow anyone to leave Berlin without special papers, which were impossible to obtain. Hitler had declared Berlin a fortress, just as he had with Breslau to the east. It had been reduced to rubble, its citizens raped and murdered, the lucky ones sent east into slavery. Berlin would also be a fight to the death, a German death.

By the time he got to the murder scene, the rain had stopped, leaving pools of water blacken by soot, the gleam of a nearby fire making the water seem alive with twinkling imps.

Before the war, Gendarmenmarkt had been a bustling shopping center in the Mitte district. A statue of the German poet Friedrich Schiller usually dominated the center of the square, flanked by the French and German cathedrals. The old *Schauspielhaus* theater served as the background to the statue. The French cathedral and the theater were still standing though pockmarked, but the German cathedral had been completely destroyed. The statue had been moved into storage by the Nazis back in 1939 so that they could use the plaza for public speeches. As though Schiller, the greatest German poet, approved of their stupidity.

The square now looked like a graveyard long abandoned. There was a silence that lingered over the place, as though the ruined buildings deadened all noise.

Near where the Schiller statue had been there was a crowd of people trying to peer over the shoulders of the two policemen standing guard. One policeman, a young man with light brown hair, was pushing the crowd back, trying without much success to keep them away from the crime scene. It probably didn't matter. The area hadn't been covered, so between the crowd and the rain, Stachel knew that the area was now contaminated. At least the patrolmen had thought to cover the body with an overcoat.

The other policeman, who looked like a vampire with grey hair, gave the Nazi salute when Stachel arrived. Stachel ignored him and walked over to the victim, getting down on one knee as though in prayer, and pulling back the overcoat from the victim's head.

Stachel immediately recognized the victim. Sophie Holzer, wife of August Holzer, a minister reporting directly to Goebbels. The Nazi's would be all over the case, making Stachel's life more miserable than it already was.

Her eyes were still open, as though gazing up at hell, brown hair sprayed out on the wet stone, wearing a white blouse and tan jacket, a paperclip pinned to her collar. A simple hat to protect her against the rain was lying next to her head. There were lacerations around her neck, probably from strangulation. Turning her head, he could see a long, dark welt on the back of her neck. It looked like she had been hit from behind by a blunt instrument, knocking her to the ground, where the murderer then strangled her.

Seeing the dead woman lying there in the plaza made Stachel think of his wife, Hilda, dead for two months now, killed in an American bombing raid. Was he happy that he'd never found the body, that he'd never had to see the cold lump of decaying flesh she had become? Bad enough to lose his wife, and so close to the end of the war, but having the image of her corpse stuck in his mind would have driven him mad. Though he had seen countless deaths over the years, he had never gotten use to viewing a dead body. Seeing a human being without a soul made him think that life was meaningless, a struggle towards nothing, that life was a waste. It was a road he did not want to explore because it only led to suicide.

That's what Germany had become, a country without a soul, a country determined to commit suicide.

Pulling the overcoat further back to expose her chest, Stachel saw countless knife wounds around the chest and stomach. The puncture wounds were deep, but there was little bleeding, so the stabbings were probably done after she was already dead.

There was a paper bag on the ground near her right hand. Inside Stachel found two turnips, some potatoes, and a small piece of pork. He searched her coat and found a small pocketbook. Inside was a thousand Reichsmarks, worthless currency these days, and five thousand American dollars. Why was she carrying American dollars? That would get her arrested, if not executed, as an enemy collaborator. So, the murder couldn't have been a robbery. Hell, the food was more precious than the money. Life in Berlin had come down to the basics, food and shelter. Survival.

Standing up, Stachel walked over to the younger policeman, feeling a tightness in his lower back. It had been bothering him for years, a strained muscle that had never healed.

"Coroner here yet?" Stachel asked the policeman.

The policeman glanced at Stachel, still holding his arms out to keep the crowd away. "Yes sir, Herr Uhl was here and gone. Left about ten minutes ago. Said that he had to go to an early meeting back at the Alex. Gave his apologies for not waiting for you."

"Did he say anything about the body?"

"Only that she was probably killed by strangulation. And that it happened more than four hours ago. He said he'll be free to talk after noon."

"Who found the body? Who was first on the scene?"

"I was, sir. The man standing over to the side there found the body and reported it to me."

"Were you able to look around before the rain started?"

"Yes, but only for a few minutes before the crowd came. I didn't' find anything. Not even a footprint. The rain had pretty much washed away any traces of the murderer. Haven't talked to anyone in the area so don't know if there were any witnesses. Though given the time in the night, and the blackout, I doubt there will be anyone."

"Photographer here yet?"

"Yes. Wandel. Left with Uhl. Said he'd have the developed pictures on your desk by the afternoon."

"Alright, let's get the body to the morgue." Stachel started to walk away. The crowds were bothering him. They were still pressing in, trying to get a look at the body, apparently sensing that it was someone important.

Stachel hated crowds. He always felt removed, distant, like a spectator viewing people's interactions through a lens. Ever since he could remember, he was uncomfortable when there were any more than four people around. People mingling, people wanting to be part of the herd, and all he wanted to do was hide somewhere. Crowds needed authority, crowds wanted someone to tell them what to do, crowds got nervous when someone refused to be part of the group. It was as though if someone didn't conform to the group mentality, they threatened the group and needed to be eliminated. Better to hide, better to watch than to participate. It was safer.

But he missed not having a partner. His old partner, Klein, had joined the military back in '43. He'd been working alone ever since. It was time to change that. He could always use a partner to deflect the interference that he knew would come with this ugly case.

He turned around and tapped the policeman on the shoulder. "What's your name?"

"Lakain, sir. Gunter Lakain." He was younger than Stachel had thought. No more than eighteen. Probably kept out of the military by a father with some political influence. With ears sprayed out to the side and a chiseled nose, he looked like Heydrich. His uniform hung on him like a half-sewn drape.

"You know who this woman is, don't you?"

"No, sir."

"It's Sophie Holzer. August Holzer's wife."

"Yes, sir."

"You still don't know who she is?" Stachel shook his head, looking down at the man's newly polished shoes.

"No, sir."

The crowd had started to disperse as they realized they weren't going to see the body. Why did they still consider death an event when they saw death every day? There were fools everywhere.

"August Holzer's wife. She gave some radio broadcasts a few months ago urging women and children to take up arms and defend Berlin. You know who Joseph Goebbels is, right?"

"Yes, sir." Lakain's eyes were like a cat that had just been spooked by a nighttime noise.

"August Holzer reports to Goebbels. Now, what do you think about the bag of groceries she was carrying?"

Lakain hesitated for a moment before speaking. "Purchased from the black market, I guess."

"Why? Wife of a high Nazi official. They have plenty of food. Not like the rest of us."

"I don't know, sir."

"Do you think someone in the black market killed her?"

"I don't know."

"What do you think? What's your gut tell you?"

"No, I don't think so. Not in this open space. And he would have taken the food back."

"So, what then? Why was she killed?"

Lakain danced on his feet, unhappy with the line of questioning. They're not taught to think, Stachel thought.

"Political, sir. Must be. Someone trying to destroy the country."

"The Nazi's have already done that."

Lakain looked uneasy. "A saboteur, a defeatist, a spy."

"Or maybe the Gestapo? Regardless, you passed the test." Stachel smiled and padded Lakain on the shoulder, who instantly stepped back and grimaced. "You're now my partner."

"But sir, I've been assigned to a special unit tasked to catch the people who are defacing posters. It's imperative that we catch these people. They're trying to subvert the war effort." Lakain looked like an indecisive little boy getting contradictory orders from his parents.

"No doubt an important job, but this murder takes priority. I'll clear it with your supervisor. Don't worry. Look at the good side. This is the kind of case that can make a career."

"Or end it."

Stachel laughed. At least the boy had a sense of humor. "For now, I want you to start knocking on doors. That apartment building across the plaza. Someone must have seen or heard something."

Lakain yelled a Heil Hitler and headed across the street. Stachel ignored him and walked over to the man who had found the body. Wet from the rain, the man looked in his seventies, though he was probably in his early sixties. He had the same ashen, pale face that all Berliners had these days. And he was thin, almost emaciated. Arms hugged to his chest, he stood there shivering in the cold, or was he scared? No one trusted the police anymore. As he suspected, the man knew nothing. He had been out walking, seen the body and immediately contacted a policeman. He had not touched the body or come close to it.

He doubted Lakain would find anyone who would admit to seeing anything. In Berlin right now, it was better to keep quiet, not stick your neck out, not get involved. Stay away from the authorities as much as possible. Stachel couldn't blame them Accepting reality was a good way of being labeled a defeatist. Everyone was looking for someone else to blame.

Stachel told the other policeman to stay and watch the body until it was picked up, then started walking to Kripo headquarters at the Alexanderplatz. The clouds had started to clear, and it looked like the sun might come out. Just in time for the American bombing raid. As he headed east towards the Alex, he saw a group of people gathered around two men and a boy. Probably the same people from the murder scene, Stachel thought. Sightseers. His back was bothering him again, so he stopped and stood across the street from the crowd, leaned against a building, and watched.

The men were questioning the boy, who could not have been more than twelve or thirteen years old. One man was holding the boy's arms behind him, the other man was pointing a finger at the boy, thrusting it towards the boy's face, demanding answers. In his other hand, he clutched some papers. The boy nervously shook his head, denying whatever the man said. Stachel couldn't hear them over the murmurs from the crowd. The other man lifted the boy up by his arms and started shaking him. The boy screamed out in pain, shaking his head vigorously. The man pointed at a light pole a few yards away and made a motion with his hands of tying a noose. The boy's eyes widened in terror and he jerked his head in an emphatic no, struggling with the other man's grip. More people started to mill around.

Stachel knew what was coming. He started across the street, determined to prevent it. But then stopped. The crowd was turning violent, screaming *"Tod zu den Saboteuren,"* "Death to Saboteurs!" Some of the crowd were shaking crushed pamphlets in their raised hands. The boy must have been passing out pamphlets, probably urging people to resist the Nazis. That was happening more and more these days, as the country finally started to realize that Germany was going to lose the war. And the result was always the same. Immediate execution. Stachel interfering would only bring the weight of Nazi law, the law of intolerance and fear, crushing down on him. He'd be labeled a defeatist and arrested. And the boy would still die.

The men led the boy to the pole. Another man, who Stachel hadn't seen before, came up and gave them a rope, which was already tied into a noose. The noose was draped around the boy's neck. The other end was then handed back to the other man, who quickly climbed halfway up the pole and threw the rope over, so it dropped down to the street. The man in back pulled out handcuffs and shackled the boy. He was crying, head down, his tears falling onto the pavement. Then the rope was pulled over his neck and he was lifted up, struggling, kicking his feet, as he slowly strangled. The crowd, which was about ten to fifteen people now, clapped their hands. Eventually the boy stopped kicking, gave a last jerk as though his soul had escaped, and then stopped. As the corpse swayed in the wind, the crowd lost interest and started to disperse.

Stachel stood there, transfixed, staring at the boy's feet as they turned back and forth, like a clock, like time ticking away for the German country. He should have done something, should have stopped the execution. He felt an overwhelming guilt that once again he had stood by and allowed the brutality of Hitler's justice to take its course. Over the years, as the violence grew, Stachel had carved out his own small space where he tried to do good, where he pursued murderers and brought them to justice, where he could pretend that the war didn't affect him, that eventually the country would come to its senses and the killing would stop.

The two men were walking away now. Though not in uniform, they had the strict bearing of the military. Stachel wanted to grab them but knew he could do nothing.

Maybe whoever had killed Sophie Holzer was on the side of good. Certainly, the German government, Stachel's government, had become evil. Was vigilante justice the only justice left anymore? Stachel didn't want to believe that, refused to believe that, and knew the only way to prove that was to catch her killer.

But how do you catch a killer in a city of killers?

Chapter Two

Climbing the stairs at the Alex to his second floor office, Stachel kept thinking of the executed boy and his shame that he had done nothing. He should have done something, not stood there gaping like some fool. What was the point of being a police officer if you did not upload the law? Like the Memel Incident, seven years ago, when he ran away rather than get involved in the murder of a high-ranking minister in the Lithuanian government.

Hilda and he were on holiday at the time Hitler annexed the Memel territory. Then I ran, Stachel thought, at the time justifying to himself that he was protecting his wife, knowing that actually he was afraid to get mixed up in a murder where both the Germans and the Lithuanians could have been involved. Sometimes it's better not to know too much. And that's the sentiment that led to where we are today; Germany destroyed; the perversity of our culture exposed. Will German civilization survive the war? He had his doubts. And if it didn't, he didn't want to be part of whatever replaced it.

By the time Stachel got to the second floor, he was out of breath. He knew he needed to get back on an exercise routine, but the war and his bad back had changed many habits. At times he felt like he was wading through mud. It's the heart, and he beat himself on the chest with his fist. It's always the heart that goes first.

As he stood at the top of the stairs, he heard echoing murmurs. People were huddled in small groups, whispering to each other, with either looks of relief or fear on their faces. Something had happened. He walked over to the group nearest him, three secretaries and two patrolmen, and asked what was going on.

"Roosevelt," said one of the secretaries. "He's dead. Died two days ago."

"The war criminal is gone," said one of the patrolmen. "We will win after all."

Stachel wanted to correct them. He knew Roosevelt's death would make no difference. Not anymore. But he stopped himself. Let them have their illusions. There was nothing else.

His office was ten feet by ten feet, with a big oak desk that filled the room and left little space for guest chairs or filing cabinets. Stachel needed his files, he needed to be organized, his files gave him the sense that there was order to the universe, so one chair had to go so his four-drawer filing cabinet could fit in the corner. The right wall was covered with special awards he had won over the years. An Iron Cross Second Class for serving in the Great War was placed in the middle, surrounded by civilian awards given for solving homicide cases that had a lot of publicity. He could never decide if the awards were given to him for what he'd done or because it was good publicity for the force. He figured it usually was the latter.

His hat was still perched on the portrait of Hitler, hanging on the edge of the picture, leaving one eye exposed, which stared down at Stachel like a malevolent beast. He took it and threw it on the guest chair so he wouldn't forget it next time. His coffee mug, which had a picture of Hitler on it, was sitting in the center of the desk, with a folded note stuffed inside. He pulled the note out.

Please clean this mug immediately. It is an insult to the Führer!

No signature. Stachel threw the note in the trash. He had no intention of cleaning it. It would stay dirty, growing moldier every day, until the Führer was dead.

Stachel had a theory, not shared by most of his peers. Examining the scene of the crime, talking to witnesses, getting statements was all necessary, but the key to finding the murderer was to get inside, to understand what drove him to such a desperate act. The murderer was a human being, not some evil spirit, as so many people believed. A human being that for the most part was just like everyone else, except something forced them over the edge. When Stachel understood that catalyst he would have his murderer.

He first needed to know the cause and time of death, but Uhl, the coroner, had said he wouldn't be available until after noon. The photographs that Wandel took wouldn't help him. He had already seen everything he needed to see, which was basically nothing since the crime scene had been hopelessly contaminated.

So, he had nothing to do but wait, wait for the coroner, wait for Lakain. And think. Think of the horrors that Berliners dealt with every day now, think about the country's crimes, think about what would happen after the war ended. He didn't want to think anymore.

God, he hated political murders. There was always so much unspoken, so much hidden, so much anxiety about who knew what, that it was difficult to get to the truth. He was like a mouse, peering out from the hole he had nibbled in a piece of savory cheese, knowing that out there was a trap waiting to kill him. He knew that if he didn't solve the Holzer murder quickly, he would be in trouble. The Nazi's were starting to panic and anyone who they felt was not doing everything possible to define Germany became a target for the concentration camps or liquidation. It was part of the madness of the regime that even as the camps to the east were being overrun by the Russians, they were still sending people to the camps near Berlin.

He suddenly realized there was a shadow covering his desk, and he could tell by the width of the shadow that it was his boss, Horst Gottlieb. Goes from bad to hell, Stachel thought, as he looked up. Slim and tall, well over six feet, with light blond hair cut short in a Nazi buzz, the image of the Aryan except for the feet that could belong to a ballerina. Wearing a double-breasted brown suit instead of his military uniform, Stachel wondered if Gottlieb was trying to look like Goebbels. Maybe there was another organizational change and the Kripo now reported to Goebbels instead of Himmler. It wouldn't surprise Stachel. The maniac at the top wouldn't do anything that made sense.

Gottlieb was leaning against the door frame, arms crossed, smiling like an imp gloating over his next victim.

Gottlieb might be a lousy boss, a Nazi stooge, but Stachel had to admit that he was very good at managing up. He instinctively knew who to grovel to at any moment. It won't be long now before he'll be groveling at the end of a gun.

"Well," Gottlieb said, in a grasping voice that spoke of too many cigarettes. He picked up Stachel's hat and carelessly threw it on top of the file cabinet. Sitting in the guest chair, he leaned in and tapped his hands on the desk. "You heard about Roosevelt?"

"Yes," Stachel said with a wave of his hand. "Old news."

Gottlieb looked perturbed that Stachel already knew about Roosevelt. Wanting to always feel in control, Gottlieb was uncomfortable when his reports knew things before he told them.

They both stared at each other for a minute, neither wanting to start the conversation that both were thinking of. Finally, Gottlieb spoke.

"I just heard. Another murder. Hardly a surprise these days. Do you know who it is?"

Stachel copied the same smile Gottlieb had a moment ago. "Sophie Holzer."

Gottlieb leaned forward, hands now on the desk, his face suddenly pale. He looked like that mouse that poked his head out and strung the trap. "Who did you say?"

"Sophie Holzer. August Holzer's wife. Strangled and then stabbed."

Gottlieb stood up and started pacing the room. But he could only walk a few steps before having to turn around. Like a soldier guarding his assigned territory, except his territory was only three yards wide.

"This can't be." Gottlieb stopped, closed the office door and sat down, then looked at Stachel, a whining look on his face. "Is she dead? Did you make sure?"

Stachel rolled his eyes and looked up at the ceiling for a second.

"Of course she's dead. She was stabbed in the chest multiple times. I've got a patrolman looking for witnesses right now. One thing though." Stachel paused for effect. He wanted to prolong the look on Gottlieb's face for as long as possible. "She had five thousand U.S. dollars in her purse."

"What did you say?" Stachel gloated as Gottlieb's face turned from fear to horror. "How can that be? Where could she get that kind of money?"

"Where could anyone get that kind of money? I don't know, but it looks like something's going on, something at the top."

Gottlieb stood up and started strutting back and forth again, hands clasped behind his back. He leaned against the wall, looking up at Hitler's picture.

"This patrolman," he said. "Can he be trusted?"

"How would I know?" Stachel said, throwing up his hands. "There's not a lot of us left in homicide. I'm going to need help."

"And you'll get it. Who else do you want?"

"No one right now. I'll work with this guy Lakain. He's green but that's good because he'll do what I say. I don't want someone who will second guess everything."

"This is going to get ugly. We need to find out where she got the money. Quickly. Does he know?"

"Who's he?" August Holzer? Goebbels?"

"Both."

"I assume not. I haven't told anyone."

"Well, when Holzer finds out you can bet he'll go to Goebbels and ask for the Gestapo to get involved."

"Fat chance of that. Himmler and Goebbels hate each other."

"Murder makes strange bedfellows. Especially this murder. Trust me."

Gottlieb was always saying trust me, always acting like wise counsel, like he knew more than Stachel, knew the bigger picture. Without thinking, Stachel rubbed his eyes, trying for a second to believe that Gottlieb wasn't there, letting the moment pass, because his immediate response was to say that it was trusting authority that got Germany where it was today. But he wouldn't say it. He had learned the hard way that it only got him in trouble.

"Tell the Gestapo no," Stachel said, as though it was an easy thing to do. "We don't need them. Besides, they'll just torture and kill every witness we fine."

Gottlieb walked across the office and put his hand on the drawer handle of the file cabinet.

"I need you to drop everything else and focus on this. What other cases do you have?"

"Only the Wicke case right now."

"The wounded soldier home on leave? Could they be connected?"

Stachel shook his head. "I don't believe so, but I want to talk to Uhl."

"Well, if they're not connected, give it to Ecker."

"No way. You know he'll do nothing. He's all talk. He doesn't care anymore if someone gets killed. Of course, why should he? Why should any of us? The city's a graveyard."

"Give your files to him anyway. That's an order."

Stachel sat there staring at Gottlieb, who was looking down at the desk. It was always like this. Gottlieb giving orders and Stachel ignoring them. And Gottlieb knew it but was afraid of a direct confrontation. His authority was a masquerade. Push and the mouse ran back into his hole.

"I can handle this. Just make sure people stay out of my way."

"That's probably impossible. What did the coroner say?"

"Don't know. Uhl was gone by the time I got there. Besides, I want Bennett on this. Uhl can't investigate a pile of dirt."

"Well, he's the only coroner we have now. Bennett disappeared."

"To where? He's the only one in that group with a brain."

"Who knows? He's either fled west or he's dead. Maybe he committed suicide. There's enough of that going around right now. I want to be there when you meet with Uhl."

"Apparently he was busy all morning. Left a message that he'll talk to me this afternoon."

"Well, let me know." And Gottlieb walked out, looking to his left and right, as though there was someone hiding outside the office, about to pounce.

Stachel took the Wicke files and stuffed them in his desk. He had no intention of giving them to Ecker. Screw Gottlieb.

Chapter Three

S tachel started planning out his next steps. He pulled out a pad of lined paper, noticing that it was the last pad he had. Even paper had become scare. Writing small, precise letters, he started a list. Review photographs, update from Lakain, meeting with coroner, meeting with August Holzer to get background on his wife, interview her acquaintances. At that point he hoped to have a good picture of the victim and a small list of suspects.

At eleven Wandel came by and left photographs of the crime scene. No sooner had he left than Gottlieb was at the door again, leaning against the frame as before. He wanted an update before the meeting with the coroner, Matthaeus Uhl. Sitting once again in the guest chair, hands clasped together on the desk, looking like a priest before a supplicant. Stachel pushed the photographs across to him. Gottlieb looked at them quickly, then placed them back on the desk, face down.

"That's enough," he said. "Murders always depress me. Any leads? Did your partner find any witnesses?"

"He's not my partner," Stachel said, raising his voice. Lakain was nothing more than a boy. If not for the war, he would never be in the police department. Not at his age.

Franz Klein would always be Stachel's partner. That was a team he was proud of. They complemented each other and almost always solved a case in record time. Those days were long gone and calling Lakain his partner would never bring them back.

"No leads yet. Come on, it's only been a few hours. I'm still waiting on Lakain to get back to me on what he's found."

"This was obviously a robbery gone bad. Maybe a Jew who's been in hiding trying to get that food."

"How do you know that?" Stachel could sense that his patience was already stretched. He could see where this was going. Find someone, anyone, that fits into the Nazi view of the world. He imaged that Gottlieb had already been on the phone talking to his superiors, calling August Holzer, calling anyone who would listen. And he'd bet that August Holzer was going to try and steer the investigation away from the black market. Something wasn't right there. If he could figure out why she's been to the black market, he'd be halfway to solving the case.

"What else would it be? It must be a robbery. That's where you need to focus your efforts."

"But there are no Jews left in Berlin. They're either dead or in a concentration camp. The Nazis have made sure of that."

"Well, Goebbels and Holzer agree with me." Gottlieb gloated, wanting Stachel to recognize that he had access to senior leadership.

"You've been talking to Goebbels?"

"Well, not directly. Holzer said he did. I told you this was an important case."

"So now Goebbels is a detective? Catching murderers is another one of his fairy tales?" Stachel stood up and walked over to the window, his back to Gottlieb. No one seemed to care anymore about the truth. Maybe this would be his last case and if so, he might as well use it to make a statement. Try and make up for all the Nazi lies he'd suffered through. And for years of looking the other way. "I'm going to catch this killer," he said, speaking to the window, keeping his back to Gottlieb, "but it will be the actual killer, not someone cherry picked by Goebbels."

"Or by Himmler," and Gottlieb laughed. "I told you they would cooperate. Goebbels called him and demanded that the Gestapo get involved."

Stachel turned around and sat back down in his chair. "I'd think Himmler would be happy that someone was causing trouble for Goebbels. Hitler's henchmen spend more time fighting each other than fighting the enemy."

This day was getting worse every minute.

Stachel continued. "And I won't work with the Gestapo. If they get involved, we'll never catch the killer. They'll just pick someone they don't like and execute them. Case closed."

"You'll work with whoever we want you to work with."

So now it's *we*, Stachel thought, as though Gottlieb was a member of the inner circle.

Gottlieb paused. "Look, Himmler has asked that Rudolf Plettner attend the meeting today."

Stachel stared across at Gottlieb, trying to decide if he should call him a fool or just be done with it and strangle him. "And you've agreed of course."

"Yes."

"Thanks for letting me know," Stachel said. "Again, the Gestapo adds no value. I'm trying to catch a murderer, not kill people for fun and profit."

Stachel grabbed some of the photos and threw them across to Gottlieb. "Here, give Plettner these. That will keep him busy for a while. The Gestapo seem to love murder so much, he'll enjoy looking at them." He started to look at his watch, then remembered that he had broke it a few weeks back. And it was impossible to get it fixed. He looked at the clock on the wall, with its Gothic letters, the picture of an eagle holding a swastika in the middle, covered in a thin layer of dust.

"It's time," he said. "Don't want to keep the Gestapo waiting."

The conference room was starting to look like the streets below. Good German efficiency thrown in the trash. The garbage can in the corner was overflowing with paper, two chairs had been turned over, as though a soccer match had been played in the room earlier that day. The coroner, Matthaeus Uhl, was already there, sitting in the middle of the table, making some notes on a pad of paper, ignoring the disorder around him. Stachel righted the two chairs, then sat down across from Uhl. Gottlieb sat at the end of the table.

Uhl was in his fifties, though he looked much older, his face stretched like it had been through a vise.

"Matthaeus," Stachel said, "though I think it's obvious, I called this meeting so we could have a quick review of the Holzer murder and what you've found so far. I assume you've had time to examine the body."

"Yes, but the results are preliminary. It will take a few days to complete a thorough examination, assuming I have the manpower to do that." Uhl glanced over at Gottlieb, hoping he would get the hint. He was ignored.

"We understand, but this case is important given the victim so I felt we couldn't wait. Also, I want to consider if the Wicke murder is connected."

"Wait," Gottlieb said, holding up his hand. "We must wait. We can't start the meeting without Plettner."

"Who's Plettner?" Uhl asked.

"Someone you don't want to know," Stachel said.

They waited a few minutes in silence; Gottlieb calmly looking out the window at the overcast sky, Uhl continuing to review his notes, and Stachel trying to figure out a way to get the Gestapo off the case. He'd been successful in the past at keeping them out of his murder cases. What he needed right now was an Allied bomb to fall at the head of the table. But it was the afternoon, and the Allies only bombed in the morning. They never seemed to do what you wanted.

Plettner finally arrived, throwing his overcoat on a chair and sitting at the other end of the table. He didn't apologize for being late and he didn't introduce himself.

"Well, let us begin," he said, slapping his left hand on the table. He was a thin man, maybe thirty years old, with a face that looked like it had been carved out of stone; all angles and lines. There was nothing smooth or soft about the man. Stachel immediately hated him. As soon as Plettner had arrived, tension hung over the room, like someone had painted the room in tears. Uhl wouldn't look at Plettner, and Gottlieb wouldn't look at anyone else.

Uhl coughed once, then held his papers out in front of him and started speaking.

"As Hauptsturmführer Stachel said, I'll first review the Holzer murder. Sophie Holzer, wife of August Holzer, was killed last night, probably between one and three in the morning. She was hit with a blunt instrument in the back of the head, though not hard enough to kill her, only to stun. Then she was strangled from behind. Her larynx was crushed. Given that the contusions on her neck were spread out in a fairly even pattern, it appears the killer used his forearm. Which means he must have been very strong. After she was dead, he stabbed her twelve times in the chest with a five-inch knife."

"In a rage?" Stachel asked.

"No, that's the peculiar thing. The knife wounds were done methodically, like someone slowly sticking a pin in a pin cushion. If the killer had been in a rage, there would have been bruises around the knife wounds."

"Any pattern to the wounds?"

"Not that I can discern."

"Are you sure she was dead when she was stabbed?" Plettner asked.

"Yes, there was little bleeding around the stab wounds. If she had still been alive, even unconscious, there would have been much more bleeding."

"And as far as we can determine," Stachel said, looking at Plettner, "nothing was stolen. Her purse and pocketbook were still there and there was a bag of groceries next to her body. There was one thousand Reichsmarks and five thousand U.S. dollars in the pocketbook. We believe the food was purchased at the black market."

Plettner leaned in, looking at Stachel as though at an insect, suddenly very interested. "Five thousand U.S. dollars? Where did she get that and why would she have it?"

That's one thing we need to find out. Presumably August Holzer will be able to explain the money."

"And the food wasn't taken." Plettner said. "Don't you think that's odd?"

"Given the situation in the city, yes, I do. Maybe the murderer was surprised and didn't have time to pick up the bag. That assumes robbery was a motive."

"Of course it's a robbery. Any signs of a struggle? Did she put up a fight?"

"Nothing I saw at the murder scene. Matthaeus?"

Uhl shook his head. "I've examined her mouth and fingernails for pieces of skin. Nothing. And there were no scratches on her body. That's the reason I believe that she was knocked out when she was hit on the head."

Stachel looked around the room and asked if there were any more questions. No one answered.

"Good, so if no one objects, Uhl, please review the similarities between this murder and the Wicke murder."

"Justin Wicke, a soldier, private, who had been in Berlin recuperating from a gunshot wound to his right shoulder, was killed a week ago."

"Also in the Mitte district?" Plettner interrupted.

"Yes, but not at the Gendarmenmarkt. Farther north, near the Spree river."

"How long had the soldier been in Berlin?"

"A month, according to the doctor who treated him."

"If he could walk, why was he not sent back to the front?" Plettner said.

Stachel shrugged his should that he didn't know and didn't care. It was a stupid question.

Uhl continued. "Wicke was knifed in the back."

"And no evidence that Wicke had dealings with the black market," Stachel said. "At this time, I don't believe the murders are connected. He was found in an alley, so presumably the killer snuck up on him from behind."

"But he must have put up a struggle," Plettner said. "As a soldier he was physically fit. I find it difficult to believe that he could have been killed without putting up a fight."

"He had put on weight since being back in Berlin," Uhl responded.

"Probably the only one who has," countered Stachel.

Uhl smiled and went on. "His right arm was in a sling."

"Likely or not, he was a German soldier," Gottlieb said. "He should have heard the killer and been able to fight him off. Undoubtedly it was his lack of exercise that did him in. That should be a lesson to all of us to stay physically fit, as the Führer has ordered."

Stachel couldn't help but lean back in his chair to let everyone see his girth.

Plettner looked around the table, looking like a sniper sighting a victim. "You all do realize the importance of this? Sophie Holzer was not just anyone. We can't allow this to go unpunished. As I said earlier, this is obviously a robbery. A Jew or a communist who's been in hiding. Undoubtedly they didn't know who they tried to rob."

"That was my view to," Gottlieb said. "But Hauptsturmführer Stachel thinks otherwise. I think we should start rounding up suspected communists. One of them will know who did this."

"Are there any communists left in Germany?" Stachel asked. "I thought Hitler killed them all."

There was a moment of silence.

Plettner was drumming his fingers on the table, waiting for Stachel to continue, probably hoping that he would say something else to incriminate himself. The Gestapo loved to arrest people. Finally, when Stachel didn't say anything, he spoke.

"Though a robbery, it is also the work of a defeatist. Someone who doesn't believe we will win the war."

"You mean I have to find someone who accepts reality," Stachel said. "That makes it easier. Not many of those right now."

"Quiet," Gottlieb said, "as Sturmbannführer Plettner has said, this murderer must be caught quickly, and he must be executed as an example."

"Well said," Stachel shrugged and crossed his hands over his stomach.

"I agree. Holzer's killer must be caught now, before the public hears about it. I give you three days. After that, we will be forced to take over the case."

Maybe he should strangle both of them, Stachel thought. They can go to hell arm in arm, like two little gay Nazis. Of course, he could just wait and have the Russians do it.

With the city falling apart around him, how was he ever going to catch the killer?

Stachel spoke. "We are interviewing people who live around the crime scene and will talk to co-workers and friends of the victim. And after this meeting, I will be meeting with August Holzer. Though we have no leads at this time, I am confident that with good police work, something will turn up eventually."

"Eventually isn't good enough," Plettner rose and grabbed his overcoat. He looked at Gottlieb. "I want daily updates on your progress. Top priority. If necessary, assign additional men to the case. Is that clear?"

"Yes sir," Gottlieb, giving the Nazi salute. "It already has our top priority. And I will take personal responsibility for making sure you are updated."

Plettner started for the door, then turned and looked at Gottlieb and Stachel. "Reichsminister Goebbels has a staff meeting tomorrow morning. He would like you to attend. Unfortunately, I will not be there. You will update me immediately afterwards."

"Me to?" Uhl whined.

"No, not you. Though give me a copy of your report." Plettner reached out his hand and Uhl nervously handed the papers he had.

"This is everything," Uhl said, "but they're my only copies."

"Sturmbannführer Plettner," Stachel said, "let us make a copy and send it to you before end of day."

"Fine," Plettner said and handed the papers back to Uhl. "Again, this must take top priority. The Gestapo is very busy right now supporting the war effort. I'd like to think you can solve this case so we don't need to get involved." Plettner walked out of the room, leaving the door open behind him. The threat of those last words was not missed by anyone.

Gottlieb stood up, visibly angry, and looked over at Stachel.

"You heard him. We need results. You have Lakain. I asked you earlier. Do you need anyone else?"

"No, we can handle it." Stachel slammed his hands down on the table and pushed himself up. "Well, let's not stand around talking. I have a date with August Holzer."

"And I will be coming with you to make sure you behave. Holzer is an important man, and we want him on our side. I didn't like some of the comments you made to Plettner."

"I'll behave," Stachel said, bowing his head so he looked like a small child being reprimanded, hiding the smile on his face.

"Your view of behaving makes me want to surrender to the Allies."

"That's treason," Stachel said, laughing. "Seems like everyone's doing that these days."

They left the office together. Gottlieb leading the way and Stachel close behind. Uhl remained at the table, nervously shuffling his papers.

Chapter Four

T hough the Chancellery had been largely destroyed by the bombing raids, Holzer's office on the first floor had somehow survived. When he entered, Stachel felt he had gone back in time, before he war, when the world had seemed a saner place. Though he knew that lurking behind sanity was the beast.

Holzer's office was fitting for a man who reported directly to Goebbels's. It was at least four time the size of Stachel's office, paneled in a dark mahogany wood, with the standard Führer picture alone on the left wall and pictures of Holzer shaking the hands of various high-ranking officials. The wall of shame, Stachel thought. What was it with the Nazis and mahogany? Were they all so depressed that they needed dark wood to feel at home?

The room was centered by a conference table that sat six people. In the back, framed by two gilded windows with thick red drapes, was Holzer's cherry wood desk. It dwarfed the man sitting behind it. Holzer was in his late fifties, graying at the temples, wearing a black double-breasted suit and tie. The man and office fit like a straitjacket. Dismal, depressing, lacking any feeling. He wore no insignia other than a simple black armband with a swastika. Holzer's hair was oiled and combed back.

Between the suit and hair, he looked like a little Goebbels, except he was probably six inches taller. His eyes were little slits that peered out at a world of lies. Maybe he walks with a limp. The good little Nazi, toadying up to his superiors. Gottlieb and Holzer should love each other.

Stachel's back was killing him. Too much walking, too much tension. He needed to sit in one of the guest chairs in front of Holzer's desk, but they weren't offered. Holding their hats in front of them, they both waited for Holzer to speak.

"My wife was the love of my life," Holzer said in a monotone, looking down at his desk. When he looked up, he ignored Stachel and spoke directly to Gottlieb. "I hope you both understand how terrible this is. Whomever did this must be caught and punished. It is a direct attack on the Fatherland."

"He will be," Gottlieb said and made a short bow. "All available resources will be on this case. It will be our top priority."

"With your help, of course," Stachel added.

"Of course, gentlemen. I will do what I can," Holzer said, waving his hand through the air as though batting an insect that was bothering him.

Stachel figured he might as well start right in with the questions. He sat down, leaving Gottlieb standing. He had long ago learned that preliminaries were wasted on men in power. Their ego didn't allow for small talk. "Did your wife have any enemies? She had become a public figure with her radio broadcasts. Did she receive any threats because of them?"

Holzer looked across at Stachel, sizing him up, clearly unhappy by the questions. "Of course not. She was doing what every good German mother would do, help in defending her country. I can't believe any loyal citizen would be against that. This murder must be the work of a communist or a disgruntled Jew. Someone who has no right to be called German. It couldn't be a German citizen."

Enough to die on, Stachel though as he leaned against the chair back. The throbbing pain in his lower back increased with every word Holzer said. How was he going to stop these people from solving the murder when the investigation had just started? What would they do if the murderer turned out to not be a communist or a Jew?

"We don't believe this was random. She was carrying a package of food with her and it wasn't stolen. So we don't think the motive was robbery. It looks like the food was purchased on the black market." He held back mentioning the money. He wanted to surprise Holzer later and see how he reacted.

"That's nonsense. Why would she use the black market? The Führer makes sure we have everything we need. I tell you it was the work of a defeatist."

Still standing, Gottlieb reached down and put his hand on Stachel's arm. "Sir, we agree with you. Hauptsturmführer Stachel has to explore all angles and is only trying to get some facts that might lead us to the killer."

Stachel shook Gottlieb's hand off. "But why was she out at that time of night?"

Holzer stood up, hands clasped behind his back. Stachel was surprised that he barely came up to Stachel's chin. Maybe he had an operation so he wouldn't have to look down on his boss.

"Everything we do here in the ministry is important to the war effort. Without us the people would lose hope. And my wife was part of that effort. She gave hope, she gave meaning to women and children that they could do their part to defend the Fatherland. We cannot allow this country to fall to the Bolshevik beasts."

Holzer sat back down. Use to reading witnesses, Stachel could tell that Holzer's emotional outburst was fake.

Stachel let out a sigh as Gottlieb finally sat down. It unnerved him having Gottlieb standing there, like a sentry.

And I have no idea why she was out at night," Holzer continued. "I doubt it's important."

Stachel could see he was probably not going to get anywhere with this prig of a man, stuck up with his own self-importance. This is what Germany had come to. Little men like Holzer trying to pretend they were saving the country, saving Europe, when all they were really doing was destroying it.

"Sir, we found five thousand U.S. dollars on her. What was she doing with that kind of money? And where did she get it?"

Holzer leaned back in his chair and stared up at the ceiling. He looked like he was reaching out to God, or more probably the Führer, for guidance.

"I don't know what you're talking about," Holzer said, still looking up at the ceiling. "You say she had five thousand dollars. Was it real? Did you check to make sure it wasn't counterfeit? Since no one would have reason to have the money of our enemies, it must be fake."

"We have not checked if it was counterfeit, but we will. It looked genuine to me. But that's beside the point. Counterfeit or real, why did she have it?"

"I don't know." Holzer was looking over their shoulders at the office door, hands clasped on top of his desk. "Don't be fooled by what you hear from some people. They are defeatists. Germany will win this war. We must win! Did you not read the Reich Minister's article last week? We are all fighters for the Eternal Reich and must stand strong against the enemy. The Allies cannot continue the fight for long. Losing would mean that God has abandoned Europe to the atheists."

Have the Nazis fallen back on religion now, after spending the last twelve years attacking the church and creating the dogma of National Socialism? These people were mad and refused to accept reality. Realizing he wasn't going to get anywhere now with why Sophie Holzer was out at night, Stachel decided to refocus on if she had any enemies.

"Your wife worked, didn't she? My understanding is that she was the head mistress at a boarding school for girls. Is that correct?"

"Yes, the Hortense School for Girls. A very prestigious school that only takes the best girls from the best families."

"Was anyone there upset with her?"

"I wouldn't know. She never talked about the school at home. As I never talked about the ministry."

"One last question. Where were you last night?"

Holzer stood up and leaned across the desk, making eye contact with Stachel. "That's enough. I know what you're getting at. I did not kill my wife. I've told you where to look. You're wasting my time with these kinds of useless questions."

Stachel was about to stand up, when Gottlieb leaned over and pushed him back in his chair, stuttering as he spoke. "Sir, or course we know you didn't kill your wife. That was not the intent of the question."

"I'm not an idiot. The question is to establish whether I had opportunity to kill my wife. I consider it an insult."

"We withdraw the question. The Reichsleiter is not a suspect."

"Useless perhaps," Stachel said, "but it's a process we follow. Anyone we talk to is asked the same question."

Holzer continued standing, grabbing the hanging drape and fingering it as he talked, like a woman stroking her hair. "Very well. I'll answer, but only to aid your investigation. I was at home. We went to bed around ten and when I woke up around six, she was gone."

"Do you sleep together? Do you share the same bed?"

"What kind of question is that?"

"I mean that busy men, like you, often sleep separately because of the demands on their time. I've heard your boss doesn't sleep much and calls people at all hours of the night."

"Well, that is none of your business and I won't answer your question." Holzer looked over at Gottlieb, trying to get him to speak up and interrupt Stachel. "She apparently left in the middle of the night. I didn't wake up. Why she left I don't know but given what you said about a package of food, I assume it had something to do with it. Though why I can't say.

"But, again, why was she out buying food in the middle of the night? Any why the five thousand dollars? Please, you must know something."

"I tell you I don't," and Holzer pounded his fist on the desk. "She had no reason to deal with the black market. How do you know the food wasn't planted by the murderer?"

"We don't. I admit that's a good question."

"Find her killer. That's your job. When you find him, you'll know why the food was there and why she had U.S. dollars. Not the other way around. I see no reason for continuing this discussion. And I don't much care for your insolence." He turned to Gottlieb and pointed two fingers in the air, aping Goebbels. "I will report this to the Reich Minister. Why is this man on the case? Surely you have someone better."

"He's our best man. Hauptsturmführer Stachel has over…"

"If he's your best man, then maybe this case should be turned over to the Gestapo."

"They're already involved," Stachel said, shrugging his shoulders. "I'm only doing my job, following the process we always follow in an investigation. If you truly want your wife's killer caught, you should help, not hinder me."

"Hinder you! I've just told you where to look for the killer. What further help can I give? Now get out, both of you.

Holzer activated his intercom and asked his secretary to come in and usher them out. He then sat down at his desk and started going through some papers, ignoring that Stachel and Gottlieb were still there.

The secretary, an old man in an SS uniform, motioned for them to follow him. Stachel reluctantly stood up, stared at Holzer's head, which was bowed over his papers, and followed the man out. As he got to the door, he realized that Gottlieb wasn't following him. He was standing in front of the desk, looking at Holzer, clearly wanting to say something but not wanting to interrupt the man.

Holzer looked up. "I've heard you both will be attending the Reich Minister's meeting tomorrow. Remember, he is less forgiving than I."

Stachel gave a snort of disgust and left. As he walked down the hall, he was thinking of how he could turn up some dirt on Holzer. If only to satisfy himself that the Nazis were all idiots.

He let out a sigh of frustration when he remembered that he had to attend Goebbels's staff meeting tomorrow. It would be more of the same evasions, only this time with a room full of party hacks and a man, the poison dwarf, who could have him executed for looking the wrong way.

Chapter Five

People often dreamed about being able to listen to the meetings of the rich and powerful. But not Stachel. He wanted to stay as far away as possible. That morning he had tried to talk Gottlieb into letting him out of the meeting.

"You can handle it. You know I'll just cause trouble if I'm there."

They were standing in the hallway of the Alex, just outside Stachel's office, whispering so that no else would hear. Gottlieb was poking him in the chest with his index finger.

"You will come, if only so I can see you suffer. For once, I'll enjoy myself."

Cars were scare in Berlin, not only because of the lack of petrol, but also because it was impossible to navigate many of the streets. Between debris and craters left from the Allied bombing, the only place to walk was a thin path through the center of the street. So Stachel and Gottlieb had to walk from the Alex at Alexanderplatz to the Reich Chancellery. It took them a good half hour, during which they did not talk to each other. Stachel couldn't help noticing the suffering around him, while Gottlieb seemed oblivious to it.

Once at the Chancellery, ruined by repeated bombings, they were ushered through the garden and down into the

Vorbunker. There was a hallway running down the center, with rooms branching off to the right and left. There were soldiers everywhere, crowded into the small space, the sweat of anxiety and fear on their faces.

Stachel kept looking around as they walked down the middle of the bunker, past the dining room to a small conference room. He had never been so close to Hitler before and was afraid of running into him.

The conference room was in the center of the *Vorbunker* had no windows. There were exits on all four sides. The left led to rooms where Stachel could hear children's voices. An oak table that seated eight and extra chairs that lined both sides of the walls was the only furniture. Except for a picture of the Führer, there were no pictures on the walls, though it looked like there were pictures hanging at one time. Probably looted from occupied countries and now hidden away somewhere, Stachel thought.

Though there were six people at the table, Gottlieb and Stachel were told to sit against the wall, like they were insects allowed only to observe their superiors.

They're the insects, the parasites, Stachel thought. They've burrowed their way into the country's skin and left open festering wounds.

The meeting hadn't started yet. There was a photographer in the room, apparently taking a promotion picture of Goebbels for the latest edition of *Das Reich*. Undoubtedly a picture to show the public the heroic leader working tirelessly to defeat the enemy.

The poison dwarf, Joseph Goebbels, Reich Minister of Public Enlightenment and Propaganda, posed for the camera, carefully hiding the metal brace and elevated shoe he wore because of his short right leg. He looked small compared to the men around him. Thin, with a hawk-like nose and creases running down his face, he looked every bit the predator he was.

After the photographer left, Goebbels moved to the front of the table and sat down, informing the others by his action that the meeting was to begin. Holzer sat on his left; Otto Dietrich, Reich Press Chief of the Nazi Party, on his right; Heinz Lorenz, deputy to Dietrich, and Dr. Robert Ley, Leader of the German Labor Front, were also seated at the table. Sitting at the far end, opposite Goebbels, sat Lieutenant General Helmut Reymann, in charge of the defense of Berlin. Goebbels crawled out of Hitler's bunker below for this staff meeting every day. Mainly they discussed what half-truths and diversions they would tell the public about the defense of Berlin. *Das Reich*, the party newspaper, was all propaganda now. Other than the Wehrmacht communiqué, there was little positive news to tell the public.

"I have the article from the military," Goebbels said, holding a piece of paper in front of him. "Fighting is still going on at the Oder. Our troops are holding strong against the enemy."

"We will hold them off," said Dietrich. "With time, the Allied coalition is bound to fall apart."

Reymann glanced over at Dietrich and shook his head.

Goebbels ignored the remarks but looked angrily at Reymann. Stachel had heard that they were not getting along. Reymann disagreed with Hitler's Nero Degree, the destruction of Germany's infrastructure to slow the enemy down, and in Goebbels's view, was slow in implementing the policy. Stachel figured it was only a matter of days before Reymann was dismissed and someone else designated to lead an already hopeless task.

The two stared at each other for a moment, while everyone else at the table looked down, then Goebbels broke and looked around the room. "We must have an article in tomorrow's paper that more food and coal will be arriving within a few days and that extra rations will be distributed."

"Is food coming in?" asked Holzer. "From where? The public won't believe us."

"Who cares from where," Goebbels said with a wave of his hand. He seemed to be doing that a lot these days. "If you tell a lie enough times, people will believe you. We must give the people hope. Bad news only undermines the war effort."

He turned and looked at Dr. Ley. "I want an article about the Allies not getting along. As Dietrich said, something about the Americans and British joining us to defeat our joint enemy. It is obvious that an alliance of Capitalists and Communists will enviably fall apart."

There was a shuffling of bodies. No one wanted to mention the subject that was on everyone's mind, the subject that could get you shot, the subject of a retreat south to Bavaria.

Goebbels turned to Holzer. "And what of your wife's murder?"

Holzer rested his hands on the table and looked over at Stachel with a petulant and unhappy stare. "I have heard nothing. This detective, Stachel, doesn't seem to take direction from his superiors."

Goebbels looked over at Stachel. He was staring right through him, as though there was something concealed on the wall behind him. Or Stachel feared he was lining him up for the firing squad. "Yes, well, anyone who stays in the Kripo and doesn't join the military is suspect. Are you a defeatist?"

Gottlieb stood up and motioned Stachel to remain seated. "Someone must remain behind to ensure that defeatists and saboteurs are captured and punished. Hauptsturmführer Stachel is one of my best men and is diligent in pursuing the enemies of the Third Reich."

"Can't your man answer for himself?"

"Of course he can." Gottlieb motioned for Stachel to stand up.

Stachel wanted to tell everyone in the room to go to hell. He was not their pet dog, expected to bark on command. Right now, survival was more important than integrity. But he remained seated as a silent act of defiance. "Reich Minister, the enemies of the state are everywhere. We will catch this man as quickly as possible. He will be punished."

"Of course, of course," Goebbels said with another wave of his hand. He turned to Holzer. "Reichsleiter, do you have anything more to add?"

"I keep telling him that it was obviously a robbery, but he won't listen. He insisted on asking me personal questions, as though I was the one who killed my wife?"

"I am only trying to get a complete picture…" Stachel started to say but was silenced by Goebbels's stare.

Goebbels turned to the rest of the table. "Sophie Holzer's murder proves that our enemies are everywhere. That they are ruthless. We must also be ruthless. Our enemies must perish, will perish, before the might of the Third Reich. And we must continue telling the public to watch for defeatists and saboteurs. We must give examples. Like reporting about people imprisoned or executed for saying the war is lost. Wasn't someone hanged for distributing defeatist pamphlets? That's the kind of example we need to remind the public that punishment will be swift."

"It was a child, sir, a young boy, Dietrich said. "Letting people know that a child was executed might not be a good thing. I agree that we need to show an example, but killing children…"

"That is exactly what we must show," Goebbels said, pounding his fist on the table. "We must meet fanaticism with fanaticism, death with death. We must show the people that we are stronger than the enemy and that we will go to any lengths to win this war and save Germany."

"Should we put anything in about my wife's death?" Holzer asked.

"No, of course not. We must keep the news positive."

Goebbels shifted in his chair, obviously uncomfortable with what he would say next. "Now, about the Alpine Fortress, the National Redoubt. Rumors are spreading that we are planning on leaving Berlin and fleeing south. It's nonsense and we must put a stop to it. It's defeatist talk and undermines the people's will to resist."

"But it's true, isn't it?" Lorenz said. "There are plans being drawn up to continue the struggle from Bavaria."

"Himmler's wishful thinking," Goebbels said. "The Führer has personally told me that he has no intention of leaving Berlin. We must fight to the end, for the greater glory of Germany, of Europe, and for our Führer. There will be no stab in the back. The Führer has not given up on the German people, we cannot give up on him. I am writing another article for *Das Reich* about the need for continued struggle against our enemies. Only if we stand united can we win. And we will win because we must win. The fate of European civilization rests with us. The article will come out later this week. August, I ask you to read my draft, which I will have ready by tomorrow."

"Of course," Holzer said, bowing his head as though the request was an honor.

"Anything else? If not, then this meeting is adjourned."

Goebbels stood up, his index and middle fingers thrust out to the side. "Stay the course. I trust all of you understand the importance of what we're doing. We must keep the people believing that we will win this war, that it is not possible for us to lose. In some ways, what we do is more important that what the generals do. The Führer will not listen to any talk about defeat."

Goebbels looked around the room, silently making eye contact with each person. "I know that the stress of the last few months has brought us to the breaking point, but we must remain strong, we must not give in to weakness. Only through strength can we win, only through strength can we lead the people to victory."

He placed his hands on the table, fingers spread out, and looked over at Holzer. "I want daily reports on this murder investigation. The killer must be caught quickly and made an example. I am thinking of a public execution and it must happen soon. If this policeman does not produce results," and he pointed at Stachel, "than we need to hand it over to the Gestapo."

Stachel shook his head. "They're already involved. A man called Plettner."

"A good man. He will keep you in line. Put some fire in your belly."

Goebbels looked across at Reymann and asked him to follow him. They would meet separately to discuss the defense of Berlin.

While the others stood up, Holzer still sat, staring straight ahead. Stachel remained seated, watching Holzer, reminding himself that he must be careful of what he said, that these men were so caught up in their fantasy world of winning the war that they would lash out at anyone that tried to bring them back to reality. But surely, they had to know that death was close, that the war was lost and punishment by the Allies would be swift?

As Goebbels said, they were all fanatics, and fanatics will do anything to protect their version of reality.

After he was back at the office, Stachel asked around if anyone had seen Lakain. He hadn't seen him since yesterday morning when he told him to look for witnesses and was starting to worry that Lakain had finally woken up and fled the city. Or in hiding. With all the refugees from the east, it was easy to lay low. One secretary mentioned that the boy had been in earlier looking for Stachel, so that made him breathe easier. He asked her to go find him while he retreated to his office to wait.

Sitting at his desk, looking at Hitler's picture on the wall, Stachel couldn't remember when he had finally realized the Nazis were nothing more than criminals. The guilt that he had voted for Hitler back in '33 because he said he'd bring back respect for law and order and not recognize the Versailles Treaty appealed to Stachel, as it did to many. But after the Reichstag fire, the real Nazis came out. Mass arrests, concentration camps, every year another law to worsen the fate of the Jews, the annexation of the Sudetenland, all worried Stachel, but it wasn't until the invasion of Poland that Stachel knew that it was all a lie. Hitler and his cronies would bring the country to ruin.

All of a sudden, he realized that Lakain was sitting across from him, legs crossed, trying to look calm, wearing a uniform spotted with stains. Any other time, Stachel would have reprimanded him for entering unannounced. He's a boy, nothing but a boy trying to be an adult. He wanted to ask him his age but was afraid to because he knew he wouldn't like the answer.

In a halting voice, Lakain explained that he had knocked on every door in the apartment building across from the plaza. About half the apartments were apparently vacant since no one responded to his knock. The ones where someone answered had all denied seeing or hearing anything.

Stachel interrupted and told him that that meant nothing. These days, anyone in their right mind would hide from authority. The ones who did talk to Lakain would, of course, say they saw nothing. No one wanted to get involved. All people cared about was food, heat, and praying a bomb didn't kill them.

"Go back and check those empty apartments again. If you need to, break the door down. It's likely that if someone saw something that night, the last person they'd want to talk to is a policeman."

Lakain said he didn't agree. "We are only upholding the law, protecting the public. Surely, anyone who isn't guilty wouldn't hide from us."

Stachel looked down at his desk, using his index finger to push a pencil back and forth. Why me? Why do I always get the naïve ones? How can anyone these days think that the police are upholding the law? The warped law of the devil.

"Was there anyone you talked to that acted suspicious? Anyone act like they weren't telling you the truth, that they were hiding something?"

Lakain thought for a minute before answering. He had his hands clasped behind his head; his arms spread out as though he was about to take flight.

"Maybe one. A man called Pantel. He looked nervous and wouldn't look at me. Kept shifting his eyes to the side. One of his neighbors told me that Pantel was often up late at night, so if anyone had heard something, it would be him. But Pantel told me he'd been asleep the whole night."

"Well, talk to him again. For now, you focus on Pantel and checking out those supposedly vacant apartments."

"And what will you be doing?"

Stachel wasn't about to tell him that he considered August Holzer a suspect. He couldn't trust Lakain to keep his thoughts to himself. Besides, it was presumptuous of Lakain to ask him what he was doing. Stachel was the senior officer, he was in charge.

"I'm pursuing other angles. And that's all you need to know for now. Get back to that apartment immediately. With our luck, that Pantel guy saw something and has now fled."

Time to check up on the Holzer's.

Chapter Six

When Stachel got home that Sunday evening, he was exhausted, hungry, and his lower back was acting up again. The only thing to eat were two moldy potatoes and some crusty lettuce that his neighbor had given him yesterday. She kept a small garden behind the building, and it was often the only way to get fresh vegetables. When he turned on the ceiling light, it flickered momentarily. He feared that the electricity was about to go out again. But the light held, so he went into the kitchen and sighed in relief when water came out of the faucet. He set the potatoes in a pot of water to boil, poured a glass of water, and walked back into the main room.

He had been squatting in this apartment since his wife had been killed. A direct hit on their apartment building two months ago, when Stachel was out, had instantly killed her, and everyone else in the apartment. The people who lived there previously had probably escaped to the west before Hitler had announced that the city was a Fortress, and no one could leave.

His apartment now was one room, with a kitchen and bathroom down a hallway to the left of the front door, one window looking out on Marienstrasse. A double bed filled the room, one end table to the side with lamp, and a small table, which doubled for dining and as a desk, against one wall. Two wooden chairs that creaked whenever Stachel sat in them were pushed up against the table. To the right was a grated fireplace that was filled with the remnants of the coal he had burned the night before. He hadn't been able to pick up any more today. The temperature was supposed to be around freezing tonight, so the apartment would be an icebox by morning.

Minus the fireplace, it looked like a painting from Van Gogh, except it was dark where Van Gogh's painting had been full of bright colors.

He fell into a chair and took a sip of water. Schnapps would be better, much better, but the only way to get liquor was from the black market, and Stachel refused to deal with them. The only thing he had left these days was his integrity and he wasn't going to let anyone take it away.

He ate his meal slowly. His body had adapted to the few rations received each day. He knew he'd get sick if he ever had a proper meal.

It was only eight, but he was so tired he laid down in the bed and tried to get some sleep. He knew he'd be awakened by three by the British daily bombing raid. Sleep didn't come, so he laid there, squinting up at the cracks in the ceiling, following them into the corners of the room and down the walls. He wondered if the building was about to collapse. Like the country, falling apart.

The meeting with Holzer from the day before still bothered him. The man was hiding something, Stachel knew it, and in Hitler's Germany, there was always someone who knew what you were hiding. And it was usually the Gestapo. They documented everything. Someone like August Holzer would have a nice fat file. The question was how to get it. Though both reported up to Himmler, these days the police rarely knew what the Gestapo was up to and would become immediately suspicious if Stachel asked them for Holzer's file.

He needed a way to get to them without anyone knowing, and the only way to do that was through his friend Hugo Baer.

Baer was a former police officer who had joined the Gestapo a few years back. He needed the extra pay, he told Stachel. It had nothing to do with ideology. Personally, he didn't like the group, and had grown disillusioned with the Nazis, like Stachel, but his family came first. It was hard keeping three children's bellies full on a policeman's salary.

Stachel reached for the glass of water next to his bed and started to take a drink but tasted only the final drips of an empty glass. He threw the covers off, groaning as he sat up, rubbing his hands through his hair, making him look like he'd just seen a ghost, the ghost of his wife Hilda. He reached over to turn on the lamp and heard the pop of the bulb dying. He didn't have a replacement and knew it would not be easy to find another light bulb in Berlin. Holding his left hand out, he shuffled into the kitchen. God, he was getting old. He could barely see in the dark anymore. He turned the faucet at the kitchen sink. Nothing now. There was some water rimmed on the spout. He touched it with his finger and then licked the drop of water with his tongue, savoring it as though it would be the last drink he would ever have. He walked back and sat down on the bed, empty glass in his hand. Where was the enemy when you needed them? Surely the Russians should have started their final assault by now?

His stomach started growling like an air raid siren. He bemoaned the fact that even with his meager diet, he still hadn't lost any weight. He still had the flab of his fifty years. And he never seemed to get any sun anymore. Berliners had all turned into *schlafwandlers*, pale, thin, wandering the city, covered with the dust from the rubble of fallen buildings.

That's the only good thing about the Nazis. They made us all go on a diet and made sure we'd never get skin cancer.

He realized he was still holding the empty glass. When he went to place it on the side table, he knocked over the picture of his wife. He grabbed the picture before it fell to the floor and cradled it in his hands, wishing she was here now. She would calm him, give him hope, give him an escape from the horrors he saw every day. Life is made up of the habits of daily existence, and he had lost those habits when his wife died.

"I believe I am going mad," he said to his wife's picture. "You know I've never trusted authority and now I'm knee deep with some the worse monsters this country has ever created. In trying to find a murderer, I must work with murderers. And you know I can't play that game."

Still holding his wife's picture, he walked over to the desk and set the picture down. It helped him deal with his grief to talk to his wife now and then. And it had to be out loud. Talking to her silently didn't help. The sound of his voice helped him believe she was still alive, though he knew it was only a symptom of his denial.

He had kept some of her clothes that had survived the bombing. They were hanging in the closet. Occasionally, he would touch them, feel the silk of her dress, the frills on her blouse, the smell of her perfume.

Why couldn't he have been the one at the apartment that day? It was a Sunday and he had gone out to queue for their daily food rations, holding a red card for butter and a green card for meat. Normally, it would have been her, but that day he had told her to rest, he would get the food. It was afternoon, so no bombing raid was expected, but someone must have screwed up because an American raid appeared. By the time the air raid sirens sounded, the planes had already dropped their bombs and left. He returned to find his building in ruins, a direct hit, everyone inside vaporized.

It was Hitler's fault for starting the war, and Stachel's fault for not trying to end it. He had done nothing to stop the madman's dreams.

There was a knock at the door. It was now nine-thirty at night. He cautiously got up and moved towards the door as he heard another knock. But the knock wasn't loud, wasn't the brute force of the Gestapo, the sound of fiends trying to knock the door down. It was light, more a tap than a knock, with the knuckles rather than a fist. Besides, the Gestapo came later in the night, when there would be on witnesses and the victim was asleep. Not at nine-thirty.

When he opened the door, he let out a sign of relief, then wondered if maybe it was worse. It was his wife's sister, Sommer, clutching her overcoat around her with one hand, about to knock again with the other. He should never have told her where he was living.

"Thank God, you're here," she said, pushing her way into the room. "I've been looking for you for the last two days."

"I've been busy."

Sommer was shorter than her sister and had her light brown hair pulled back in a bun, a streak of dirt across her left cheek. The slightly upturned nose was the only similarity between her and her sister. Though she only came up to Stachel's shoulders she had a way of carrying herself, always erect, always looking straight ahead, always resolute, that made her seem taller. Once she wanted something, she wouldn't stop until she got it. Hilda, his wife, though also stubborn, knew how to quietly get what she wanted.

Besides, she still believed in the Führer.

"I've left messages with your neighbor, Minna. Didn't you get them?" Minna was Stachel's next door neighbor, the one who had given him the lettuce. She had become the de facto landlord of the building and watched over Stachel as though he was her husband. She had three children, all young, and last she had heard, her husband was still fighting in the east. But she hadn't heard from him in six months and now accepted that he was probably dead.

"I did, but like I said, I've been busy."

"Too busy for your sister-in-law?" She sat down on the edge of the bed, looking around at the unkempt apartment. "This is no place for you. Why don't you come live with us? We can make room somehow."

Stachel knew that the comment was not made of benevolence. Live with them and then she'd have him close by, where she could watch him, where she could make her demands at any time.

"No, I'll stay here. It becomes me," he said as he picked up a newspaper he had thrown on the floor the other day.

"Do you miss Hilda?"

"Of course. Every hour of every day."

"You know, Hilda and I were very close."

Something I always regretted, Stachel thought.

"She told me once about your plans to retire to the country after the war and open a pastry shop. Hilda was always such a good cook. Did you know she got most of her pastry recipes from me?"

"Yes, I knew that. Does it matter? That plan, that dream, is gone."

"It doesn't have to be. After the war, I could make the pastries."

"What, you'd move your family to the country?"

"Well, we wouldn't move to the country. Hans likes the city too much. But I could bake them here and have a delivery service take them to your shop."

"They'll already be stale by the time they got to me. That won't work. The dream's gone. I don't want to think about it anymore." Stachel was now straightening a picture on the wall of Hilda and him hiking in the Black Forest about ten years ago. They were happy then. Stachel had a good job. They talked about having children. Now, the job was a nightmare, the children never happened, and she was gone. He turned from the picture and looked at Sommer.

"Out with it. Why are you here? I know you. You didn't come to talk about your sister. You two barely spoke to each other the last few years."

She looked at him as though he was about to assassinate the Führer. "Don't talk like that. I'm the only family you have left." She paused for a minute, grasping her hands in her lap, now holding a handkerchief that she used to dab at her eyes, as though she was crying. "I need your help."

"Why else would you be here?"

She looked down, now clutching her overcoat with both arms, "We need food. My son, your nephew, is sick. He's weak and hasn't had a decent meal in months."

"You get your rations, don't you?"

"You know that's not enough. A few small rotten potatoes, some sugar, coffee, maybe a sliver of pork every few days.

Your nephew is dying. He's caught something. Probably some disease dropped by our enemies to infect us all.

"Have you seen a doctor?"

"Doctors are useless. What can they do? They just say they have no medicine. You can get some, right? You're a policeman. You must have means. Medicine. And some extra food."

Stachel threw up his hands as he sat down at the desk. Without thinking, he took his wife's picture and turned it face down on the desk. "You know I can't do that. I have no authority to get what doesn't exist."

"Don't lie to me. People are saying that you all live pretty well at the Alex and Prinz Albrechtstrasse. Hoarding food, keeping it from the public, letting us all die." Her voice was vicious, as though she was throwing knives at him with every word.

"I can't speak for the Gestapo, but I assure you we have nothing at the Alex."

"So you won't help your nephew?"

"I can't. If I could do something, I would. I can try and find a doctor. But I doubt they'll have the medicine your son needs."

She looked up at him. She started crying and her tears washed some of the dirt from her face. She wiped away the tears, leaving a mark of dirt on her fingers.

"You're a man in authority. You can get anything these days."

"Yeah, in authority. That just puts me one step closer to the guillotine. But again, I'll do what I can."

Stachel thought she was going to say something more, maybe lash out again, but she let out a quiet whimper of resignation instead.

"Alright. Thank you. Can I come back tomorrow?"

"Yes, if I'm not here, leave word with Minna."

She stood up, walked over and briefly hugged him, then left without saying another word. Stachel sat at the desk, rubbing his face with his hands, as though trying to erase what he had just agreed to away. Maybe suicide was the best way out of this hell. He had heard that at the last performance of the Berlin Philharmonic, they had handed out poison pills to everyone when they exited the building. What would he do if he had one of those pills right now? Would he take it? Take the easy way out. Or save it for later, like a fine bottle of wine he was saved for a special occasion. Better he didn't have one of those pills. It was too tempting.

The only thing keeping him going now was the case. It was tempting to think that maybe he could arrest August Holzer for the murder of his wife. Take down one of the Nazi criminals. He needed to get to those Gestapo files. It was ten o'clock, but he knew Hugo Baer would still be up. No one slept much in Berlin these days. And maybe Baer could help him get the medicine for his nephew.

He reached for the phone on the wall near the front door, hoping it was working, that the lines had not been knocked out. It was. He righted his wife's picture as he dialed Baer's number from memory.

"Yes?" He recognizes Baer's voice, though it was only a whisper.

"It's Stachel. I'm sorry for calling so late."

"The children are asleep, as is Marlis."

"I know, I know. I'm sorry, but it's important. I need access to some Gestapo files."

"Our files? Why?"

"I can't tell you, but it's because of a murder investigation. Can you help me?"

"What, you want me to get you files on someone who's name I don't know?"

Stachel laughed, though he knew Baer wasn't making a joke. "Of course not. Can you get me into the file room? The one in the basement of Prinz Albrechtstrasse."

"That's only a small room. All our files aren't there."

"I'm sure, but I assume any recent files would be there. I don't think I need to go back too far."

Stachel could hear Baer sigh. "Look, I shouldn't tell you this, but the files are not exactly guarded these days. The building has been mostly abandoned because of the bombings."

"So there's no one guarding the room? I can just walk in. Isn't the door locked?"

"There shouldn't be a guard. The lock on the door broke weeks ago and no one's bothered to get it fixed. The file cabinets have never been locked."

"I'm surprised they haven't started burning their files."

"They will, once they finally accept that the war is lost. Though late at night there shouldn't be anyone in the building, be careful. The Gestapo is very sensitive about its files and won't be happy if you're caught snooping around in them."

"Thank you. I'll watch myself. But I don't think they'd arrest a policeman."

"Don't bet on it."

Baer hung up just as Stachel realized he'd forgotten to ask him about a doctor and the medicine. But he didn't want to call him back again at this late hour. It would wait until tomorrow.

Chapter Seven

Sunday night was crisp and cold, with a full moon that bathed the street in pale dappled light that made the building debris look like artwork from some demented sculptor. Wind from the west had cleared the air of the smoke from fires. Walking down the Wilhelmstrasse towards Prinz Albrechtstrasse, Stachel had a moment of optimism. Germany would surrender, the destruction of Berlin would not happen, the country would survive and prosper once again. Of course, the full moon also meant the British would have a clear view when they dropped their bombs around three in the morning.

Stachel considered waiting until after the raid to head over to the Gestapo office. Nazi buildings were always a target. Apartments were collateral damage. But that risked still being there in the morning when the city stirred awake. So, he felt it was safer to go in the middle of the night when everyone would be home trying to get some sleep before Meyer's Trumpets, the air raid sirens, sounded.

He had to find out more about Holzer, had to quickly either eliminate him as a suspect or find a motive for wanting his wife killed. And he couldn't talk to anyone. It would quickly get out that he was investigating Holzer and that would give

Goebbels an excuse to throw him off the case and possibly have him arrested.

Gestapo headquarters was a great stone façade residing on the border between the Mitte and Kreuzberg districts, in the heart of Berlin. It had been largely destroyed by Allied bombings, but the files were all in the basement and Stachel hoped that room would still be intact. The building was dark and silent, most of the windows broken, looking like a beast from hell. If it had two lit windows on the top floor, with the front door a gaping maw, it would look like Magog waiting to swallow its victims.

When Stachel walked through the front door, he was surprised to find a guard in the foyer, sitting at a desk in the dark, leaning back against the wall. So, Baer wasn't correct, at least, not of the entrance. The soldier kicked his chair forward and turned on a small desk light. He took a quick look at Stachel's badge and then waved him through. He never said a word, never asked Stachel why he was there in the middle of the night. A soldier going through the motions, lost without someone to give him orders.

You walked down a few steps to the main entrance hall, which looked like a poor imitation of a Gothic cathedral. He went down a main staircase and to his right and down some steps to the basement. He knew the file room was down the corridor to the right. There was no one around. Turning the doorknob, he could tell it was broken. It jiggled, like it was hanging to the door by a single thread.

It looked like no one had bothered to clean the file room in a while. The archives were dark and musty from the debris that had fallen from the ceiling when bombs hit the building. There were four rows of wooden shelves, with filing cabinets along both side walls. The shelves were stuffed with folders, with an alphabet tag on the side of each shelf. Above each aisle hung light bulbs, casting the room in a hazy light that barely penetrated the dark. A library dedicated to documenting death. He felt like he was in some medieval catacomb littered with the bodies of dead monks. Except these monks were all murdered.

He found the 'H' row and eventually, after some digging, found the area for 'Hol.' But there was no file for Holzer. He checked to see if it had been misplaced but couldn't find anything. The Gestapo had to have a file on him. They had to. They watched everybody, and especially someone as high up as Holzer. So, either the file had been removed or it was somewhere else. And given the state of the archives, Stachel didn't believe anyone had been here for some time, so it was likely still here.

He noticed that the shelves started with A and ended with Z. So, what were the file cabinets against the walls? He wandered over to the cabinets on the left and noticed that they were labeled by department, rather than alphabet. Walking down the aisle, he found three cabinets that were marked Ministry of Public Enlightenment and Propaganda. Goebbels's department. He started with the first cabinet, first drawer and worked his way down and over.

Two of the cabinets were dedicated to Goebbels, to his numerous dalliances, reports about his family, his relationship with his wife, his six children, and copies of every speech and article he had written. He wondered if Goebbels had any idea that everything he did was being documented, probably on Himmler's orders. Stachel wanted to look at the files, see what one of the devil's disciples was up to, but fear of being caught, of lingering to long in the room, kept him focused on his objective. In the third cabinet, top drawer, he found a file on Holzer. It was thicker than most of the other files, but there was only one folder. Either the Gestapo didn't think he was that important or they couldn't find enough dirt on him.

Still, the file was thick and would take time to go through, more time than he wanted to spend in the archives, knowing that he needed to be out of the building before morning. But he couldn't risk taking the file. If someone else went looking for it and realized it was gone, it would set off alarms throughout the Gestapo, and one of the first people they'd check with would be Stachel, given the Holzer murder. So, he had no choice. He would have to chance it and go through the file here.

In the back of the room, against the wall, were a row of plain wooden desks. Stachel sat down at one in the corner, as far away from the door as possible. The light wasn't good, so he had to keep holding each document up to read it. The folder contained information on both August and Sophie Holzer, though of course more on him than her. The only interesting document he found on her was one dated a month ago, a scribbled note that she was not comfortable with her radio broadcasts, had mentioned that she didn't want to do them anymore, and a final sentence about a rumor that she was planning on fleeing to the west and surrendering to the Americans. Apparently, the Gestapo didn't think much of the rumor, since they didn't investigate further.

But on August Holzer there were plenty of documents. Apparently Holzer had upset someone at the Gestapo, since there were numerous notes going back at least a year suspecting that Holzer harbored defeatist sentiments. There was even one note wondering if Holzer was involved in the Hitler assassination attempt, though it didn't give any reason for the thought. There must not have been anything to back it up, since if there was, Holzer would have been interrogated. And there was nothing in the folder that said the Gestapo had even talked to him. Just numerous suspicions that he was not to be trusted. Of course, the Gestapo didn't trust anyone, especially anyone from the propaganda group, given the ill will between Goebbels and Himmler.

Stachel kept digging through the files, looking for something specific, something that would help him, and he admitted to himself, some dirt on Holzer that he could use. But there was nothing, nothing except misgivings that he was not totally behind the war effort. Looking at his watch, he realized he had been in the archives for two hours, much longer than he had wanted. He closed the folder and put it back in the cabinet. It was now three in the morning.

He headed back up to the first floor. When he went pass the soldier at the front door, he was stopped and was asked what he had been doing in the building. Stachel again showed him his police badge, explaining that he had been asked to examine the structure of the building and that Himmler was thinking of moving back in. He figured that the more outlandish an idea he told the guard, the more likely he was to be believed. The guard was taken back by his statement, asked him if it was really true, to which Stachel said he didn't know, he was just doing what he was ordered to do. The guard was so worried about Himmler that he didn't ask why a police detective was assigned to inspect the building.

Back on the street, he started working his way home. The British were late, but he knew they'd show up soon, and he didn't want to get caught in a bomb shelter with people he didn't know.

Stachel knew what his next step was though he didn't like it. He needed to confront Holzer with the rumors about his marriage, about the rumor of his wife deserting. Was that what he had been hiding? Did he find out his wife was going to surrender to the Allies and have her killed? Bringing up that subject was dangerous. Holzer could easily have him arrested and shot.

Sophie Holzer planning to leave would explain meeting with someone in the black market to obtain food. Their servants would undoubtedly be watching the kitchen, so stealing food from the household would be risky. He wanted Holzer to be involved, wanted Holzer to have ordered his wife's death. Having a high-level Nazi leader arrested and executed was something Stachel would love to see. Yet if it came out that she had been planning to flee the city, the Nazis would consider it just punishment. She would be labeled a defeatist and Holzer would probably be congratulated for getting rid of her.

Wouldn't it be nice to bring down one of the people who had helped destroy the country? It would be Stachel's final triumph.

He was chasing dreams now. If Holzer wasn't involved, then he had no suspects. The killing could be random, could be a simple robbery that went bad. He needed to check in with Lakain, find out if he had found anything from interviewing the witnesses.

He got home just as the air raid sirens started. He should go down to the cellar, but he really didn't want to be around people right then. He'd risk it and hope that God would take pity on him and let him survive another day. Surely God would want Stachel to punish an unrepentant Nazi?

Chapter Eight

Monday, April Sixteenth. The sky was still dismal, thick and low like the sloping forehead of a Nazi stooge. Hovering around freezing, Stachel cursed when he got up that he hadn't found time the day before to find any coal. He told himself that he needed to deal with the necessities of survival, or he'd never live long enough to finish this case. He'd barely gotten more than two hours sleep and every muscle cried out for a few more hours. God, it could snow, he thought as he dressed. Would snow help Germany or the Russians? He didn't know. Probably the Russians. They liked snow. He hoped it would hamper both sides. Let them kill each other until there's no one left to invade the city.

He thought of going to the Alex first thing, but then decided that he'd only run into Gottlieb, who'd want an update, or worse, Plettner, who'd scream about the daily status report. The Gestapo always seemed to be in a spiting rage these days. Like some mad dog looking for food, afraid it would be its last meal.

Instead, he'd see if he could get something to eat before heading over to the school where Sophie Holzer worked. Maybe he'd be lucky today. Down the street from his apartment, he found a small shop that had just opened and had an assortment of small cakes. Though they'd been made with the gritty powder that passed for flour these days, they still tasted good. If only he could have a cup of real coffee.

As he ate, Stachel watched a group of *Volkssturm* erecting a barricade at the end of the street. Young boys and old men, they were tripping over each other laying down barbed wire tied to railroad ties they must have gotten by ripping up some of the city's tram tracks. A soldier walked up to them and started yelling that they were wasting their time. The Russian tanks would plow through the barricade like it was butter. They'd all be killed if they tried to defend it. They listened to the solider for a minute than ignored him and went back to work. What else were they going to do? Not erecting the barricade was admitting defeat, and no one in Berlin was ready to accept that yet.

Leaving the shop, Stachel walked a block before his luck continued. One of the few trams still running came lumbering down the street.

The Hortense School for Girls where Sophie Holzer worked was in the Kreuzberg district. The tram turned down Franz-Kluhs-Strasse street, passing by the bombed ruins of the Mehringplatz column of peace. Stachel shook his head. A statue of peace commemorating war. Fitting for a dying city. The school was on Friedrichstrasse, a few blocks north of Mehringplatz. Stachel jumped off the tram and walked the remaining few blocks.

A few trees that hadn't been destroyed were struggling against the cold to bloom, the small buds the only sight that there might be life in the city after Germany's defeat. Probably the only life after the Russians get through with us, Stachel thought.

He had phoned yesterday and was scheduled to meet with the temporary director of the school, who had been appointed quickly after Holzer's death. The school building was a worn-out pastiche of various architectural styles going back hundreds of years. Baroque, romantic, classical, all woven together to create mishmash that illustrated Berlin's chaotic past.

There was a security guard at the front door, a boy who couldn't have been more than twelve years old. Stachel had to show his Kripo ID. He figured the boy had no idea what it was but let him through because the badge looked official. Stachel couldn't figure out why the school bothered with security. When the Russians came, did the school expect them to show IDs before storming the building? Then Stachel reflected that security was probably there to keep refugees from getting inside. Another example of Berliners not helping other people. People now only cared about themselves and their families. Everyone else was not their problem. Germans had experience at looking the other way.

The new director of the school, Liesa Von Schwager, was a short thin woman with graying hair pulled back in a bund. She was dressed in a light red dress, buttoned at the top, with a white lace collar. She wore no earrings, though in addition to her wedding band, she wore on her right hand a silver ring that was clearly expensive. A woman who believed that appearance was the key to authority. She stood up and shook Stachel's hand then sat down, her back straight and her hands clasped and resting on the large oak desk. She acted as though she was from the upper class and was talking to someone below her. But Stachel knew too many Germans had added the Von to their name regardless of their social background. Besides, many of the rich had supported Hitler's rise to power. It seemed greed and wealth were wedded to each other. None of them cared a damn about the country.

"It's terrible what happened," she said, shaking her head. "I can't believe it. It's hard to realize that the person you talked to only a few days ago is gone forever. You'd think that we'd all become use to death these days, but it's still a shock when it happens to someone you knew and saw all the time." She hesitated before saying the word death, as though speaking it brought it closer.

"Death is never easy," Stachel said, using a stock phrase he often said. He shifted in his chair, his rumbled suit was bunching up on his back and made him think someone was holding a gun to him. "As I mentioned on the phone yesterday, I am in charge of the investigation into Sophie Holzer's murder. I'd like to speak to you and anyone on your staff who knew Sophie."

"Please," Schwager said, "call her Mrs. Holzer. For the sake of the children, we never called each other by our first names. It instilled in the children a certain level of respect and authority which we've found difficult to maintain these days."

Stachel nodded that he understood. "How well did you know Mrs. Holzer?"

"Fairly well. I have reported directly to her since I joined the school eight years ago. She was very demanding, but I respected that since the opposite would show a lack of discipline."

"And did you get along?"

"That's beside the point. I reported to her and did what I was ordered to do. I never considered it anything but that. Besides, why would we not get along?"

"That would be for you to answer. I'm just trying to understand Mrs. Holzer's relationship with everyone at the school. I'm trying to figure out why someone would want to harm her."

"But I heard that she was killed in a robbery. Isn't that correct? If a robbery, then it wouldn't be by someone she knew."

"It's possible, but it's only a theory." Who would have told her that? Had she talked to August Holzer? "Did she have disagreements with anyone in the staff?"

Von Schwager looked down at her hands, which were now in her lap. She struggled for a moment, making sure she chose her words correctly. "Mrs. Holzer was very strict and disciplined about everything that went on at the school. She did not tolerate sloppy work or sloppy thinking. When she felt that someone was not meeting her standards, she spoke up, often in public, and often to the embarrassment of the person. Though she cared deeply that all the teachers had the proper authority with the children, she never understood that ridiculing someone in public achieved the opposite. I tried to tell her a few times, but she wouldn't listen."

"How did the staff feel about this?"

"Not very well, as you can image, though I never asked around. But I sometimes overheard things they said to each other. I would say that everyone respected Mrs. Holzer, but not many liked her."

"Anyone dislike her enough to want to do her harm? In your opinion, of course."

"No, I don't think so. I think that everyone understood that with our enemies so close, her discipline gave them something to cling to. With her death, there's been a feeling of hopelessness here, that their world has ended. And the children all fear what will become of them. I've been trying to keep them positive, but it's hard when you have to cancel a class and herd the children to the cellar. I've considered shutting down the school temporarily, until the war is over, but many of the parents say they want us to continue, that it gives the children a sense of normalcy."

"What about the radio broadcasts that Mrs. Holzer did? How did people feel about that?"

Von Schwager shook her head. Her face looked like she had just bitten into a rotten piece of fruit.

"Oh, they were very much against it. Asking children to fight the Russians seemed nonsense. It wouldn't make a difference. Some teachers said it was as though Mrs. Holzer wanted to kill off Germany's future. But no one would have killed her for that. At least, I don't think so."

"Did Mrs. Holzer ever mention that she had second thoughts about the broadcasts?"

Von Schwager stood and walked over to the window, her back to Stachel, staring out on the street. "Last week she did mention to me that she wished she hadn't done the broadcasts. She didn't say directly, but I thought that she had been forced to do them. It was only that one time. She never said anything again."

"Did she ever talk about her husband, August Holzer?"

Von Schwager turned and looked at Stachel, then sat down. He could smell her fear, a smell of rotting corpses, of a fire out of control, of a hopeless future.

"Rarely. I sensed the marriage wasn't going well. You could tell when she had had an argument with her husband. She was more reserved, and that seemed to happen more often lately. But her reserve could also be that she was worried about the war. I don't know."

"Did she talk about leaving Berlin, about heading west and surrendering to the Allies?"

Von Schwager looked shocked and shook her head vigorously. "No, of course not. I don't think she would ever leave the children. Who would say something like that?"

"It's just a rumor, nothing more. I'm sorry, but I have to follow up on everything I hear. If anything, to prove the rumors wrong."

"Well, it is wrong. I mean, I don't actually know, but again, I don't think she would leave the children. It's just not like her. Of course, no one is behaving normally these days."

Stachel couldn't think of anything else to ask her for now. Stachel stood up and asked her if she had anything more to add. She said she didn't, but she would contact Stachel if anything came up.

"Can you give me a list of the staff? I'd like to have a room, with a desk and two chairs, where I can interview each staff member."

"Do you need to? It would upset them."

"Yes, I'm afraid it's necessary. They might know something."

"I doubt that. Mrs. Holzer never confided in the staff, but we'll help as much as we can. You'll have to schedule the interviews around their class schedule. I don't want the children to know about this. It would just upset them. And they already have enough to deal with when they leave the school and head home."

Three hours later, Stachel was back on the tram. He couldn't find a seat, so was standing, holding a strap. He had talked to three teachers after Von Schwager. And tomorrow he would talk to the remaining four teachers. All had essentially confirmed what Von Schwager had said. Sophie Holzer was respected but not liked. Though no one said it openly, Stachel had the sense that they were relieved that she was gone. A few mentioned that they were uncomfortable around her, that she was a little dictator, but that was hardly a reason for murder.

What did Stachel have at this point? Nothing. August Holzer was his only suspect. Could it be someone from the black market? Or someone random, someone who had seen her buying food and killed her for it? There were enough hungry people in Berlin to make that plausible. But then, why was the food not taken? And that didn't explain the five thousand U.S. dollars. What possible use would she have for those dollars other than to bride officials?

Stachel had nurtured a contact over the years, a man named Stehen, who wandered around the fringes of the black market. From time to time, he gave Stachel information in exchange for food or cigarettes and the promise that Stachel would look the other way at whatever Stehen was up to. If he was still alive, Stachel needed to contact him and find out what he knew. Quickly, since he could already feel the hot breath of Goebbels and Holzer fanning the back of his neck.

He thought back to when he had an experienced partner, someone he could work with, someone to bounce ideas off of, someone he could share the uncertainty of an investigation. Now, all he had was Lakain. A young man oblivious to the world, a boy who had grown up with the spite of National Socialism bouncing around in his head.

There was a time when Stachel felt good about what he was doing. Making Germany safer, protecting the public, upholding the law, was a noble profession and he was proud of the part he played. That pride started to fall apart when Hitler's true intent began to show with the occupation of Czechoslovakia. Before that Stachel had given the Führer the benefit of the doubt. He had reunited the German people under one country, he had made people proud to be German again. Though Stachel didn't always agree with Hitler's means, he believed that the end result was good for Germany. He didn't like the non-aggression pact that Hitler had signed with Stalin, but he accepted that the Führer knew what he was doing. But with the invasion of Poland, Stachel began to realize that Hitler had larger plans. Stachel's blind trust in his leaders had ended then, but it wasn't until his partner, Franz Klein, had left the police force and joined the army, that he realized that he no longer loved his country. That had been early in '43, though Stachel could no longer remember the exact month. It was after the news about Stalingrad. For the first time, Germans started thinking that maybe they would lose the war. Klein, in a fury of patriotism, joined the army and was sent to the Eastern Front.

Stachel and Klein had been a strong team. They complemented each other. Stachel was the rational one who followed the process and made sure that the proper evidence was collected and documented so that when they caught their suspect, they would get a conviction in court. Klein was less disciplined. He took risks, he followed hunches, and he often didn't care if he was following the letter of the law.

And they were always at odds. Stachel because he wanted to follow the process and ensure arrest and conviction. Klein because he was inpatient with the process. "I already know who the killer is," he'd say, "you pick up the pieces."

That infuriated Stachel. He was the senior partner, Klein should show him the proper respect, Klein should learn from Stachel's experience. But instead, Klein treated Stachel as his junior. "I work with you, not for you," he'd say. But though there was conflict, they both believed that they were stronger together than apart. They were the most successful homicide team in the Kripo and often were given special commendations. Stachel had been proud of the awards and the recognition. It helped reinforce the importance of what he was doing. Klein didn't care. He knew he was good at what he did; if people didn't agree that was their problem. His office was bare, no personal items to show that it was someone's office. It didn't matter since Klein was rarely there. He was always out on the street, hustling, looking for information, never afraid to follow a dubious lead.

Neither Stachel nor Klein cared for promotion. If you rose too high in the force, you only became a pigeon to the politicians. Catch criminals, leave the PR to someone less qualified. The pursue was all that mattered.

Everyone was surprised when Klein announced that he was leaving the force to join the army. It had become common for Kripo personnel to join the army. That wasn't the surprise. It was that Klein had done it. Everyone thought he lived in his own world and didn't pay attention to what else was going on. He had never talked about the war to anyone. Stachel had tried to talk him out of it, but Klein, as always, had already made up his mind and wouldn't listen.

After that, Stachel didn't get a new partner. There weren't enough people left in the homicide squad. Many had left for the military, some had been killed or wounded in the bombing raids, rarely was anyone replaced. So Stachel continued on his own, working each case, but feeling all the time that he was less successful since he didn't have Klein's recklessness to push him forward.

But he knew the madness was about to end. At least the madness of the war and the Nazis. To be replaced by the madness of occupation. He didn't want to live a slave to the Allies, live in a country that had to live with its criminal past. Sometimes, he thought he was counting down the hours to suicide.

Better to follow what Von Schwager had said. Pretend everything is normal, go on with your job and ignore the war. There will be life after the war. But it might be a Russian life.

Chapter Nine

Like it or not, Stachel had to go back to the Alex, if only to meet up with Lakain. He desperately needed some good news, something to show that he was getting closer. But his luck at finding a pastry shop open and the tram early that morning finally ran out. Just as he got to the top of the stairs, Gottlieb came down the hall, arms thrust out, like a soldier from the Great War storming the trenches of the enemy. He demanded to know why he and Plettner had not received a status report.

"He's hopping mad and blames me for your disobedience."

"I've been busy," Stachel said, holding his hands out to his side, like a Hindu god in the middle of a dance.

"Do it now," Gottlieb said, snapping his fingers. "This is urgent?"

"More urgent than catching Holzer's killer?"

"Keeping your supervisor abreast of the investigation is part of the process. Besides, if Plettner doesn't get his report, he'll take over and I know you don't want that."

"Remember, I've also got the Wicke case. I can't do everything." As soon as he said that he knew it was a mistake. Someday he'd learn to just shut up.

"You were supposed to give the Wicke case to Ecker."

"I forgot."

Stachel headed for his office, hoping Gottlieb wouldn't follow. But he could feel Gottlieb behind him, like he was holding up a magnifying glass to the sun and was burning a hole in Stachel's back.

As he sat down at his desk, Gottlieb tapped his index finger on the desk, giving him a look that if he didn't know Gottlieb was a fool would have scared him. But Stachel knew the man had no teeth. It was the people hiding behind Gottlieb that Stachel needed to worry about.

"Give me the Wicke files now," Gottlieb said. "I'll give them to Ecker."

"What? You think I have them all packaged up and ready to go. I need to update my notes and assemble everything. Otherwise, Ecker will be lost."

Gottlieb leaned over the desk, his fingers sprayed out. "I thought you were always organized, always on top of things, never letting anything slide."

"There's a few other things going on. Like I have to spend time in queue to get something to eat."

"Get someone to do that for you. You've got to stay focused on the murder."

"Who? I got it," Stachel said, snapping his fingers. "Ecker can stand in line for me. That's all he's good for." He thought Gottlieb was going to explode in flames. His face was red, his cheeks puffed out. If he'd had a gun Stachel would have ducked under his desk.

"Well, get the files together and bring them to my office. That's a priority."

"Instead of doing the status report?"

"Do the status report first, then the files. After that, I don't care what you do."

Gottlieb turned and left the office, muttering to himself and shaking his head. Well, I got rid of him for at least awhile, Stachel thought. He pulled a piece of paper out of the front drawer of this desk and wrote "status report" and the date at the top. But before he could start the update, Lakain came into the room holding a folded copy of the daily newspaper, *Das Reich*. He placed it on the desk, with the headline facing Stachel, and sat down. The headline was a lead article from Goebbels, in large Gothic letters, "Fighters For The Eternal Reich." More propaganda, more lies from the dwarf.

"Did you read this?" Lakain said, pointing at the article. "Goebbels says the Allies are in worse shape than us, that they cannot keep up the fight, that if we continue to fight, we will win."

"And you accept that?" Stachel couldn't believe what he was hearing. People would believe anything. The bigger the lie the more they believed. And Goebbels was a master at the big lie.

"Of course. Our leaders would not lie. We will win, as the Führer has always told us."

"Sit down," Stachel said, then realized that Lakain was already sitting. "What is written in the newspaper doesn't matter," and he grabbed it and dropped it in the trash bin. "All that matters is that we find this killer. That is our contribution to the war effort, to the glorious Reich."

Lakain shook his head in agreement. Stachel couldn't bear to look at him. The fool didn't even see the sarcasm. But what was he going to do? There wasn't a line of experience policemen waiting to be assigned as his partner. He had to do what he could with what he had. Like poker, a game Stachel had no interest in, you played the cards you were dealt.

"Did you find anything else? What about that Pantel guy?"

Lakain produced a folder, which he had been holding at his side, away from Stachel. "Yes, possibly some pretty good stuff."

"Well, let's have it. Give me a quick summary. I'll read your report later."

Lakain opened the folder and pulled out a piece of paper. "I already prepared a written summary. I figured you wouldn't want to look at the details."

"I always look at the details," Stachel said and snatched the paper from Lakain. He couldn't believe what he just heard. Lakain was basically saying that Stachel was lazy, that he was sloppy and careless. "We'll find the killer in the details. Give me a summary now and I'll read your *detailed* report later."

Stachel glanced at the summary. The title read "Notes from interview with Johann Pantel." He read the first paragraph quickly. Stachel was impressed. The report was typed, and it was obvious that his German grammar was good. Maybe Lakain was a fool, but at least he followed procedure and cared about what he was doing. That was more than you could say for anyone else in the Kripo these days. He took the folder from Lakain and placed the summary inside.

"Talk me through this."

"Pantel was in the military," Lakain said, "so I was able to view his military records. There was nothing in our files. And if there's anything with the Gestapo, I couldn't look at it."

Stachel motioned that he agreed. He didn't want Lakain getting involved with the Gestapo. That would only lead to more headaches. "How did you get the military files?"

"Let's just say I have a friend who owed me a favor."

"Ah, good man. There's nothing like having a friend in need." Definitely looking up, maybe he'd start calling Lakain Fritz, the nickname he used for Klein.

"Pantel was a decorated veteran of the Great War, had risen from a Private to Colonel, which I might add was not easy to do in an army that considered the aristocracy the only suitable people for officers."

"Please, leave out any opinions for now. Just the facts."

"OK." Lakain continued, perched at the end of the chair, his voice betraying how excited he was. "He was injured in the battle of Verdun and was in hospital when the war ended. In '24, he was reprimanded, though only a slap on the hand, for saying publicly that the military had been betrayed by the politicians and that Germany would have eventually won the war. The old stab in the back. He had advocated installing a military dictatorship and forcing all non-Germans to leave the country. He was quickly silenced by his superiors. Apparently, he kept his head down after that, since there was very little information from '24 on. He was never promoted after that but stayed in the army for another nineteen years. As far as I can figure out, he was not involved in any military matters since '33. He was stationed in Berlin, a high-level bureaucrat who was forgotten. He retired in May 1943."

Lakain looked up at Stachel with pleading eyes. "Can I give you my opinion now, I mean, my analysis?" Stachel motioned to continue.

"This seemed strange to me. Basically, in '24 Pantel had voiced some of the same views that Hitler used and that helped get him elected in '33. But he was never involved with the Nazis, kept his head down, a bureaucrat among bureaucrats, until he retired. Why didn't he say anything, why didn't he embrace the Nazis when the political climate changed to one more to his liking? Had his opinions changed? Or was there something else that made Pantel want to be forgotten?"

"Communist?" Stachel thought that something wasn't right here. Pantel was obviously doing something right back in the early twenties to get noticed and promoted so quickly. He says something that a lot of people were saying back then, and suddenly, he's pushed aside. But if he was forgotten by his superiors, pushed into a dead-end job, why did he stay in the military for the next twenty years? Why didn't he leave?

Lakain shook his head. "I don't think so. At least, there's nothing in the files about that."

"Was his retirement voluntary?"

"Officially yes. But remember, after the news came out about Stalingrad, the Führer did a house cleaning in the military and I think Pantel was finally forced out."

"Homosexual? Jewish blood somewhere in his past? That would explain why he wanted to stay unnoticed."

Lakain shook his head. "Probably not, but you never know."

"That's the only explanation that fits, but maybe it fits to well. I'm always leery of easy answers. There must be something else. But good job."

Stachel took the folder and placed it on the side of his desk. "So, Pantel might have motive. He probably hates the Nazis for forcing him out of the military. Maybe he wants to get even."

"But why now?" Lakain asked. "Why not back in '43?"

"Maybe he's been planning it for a while. And he thinks he's running out of time with the war about to end."

Lakain shook his head in agreement, then sat there silently, as though waiting for Stachel to say something else.

"Don't you have anything to tell me?" Lakain said.

"What would I have for you?"

"Holzer. Did you find anything?"

Stachel was taken aback for a minute. He didn't want to share anything with him. He didn't think of Lakain as his partner. He didn't have the experience. He was too young. Like it or not, he was for now his partner, maybe his last partner, but still, he couldn't keep him in the dark forever.

"I haven't written anything up yet, but yes, I did do some digging into him. It's all rumors, but I've learned that though rumors are usually negative, there's always some truth there."

"Except when we're talking about the Führer, and then the rumors are always positive."

"Our Führer is a lucky man." Lucky he's not dead, Stachel thought. "Regardless, about Holzer. His marriage was apparently breaking up. His wife might have been forced into giving those radio broadcasts a few months back and grew to resent it."

"Who told you that?"

"A fly on the wall. It doesn't matter. If the above is true, then maybe she was going to leave, head west and surrender to the Allies. That would embarrass Holzer."

"Enough to kill her?"

"Holzer doesn't seem like the killer type. More a mouse than a lion. But he certainly has the power to have her killed."

Lakain slid closer to the edge of his chair. "So what's next?"

"Talk to Holzer again, of course. Into the lion's den, or maybe just the mouse's den. But we need to be careful. Sometimes a mouse is more dangerous than a lion."

"Can I come along?"

What was this? At the murder scene, Lakain didn't want to get involved. Now he acts like he wants to take over. It wouldn't be a good idea to have him along. The next meeting with Holzer would be worse than the first. Stachel would have to confront him with the rumors, and he knew Holzer wouldn't take it nicely. Having Lakain there wouldn't help.

"No, let's continue our separate paths. Why don't you talk to Pantel again. See what he thinks of the Nazis. He must be angry at what happened to him. Draw him out. And make another round of the apartments. Maybe you'll get someone else to talk to you."

"OK, chief. I'm on it."

Lakain started for the door, but Stachel told him to stop. He took the one-page summary, wrote status report at the top, and handed it to him.

"Make two copies. Give one to Gottlieb and send the other over to the Gestapo, to a man named Plettner."

Stachel could tell that Lakain wanted to ask who Plettner was, but thought better of it, and left.

God, Stachel hated it when people called him chief. It sounded so official, made Stachel look like a man of authority, and that was the last thing Stachel wanted these days. Having authority got you killed.

Chapter Ten

As Lakain left the office, Stachel suddenly realized that he'd been meaning to contact his informer in the black market and had done nothing. He was losing his edge. With Gottlieb and Plettner breathing down his neck, Lakain's continued irrational belief in Hitler, thoughts of his wife, and above all the war, he was finding it very hard to stay focused. And his increased anxiety set his back off, a dull pain that wouldn't go away. Any attempts at stretching only seemed to make it worse.

Other the last few years most of his contacts within the *Schwarzmarkt*, the black market, had disappeared. But one informer, Stehen, was still around. Stachel had worked with him off and on for years now and found his information mostly creditable. The procedure was to dial a number and leave a message for Stehen to contact him. Then, usually within an hour, Stachel would return the call and arrange a meeting place. He made the call and left the message, telling the man who answered that it was urgent. The man said nothing beyond acknowledging the call and then quickly hanging up.

It was 6 pm and his stomach was growling. He hadn't eaten anything since the pastries that morning. And he needed to get more information on Holzer. Anything.

So, he called his friend, Hugo Baer, over at the Gestapo and asked if he'd like to meet for dinner. At first, Baer said no, saying that he was too busy, that things were crazy there. But Stachel persisted.

"The Café Wilhelm, you know it right?"

"Yes," Baer hesitated, "but what's the point? No one has decent food."

"Well, what I heard was that one of the army units deserted their barracks yesterday and left behind a cache of food. My landlady rushed there, along with everyone else in the area, but was too late. But she heard that the owner of the Café Wilhelm had gotten there first and left with a treasure trove of sausages and fresh potatoes. Fresh, Hugo, not the spoiled stuff they hand out as rations."

"Ok, let's say six thirty. And I'll get there early and pull rank and get us a table."

Stachel didn't like to hear that. Using your position in a collapsing government to get favors was dangerous. It didn't take much for a civilian to lash out these days. But before he could say anything, Baer hung up. He was going to call him back, but the phone rang, and it was Stehen. He'd meet Stachel tonight at ten, at the corner of Wilhelmstrasse and Behrenstrasse. There was an abandoned building at the corner. They'd meet inside.

The café was full of customers when Stachel got there. He paused at the front door to smell the freshly cooked sausages. The murmur of voices filled the room. People were all hunched over their food, whispering to each other. The sound of anxiety and fear, the sound of despair, of not knowing if there will be a tomorrow. At a side table sat Baer, a smile on his face, a plate of potatoes surrounding a nicely charred sauerbraten. Fortunately, he had the good sense to change into civilian clothes.

Baer was an old friend of Stachel's. He was forty-five, with reddish blond hair and ears that jutted out from his ruddy face.

Stachel sat down across from him and motioned to a waiter, an elderly man wearing a dirty apron, sporting a walrus size mustache that curled around his face. He asked for a menu and the waiter laughed.

"You get what he's got," the waiter said, pointing to Baer's plate.

Stachel said he wanted two sausages. The waiter grumbled and walked into the kitchen, returning a few minutes later with one poorly cooked sauerbraten and four red potatoes.

Stachel looked at the anemic food, pushing the sausage around like he was looking for insects. "My friend got six potatoes."

"We're running out. Be glad for what you got."

The waiter left. Stachel could see there was no use arguing.

"Hugo, how are you?" Stachel said, piercing a potato with his fork and chewing it slowly. It was indeed a fresh potato. The waxy taste melted in his mouth, bringing back memories of before the war, when food was assumed, when people thought positively of the future.

Baer didn't answer. He just sat there, taking small bites from his sausage, like he wanted it to last forever.

"Marlis and the kids, how are they?"

"Fine as can be these days."

Stachel leaned over and whispered. "Can't you get them out? Send them west, away from the Russians."

"I've tried. I went to the department, filled out the paperwork, saying that my wife was needed by relatives. But the paperwork somehow got noticed by Himmler, who immediately denied my request. That's considered defeatist talk. Of course, all Himmler seems to talk about, when he's not screaming about spies, is retreating to the south, to what he calls the Alpine Fortress."

"Is that actually going to happen? The Golden Pheasants are all going to run away and leave everyone to their fate?"

"Who knows? Supposedly the Führer is against it, but it's hard to know what's true anymore. These people seem to think there's some magic that's going to send us back in time to 1940."

They ate silently for the next few minutes, the subject they both wanted to discuss and avoid lingering between them. Finally, Baer leaned across the table, almost touching his food with his shirt, and whispered to Stachel.

"So, what happened? I assume it went alright or I would have heard something."

"Went fine. No one saw me. But did I get anything. I don't know. Maybe."

"Maybe? Out with it. I presume that's why you asked me to dinner."

Stachel pushed at his food with his fork, unsure if he wanted to involve Baer any further. It was dangerous and he couldn't live with himself if something happened to him. But then again, did it matter when the whole world had been turned upside down. They would both surely be arrested by the Allies and tried as members of a criminal government.

The people at the table next to them stood up and made a noisy exit. Immediately, two men in Wehrmacht officer uniforms sat down. One raised his hand and clicked his fingers, banging on the table with his other hand. They obviously expected to be treated as special and not ignored. Within a few weeks, they'll wish they were being ignored, Stachel thought.

The waiter came over, apologized, his voice trembling, and said that they had just run out of sausages. But they could have as many potatoes as they liked. The officer stood up and put his hand on the waiter's shoulder.

"Well, we expect you to find some, don't we? Unless you want us to close this place."

"Does it matter? After today, we won't have anything to sell, so we might as well be closed."

"Get some sausages, now." The officer sat down and smiled across at his companion.

The waiter fled into the kitchen and quickly returned with two plates, with twice as many potatoes as Stachel or Baer had gotten, and one pale sausage to share between the two men. He set the plates down on the table and hurried off, not waiting for any response. They whispered something to each other, shrugged their shoulders, laughed, and started eating.

Stachel had been watching the scene and didn't say anything to Baer before he was confident that the officers were busy with their meals and wouldn't be listening.

"That murder investigation I mentioned yesterday. It's Sophie Holzer. I was looking at the files on her and her husband."

"August Holzer? You're asking for trouble. Don't you have enough these days?"

"Plenty." Stachel looked at the soldiers and grimaced. "There's one thing I'd like you to look into. In the Holzer file, there was a note mentioning a rumor that Sophie Holzer was thinking of fleeing Berlin and surrendering to the Allies."

"Who wrote it?"

"It didn't say. And there was nothing more, so I assume no one followed up on the rumor."

"Could be," Baer said, tipping his head to the side. "Could be they did look into it and whatever they found was too sensitive to write down."

"Can you find out? Was it a baseless rumor or was it true? And if true, did August Holzer know about it?"

"And have his wife killed? Is that what this leads to?"

"It gives him motive."

Baer leaned back and looked over at the officers. They were still eating, ignoring everyone around them.

"Can I give you some advice? Lay low, stay alive, stay away from people like Holzer. People are starting to panic, acting like wild animals, and they'll lash out at anyone who frightens them."

"I can't do that," Stachel said, shaking his head. "I'm looking into the black market angle also, but my gut tells me that Holzer is involved in some way. And wouldn't it be nice to see someone like Holzer arrested."

"He's going to be arrested in a few weeks anyway. What does it matter? Besides, even if Hitler or Goebbels arrests him, they'll also arrest you for embarrassing them. You know they're both in denial right now. Bringing them back to reality won't be appreciated."

"You haven't answered my question. Will you help? Will you check on the rumor?"

"I'll do what I can, but don't expect much. Right now, everyone is busy chasing defeatists and saboteurs."

"Not everyone. Goebbels and Himmler are afraid that Sophie Holzer's murder is the beginning of an uprising. They got Plettner involved. I have to send him a status report every day."

"Plettner's involved? He's too busy kissing up to Himmler, looking for a promotion. He still thinks Germany will win the war."

"Well, then he's a fool."

"Yes, but a dangerous fool. I wouldn't mention your suspicions about Holzer in your reports."

"If I did that, I'd be a bigger fool than him. Do what you can, let me know if you find anything. I need to know quickly if Holzer's involved or if I'm wasting my time."

Baer noticed that one of the officers had stopped eating. He stopped talking and focused on his food, which had gotten cold. They finished their meals in silence. Stachel paid the bill, which was more than he made in a month. But he didn't care. Reich marks were going to be completely worthless within a few weeks.

The building where he was to meet Stehen was in complete ruin and looked like all it needed was a breath of air to send it crashing to the ground.

Stachel never knew his informer's real name, though he didn't really care. As long as Stehen got him information, he preferred not to know.

Stehen was a short man, a little over five feet tall, dirty, with stringy black hair hung down pass his ears like web noodles. But you could tell from the fullness of his face that he was eating well, or at least better than the majority of Germans. Stehen was in the back of the building, as far away from the street as possible, hiding in the shadows. He came out only when he was sure no one else was with Stachel. He was ill at ease, dancing back and forth on his feet, looking over Stachel's shoulder to Wilhelmstrasse.

"You've heard about the woman, Holzer?" Stachel said.

"I heard a rumor that someone important had been murdered. So what? People are dying every day. It's about time someone from the party joined in the festivities."

"Remember those broadcasts urging women and children to come to the defense of Berlin?"

"Stupid idea. Basically, our beloved Führer is letting everyone know how desperate he is, how badly the war is going, despite what the poison dwarf says."

Well, the woman murdered was Sophie Holzer and she's the one who gave those broadcasts."

"And that's why she was killed?"

"I don't know. I don't think so. She had met with someone from the black market just before she was killed."

"And you think that's who killed her?" Stehen shook his head and stuffed his hands in his worn overcoat. "Why someone from the black market? Why do you treat people as criminals who are helping get food to the people? They're the real patriots these days, not the damn government."

"I didn't say she was killed by someone in the black market. Only that she met someone before she was killed. I'm just pursuing all angles right now. She was carrying a parcel of food. Stuff that could only have come from the black market. I need you to find out who she met with. That person might have seen something."

"How much?" Stehen asked.

"100 Reich marks."

Stehen shook his head. "Money is useless. Two packs of cigarettes. One before I start checking around, one when I tell you what I found."

"I thought you were a patriot. Can't do this for the Fatherland?"

"To hell with the Fatherland. Survival is all that matters now."

Stachel reached into his pocket and pulled out a packet of Trommler cigarettes and tossed them to Stehen.

"I want American, not this German shit." He gave the cigarettes back to Stachel.

"Sorry, not possible anymore." Stachel held the cigarettes out, waving them in front of Stehen. "This is all we get these days. Take it or leave it."

Stehen thought for a minute, then grabbed the cigarettes. "OK, though if I hear that the police are hoarding American cigarettes, the deal's off. Give me a few days. I'll call you when I'm ready to meet again."

Chapter Eleven

Since Goebbels's house on Herman-Göring-Strasse in Berlin had been heavily bombed, he had split his time between his Bogensee villa north of Berlin and a villa on the island of Schwanenwerder, near Wannsee, southwest of Berlin. Now that Goebbels had moved his family into the *Vorbunker*, Stachel assumed the villas were empty.

Schwanenwerder was a small island and very exclusive, filled with large estates huddled around the waterfront, most stolen from Jews in the '30's. Since there was no available real estate on the island, Holzer had a house as close to his boss as possible, in the suburb of Wannsee, on the mainland, just south of the island. From his house, Holzer could peer out across the river to the island and wonder what the rich and powerful did when relaxing. It had to grate on him that Goebbels hadn't pulled any strings to get him a place there. It was a slap in the face. Goebbels way of telling him that though high up in the Nazi echelon, he was still considered an inferior.

Stachel had to requisition a car from the Kripo carpool. He encountered some resistance, being asked to explain why he wanted the car, how long he would have it, and that he would have to refill the petrol tank before returning it. Stachel explained that he had a meeting with August Holzer at his retreat south of the city, but that he couldn't possibly refill the petrol. The man said that nevertheless, he had to refill it. Stachel gave in, said he would, and figured he'd deal with the problem when he returned the car. Good German bureaucracy. Oblivious to reality.

A light rain was falling as he slowly drove his car through the city, looking for streets that were not blocked by debris. Not use to seeing cars anymore, people constantly crossed the street in front of him, figuring he must be high up in the Nazi government and it was their silent way of telling him that the public still existed, that their lives still mattered. Three times Stachel had to suddenly brake to avoid hitting someone.

At a checkpoint before leaving the city he had to show a letter he received the other day from Holzer giving him permission to leave the city. Holzer's name obviously carried some weight since he breezed through the checkpoint with only a superficial glance.

Once out of the city, he thought briefly of heading west, escaping, now was his chance. But that would be running away, and he wasn't going to do that anymore.

The autobahn, constantly bombed but quickly patched, was empty and Stachel made relatively good time, slowing down to avoid craters. But then he got lost in Wannsee. He knew the house was on the water, so he figured once off the autobahn, he would just head for the water and drive along the Uferpromeade until he found the house. But he turned left when he should have turned right, so he got lost and it took him thirty minutes to find his way back to the Uferpromeade. From there, within a few minutes he easily found the house.

Holzer's house abetted the River Havel, with a clear view across the river. Off to the left, you could see the town of Kladow. By the time Stachel got there, the rain had stopped, the clouds were parting, and the sun was peeking through, shining down on the house like it was the home of a God. Valhalla, Stachel thought, the home of the dead.

Stachel pulled around the long, curved gravel driveway and got out at the front door. A servant came out and silently pointed off to the right, to a small car park labeled for servants. Stachel thought of ignoring him and leaving the car where it was, then decided it wasn't going to do him any good to antagonize the servants, so he got back in and parked the car where he was supposed to. The servant was still standing there when he got back, a small man who's tanned skin matched the color of his coat His hands clasped behind his back, he looked at Stachel as though he was vermin.

"I'm here to see Reichsleiter Holzer."

"Are you expected? I was not informed that there would be any visitors today." The servant stared at Stachel with a cold, penetrating gaze, as though he was the owner of the house and Stachel was a vagrant.

"I'm expected. I was told to be here at ten." He held the letter out to the servant, who looked at it as though it must be fake.

"It's now ten forty-five. You're late."

"I got lost. Are you going to let me in. Or are you going to stand out here working on your tan?"

Keeping his gaze on him the whole time, the servant stepped to the side and motioned Stachel inside. He was led into the living room and told to wait.

The room had to be three times the size of Stachel's one bedroom apartment. There were two cream colored sofas in the center, facing each other, with a coffee table in the middle with salmon colored dolphin motifs. Floor to ceiling windows to the left and right looked out on the river, and between the windows, above a fireplace, was a giant picture of Hitler, arm raised, hand on his belt. On the left wall were smaller pictures of Goebbels, Göring and Himmler. All in military uniforms, all looking stern and gazing into the future, like powerful, all-knowing leaders building the future. The right wall was festooned with various pictures. While waiting, Stachel walked over and gazed at various photos of Holzer with dignitaries, mostly fellow Nazis, but also with famous civilians like Charles Lindberg.

Stachel threw his hat on a side table and sat down at one of the sofas. He had to wait a good twenty minutes before a door on the left was opened by a servant and Holzer walked in, accompanied by a SS soldier.

"My secretary," he said. "I want to ensure that this conversation is properly documented." Holzer sat down on the sofa across from Stachel, crossing his legs and resting his hands in his lap. He was dressed in another brown, double-breasted jacket. Again, trying to ape Goebbels. His secretary sat a small desk against the wall in the corner.

"Why?" he said, staring across at Stachel, mirroring the gaze of the servant who answered the door.

"Excuse me?" Stachel said. He could smell the aroma of coffee, real coffee, coming from somewhere in the house. He thought how nice it would be to taste a real cup of coffee, not the ersatz, watery liquid that was available now.

"Why are you here? I don't understand this visit. You should be out catching this killer, not wasting your time talking to me. And in case you haven't figured it out, there's a war on. My time is consumed with uniting the people to prepare for the defense of the city."

'Yes, well, to catch the murderer I need to know as much as I can about the victim." Stachel looked down at the coffee table and saw an ashtray full of cigarette butts, and they looked like American cigarettes, not the garbage cardboard that was sold in the market. "For instance, your wife gave some radio speeches back in February and March asking women and children to take up arms and defend the Fatherland. What did she think of those speeches?"

Holzer uncrossed his legs and pulled a cigarette out of his coat. He held it in his hand without lighting it, as Stachel stared at the cigarette, wishing he would be offered one. "What do you mean, what did she think? She was doing her part for the war effort, to help Germany defeat our enemies."

"But was she comfortable doing them? And why did she stop? To my knowledge, she gave no more speeches after middle March."

"That first question is stupid and I will ignore it. She stopped because other duties took precedent."

"What other duties?"

"Other duties that do not concern you."

This conversation is going badly, Stachel thought. He's evading every question. Though he knew there was no going back, he had to confront Holzer, had to get him angry in hopes that he would say something he didn't intent.

"I've heard that your wife was forced to give those speeches, that she regretted doing them, and that she was getting ready to flee to the west."

Holzer turned around and told his secretary not to write down anything from now on. He turned back to Stachel, putting his cigarette carefully on the coffee table. "If you're implying that my wife had given up on Germany, then I think our conversation is at an end."

"I'm not implying anything. I'm just stating a rumor I heard."

"There are a lot of rumors right now, mostly false. Rumors are the fodder of fools. Are you a fool, Herr Stachel?"

Stachel noticed he hadn't used his title. To the Nazis, not having a military title meant you were nothing.

"Isn't it your job to create rumors?"

"My job is to inform the people of the truth so they don't panic."

"I'm sorry to inform you, but they're panicking."

"Then they are fools. We will win the war, of that I am certain."

Stachel was biting his tongue not to say anything. Did the man believe his own lies? The Nazis refused to accept the reality of what they had created, a defeated and destroyed country. This is what happens to a country when its government believes its own lies.

"You haven't answered my question. Was your wife planning to flee?" Stachel could tell he had Holzer riled now. The signs were all there. His hands were clasped tightly together to prevent them from shaking, his face was flushed, his eyes barely blinked. The cigarette on the coffee table forgotten. He spoke slowly, eyes riveted on Stachel.

"It is because of people like you that the war effort is not going well…"

"So you admit that the war is lost. That contradicts what you just said."

"Not at all. The war is not going well, but we will win, nevertheless. The Führer has not given up. We have excellent information that the Americans and British are about to turn on the Bolsheviks and join us in our struggle against eastern barbarism."

"I've heard that rumor too. What was that you said? That rumors are false?"

"This is going nowhere. You are obviously trying to bait me. Don't bother. I've dealt with people for years who are far better at it than you."

"You still haven't answered my question. Was your wife planning to flee to the west?"

Holzer uncrossed his legs and leaned forward. "No." He then leaned back and re-crossed his legs.

"That's it? Can you elaborate?"

"It's a stupid question. Of course, she wasn't going to flee. She was loyal to the Third Reich, loyal to the Fatherland."

"Then why was she carrying five thousand U.S. dollars?"

Holzer looked over at his secretary and motioned for him to leave the room. He waited until the secretary had left and closed the door.

"It seems I am not being clear enough with you. I repeat. This line of questioning will get you nowhere. It's a waste of my time. I have no idea where she would have gotten it, or why. I believe that the money was planted, either by her murderer or by the police."

Stachel pointed at his chest. "You mean me?"

"You can infer what you want."

"Well, I don't like the inference, *Herr* Holzer." And he could see that he had probably lost his chance to get Holzer riled up. Instead, he was the one who was growing angry. Holzer had calmed down and now looked relaxed. Like he was in control and was about to spring a trap.

"*Herr* Stachel. Are we done here? I fail to see how these questions are going to catch the killer. I have told you that she had not given up on the Fatherland, that she was not fleeing. That line of inquiry will get you nowhere. We know it was a robbery. If you can't solve this murder, just say so. We will put someone else on the case. Someone more competent."

"I don't like to brag, but there isn't anyone more competent right now."

"There's always someone," Holzer said with a wave of his hand. He sat back on the sofa, calm now. "Now, what about this Pantel? Have you arrested him? Have you brought him in for questioning?"

So that was the trap. Gottlieb or Plettner must have called Holzer after reading the status report. That could only mean trouble.

"He's a person of interest, nothing more. We have no reason to suspect that he had anything to do with the murder."

"But you haven't even brought him in for questioning. So how can you know that?"

"Instinct. Experience. Label it whatever you want, but I don't think Pantel killed your wife."

"I'm not interested in instinct. Bring him in, now."

Stachel had had enough. The man was intruding on his investigation and that he would not allow. This was his investigation, and he would make the decisions, not some bureaucrat who had lost his hold on reality. Stachel had never let anyone tell him what to do, had never let anyone make decisions for him. And he wasn't going to allow it now. Let them take him off the case. If Holzer didn't care in the end who killed his wife, why should Stachel? Lies serving as the truth once again.

Stachel grabbed his hat and stood up. "I'm sorry, but that order must come from my superiors. Bring it up with Himmler, if you can find him."

Holzer also stood. "Better yet, I'll talk to Gottlieb. He'll do what I want, and I trust you will to, since you report to him."

"You'll find I'm not very good at following orders." Stachel turned and headed for the front door. The servant from before suddenly appeared and stepped in front of him. Stachel pushed him aside and went out the door. Holzer remained silent. Getting in his car, he drove out of the estate quickly, before anyone could try and stop him.

Now he had done it. Though making Holzer angry had been enjoyable, Stachel knew it was only going to bring him more grief. He should never have sent Lakain's status report to Gottlieb and Plettner, a status report that had details about Patel. That was stupid. He should have gone through the report and taken out anything he didn't want Plettner to see. The less information these people knew, the better. It was the way Stachel had always operated. Everything he did on an investigation was on a need to know basis, and right now no one needed to know.

Had Gottlieb made Lakain his spy? Lakain was young enough that he would do whatever he was told to do. Stachel knew these thoughts would only lead to paranoia. He needed to get involved in everything now, not leave anything to Lakain. This afternoon he had to finish his interviews at Holzer's school. Then he needed to get to Pantel quickly, before the Gestapo got involved, and after this morning, he assumed they would. Find out what he knew. He didn't give Pantel much chance to make it through the night.

Chapter Twelve

Returning the car ended up taking more time then he had planned. There had been an explosion and a building near the station was in rubble and on fire. The fire department had not arrived, so nearby residents had started a queue, handing pails of water from the local water pump to try and dose the fire. It was a useless exercise. But between the rubble and the people in queue, Stachel's route was blocked. Trying to find another street that wasn't blocked took him over an hour. Eventually Stachel gave up and parked the car a few blocks from the station. At the main desk, he handed the office the keys and told him where the car was, wishing him good luck getting it back to the garage.

It was past noon. Stachel needed to review his notes and think through what he wanted to accomplish before meeting with Pantel. And he knew he needed to evade Gottlieb. Maybe his day would get better. It couldn't get worse.

But just as he got to his office, and thought he was safe and his luck had changed, it got worse. Gottlieb yelled to him from down the hall and was soon pushing Stachel into his office and closing the door. Motioning to Stachel to sit in the guest chair, Gottlieb sat at Stachel's desk. Stachel badly needed a drink. This was not going to be good.

"What's up boss?" he said, trying to sound as though nothing was wrong.

Gottlieb played with a pen on the desk, spinning it around a few times, then flipping it in the air and catching it, looking happy as a parrot chirruping a song.

"You've been busy today. I haven't seen you in the office. Where have you been?"

Obviously, a rhetorical question, Stachel had no intention of playing Gottlieb's game.

"You know where I've been."

"Yes, I do. Reichsleiter Holzer just called, and he was quite angry, calling you names which I don't need to mention. He wanted you off the case and I'm inclined to agree with him. But despite my better judgment, I talked him into keeping you on with the understanding that you'd show progress within the next day. And that you'd stop questioning him."

"Given that he doesn't answer my questions truthfully, that doesn't matter."

"He wants Pantel brought in for questioning. Which I thought you were going to do, at least that's the impression I got from Lakain."

So Lakain was feeding information to Gottlieb. That would stop or Lakain would be off the case. He'd go it alone, as he had for the last two years.

"Lakain doesn't know what's going on. He does what I tell him to do. Getting information from Lakain is like getting information from *Das Reich*."

"And what's wrong with *Das Reich*? It's better than the lies the Allies are spreading. I have to believe what's written there. Not believing is to admit we will lose the war."

Gottlieb now looked worried. Clutching his hands together, he shook them up and down, like he was cradling a secret that was trying to escape.

Here he was, antagonizing Gottlieb. Stachel could only shake his head at his own stupidity. He was only hurting himself. Sometimes it was better to believe in lies.

"I take that back. It was stupid of me. Of course, you are right. But regardless, you should get your information from me, not Lakain. He's an inexperienced boy who doesn't know anything. I give him tasks, but I don't fill him in on the whole investigation."

Gottlieb ignored what he said. "Are you going to bring Pantel in? This is very important to Goebbels. He's asking me for updates every day, sometimes twice a day, and isn't happy that I have nothing to report. And when Goebbels isn't happy, unpleasant things happen. And now, because of you, I've also got Holzer breathing down my neck."

"He can't do anything. Himmler isn't going to let Goebbels stir the soup in his pot."

"Himmler won't have a choice if the Führer hears about it. And you know that Goebbels is very close to the Führer, closer than Himmler right now."

Every discussion these days always came back to the Führer. Hitler was either used as a threat or as salvation. He was either the kind and wise father who cared for his children, or a ruthless dictator who would not let anyone stop him from getting his way.

"I was just about to go talk to Pantel. Remember, he's a decorated war veteran. How would it look to the military if we arrested a veteran?"

"A veteran that no one cares about anymore," Gottlieb said with a wave of his hand. "He was thrown out of the military in '43."

"Was he thrown out, or did he quit?"

"I have been told that he was thrown out."

"By whom?"

"Generalfeldmarschall Keitel, of course." Stachel knew Gottlieb was lying. He had no access to Keitel. He was a low level bureaucrat who only had his position because there was no one else. And he was safe because he paraded his loyalty to the party to anyone who would listen. Stachel choose not to call him on it. It wasn't going to change anything.

"Look, I'm going to talk to Pantel right now. If I don't like his answers, I'll bring him in. But I want to keep him away from the Gestapo. They'll only torture the man, get a false confession, and execute him."

Gottlieb leaned across the desk, which made Stachel lean back in his chair.

"I said bring him in. We can interrogate him here. If you don't, I can't prevent the Gestapo from taking over." Gottlieb stood up, saw that Hitler's picture was crooked, straightened it, and left the office.

Stachel bent his head and rubbed his eyes, wishing he could wipe out any memory of Gottlieb. The man was a fool, a *handlanger,* a party stooge with no authority. Maybe Gottlieb wanted Stachel to believe he was in charge, but Stachel knew that Goebbels and Holzer were now in control.

Johann Pantel lived on the ground floor of the apartment building across the plaza from where Sophie Holzer was killed. The building was pockmarked from shrapnel. There were huge cracks in the foundation, running up the side of the building. It was slowly collapsing from the constant shaking of the bombs. Looking at the building from the plaza, Stachel noticed that about a third of the windows did not have blackout screens. That had to mean that those apartments were empty. If they weren't, the occupants would have been arrested immediately. The front door was hanging at an angle, the top hinge broken. The door wobbled when Stachel opened it, like the entrance to a haunted house. The foyer floor was covered in black and white tiles. Someone had scratched small swastikas into every black tile. Someone else had scratched out some of the swastikas, but evidentially had given up. Maybe someone in the apartment was thinking ahead and didn't want the Allies to think there were any remaining Nazi sympathizers in the building.

Pantel's apartment was to the left, the second door down the hallway. Stachel knocked and when he didn't get an answer, banged at the door with his fist, yelling out that it was the police. Only then did he hear a shuffling from inside.

Gestapo tactics, he thought, and was ashamed.

The door opened a crack and a tired, blinking eye peered out. A gruff voice that sounded like a car that wouldn't start asked Stachel for identification. He flipped his badge out and thrust it at the eye, telling him to open the door immediately.

"Or what? What more can you do to me?" Pantel said, opening the door and stepping back into the room. He turned his back on Stachel and on slippered feet walked over to a worn chair and sat down.

Pantel looked like a man who'd been beaten down by time, a discarded symbol of everything the Nazis had done to the country. He was a tall man, over six feet, but his frail body made him look smaller. He wore dirty wool trousers and a white shirt that was frayed at the edges. The apartment was small. Two chairs, a sofa near the window that fronted the plaza, a small bookcase with three shelves, full of books with visible creases on the spines. The walls were decorated with framed pictures and military metals. But there was no picture of Hitler, no symbols of the Third Reich. Taking a glance at the books, Stachel couldn't see a copy of *Mein Kampt*. That alone would make you a defeatist to the Gestapo.

"So you're an inspector in the Kripo," Pantel said, motioning to the sofa.

"Yes, since the twenties."

"You might be old enough. Fought in the last war?"

"No."

Stachel could tell from the disappointed look in Pantel's eye that he had just failed a test. Another man whose whole life had been caught up in the Great War and was lost after Germany's defeat. Stachel walked over and sat down on the sofa across from Pantel.

"It was a good war, not like this one. We were defending our country. Nothing more noble. And I'm sorry. I would offer you something to drink, but I have nothing. You'd think the government would take care of us veterans. Instead, we've been thrown out like so much rubbish."

Stachel had some sympathy for the man but given what the military had done recently made it difficult. The military's role was to kill, nothing more.

"I've already talked to someone from the Kripo," Pantel continued. "I'm afraid I have nothing more to add."

"Yes, I've read the report. You said you were asleep the night of the murder and didn't hear or see anything."

"Correct."

"But isn't that unusual? Not your normal routine. We've heard that you are up at night and sleep during the day."

Pantel looked at Stachel with beaded eyes. He leaned forward, gripping the chair with spidery hands that shook with anger. "Who told you that? It's a lie."

"Is it?" Stachel shook his head and looked down at the table between them. There was a small statue of Frederick the Great in the middle. He grabbed it, turned it around in his hand and then placed it back down. "I don't think so. I think you saw something but don't want to tell us. Why is that?"

"I saw nothing. Is that what we've come to? Harassing people who served their country honorable while letting criminals run free. Hitler screams that he follows in the footsteps of Frederick the Great, yet he could only follow so that he could shine his shoes. The King of Prussia would never have allowed veterans to be treated like this."

Stachel let out a sigh, twisting his hat around, feeling like he was talking to Holzer's clone. Once again, he was getting nowhere.

"Herr Pantel, we're trying to catch this killer, but we can't do it if no one will help us."

"And why should I help? Seems to me it's a good thing to kill a few Nazis these days. That idiot Hitler promised us everything. He's destroyed our country. We'll now become part of the Bolshevik empire. They'll take over Europe."

Stachel stood up and put his hat on.

"If you won't talk to me here, I'll have to take you in. Maybe some time in a jail cell will change your mind."

"I'm in jail now. Look at this room," Pantel said, standing up halfway and waving his hands frantically. "This is all I have now. I gave my life to this country and it gave me this. Living under the Bolsheviks can't be worse."

Pantel collapsed back in the chair, wiping his brow with a shaking hand. He started to sob. Stachel sat back down and waited.

Pantel continued, his voice hushed now, tears coming down his eyes, as though he was witnessing his impending death.

"I heard a noise. I went to the window but all I saw was a shadow leaning over something. It could have been a body, I don't know. Whether it was the murderer or someone who came there afterwards, I don't know. And that's the truth. That's all I know."

"Why didn't you tell us earlier?"

"I didn't want to get involved. Staying away from all of you is the best way to survive these days." Pantel looked up at Stachel and tried to control his sobbing. "I used to be somebody you know, someone important. Then the Nazis came and threw me out. Why should I do anything to help them?"

"Because you're not," Stachel said. "You're helping me, and I'm not a Nazi."

"You're a policeman in a criminal government. You're not upholding justice. You're helping to destroy it. And why wasn't the murder mentioned in that rag that Goebbels publishes? Maybe another death doesn't mean anything these days. I heard it was someone important. It must be or you wouldn't be spending so much time on it. Whatever is important to the Nazis is no concern of mine."

"It's important to me. Why Goebbels doesn't publish anything doesn't interest me. It's my job to catch killers and I'm going to catch this one."

"The Red Army will be here any day now. You don't have much time."

"Then help me catch this killer. You're right, time is running out."

Pantel got up and walked over to his wall of photographs, turning his back on Stachel, running his right hand down the wall, tapping on some of the pictures. "As I said, I was important once. But no longer, and I no longer care about this country. It used me and spat me out, so now I spit back. I've told you everything I know. Taking me in won't change anything. I saw a shadow, nothing more."

"How tall? Thin or fat?"

"Normal height," Pantel said, talking to the wall. "Around five eight or so. Probably thin, but he probably was wearing an overcoat, so I can't be sure."

Stachel stared at Pantel's back. He couldn't decide if Pantel was a witness, and a poor one at that, or a suspect. He certainly had no love of the Nazis, which gave him motive. Stachel had always felt that when a witness wouldn't look at you, it meant he was hiding something. But Stachel had a hard time believing that he was the murderer. Pantel was too old, too frail. It took strength to strangle someone. The murderer had to be someone younger, someone filled with rage at the Nazis. Pantel's rage was all spent out.

He couldn't see any reason to bring Pantel in for further questioning. He had to follow his instincts. That's all he had. He refused to let the threat of the Gestapo influence his decisions.

"Don't go anywhere," Stachel said. "Stay in Berlin. I may need to talk to you again. Do you understand?"

"Where would I go? Hitler has declared Berlin one of his fortresses and refuses to let any of us leave. And what if I try and leave. What can you do? If our government doesn't kill us, the Russians will."

"Perhaps. I'm not going to debate with you, not now, but stay where I can find you."

After leaving Pantel's apartment, Stachel headed back to his office. What was he to do now? Holzer wanted proof that Stachel was getting somewhere with the case, wanted suspects. How could he convince him that Pantel wasn't a suspect? He should have told Pantel to hide, but then there would be a feeding frenzy when they found out that he had disappeared, and that frenzy would eventually turn to Stachel. He would be replaced, and the Gestapo would take over. And he was convinced if that happened that the real killer would never be caught. But he asked himself again, why did he care? He hated the regime, felt they were getting what they deserved, and had no sympathy for Sophie Holzer. Let them all die. Yet, he couldn't give in to vigilante justice. That would invalidate everything he had done in his life. If he believed in Germany, believed that Germany still had a future, then he owed it to his country to continue with the case and catch this killer. And he was running out of time.

Chapter Thirteen

He had no sooner hung his hat on Hitler's picture then Lakain was at the door.

"What now?" Stachel said as he took off his overcoat and threw it on the one guest chair. Lakain immediately took the coat and hung it up, then sat down and started talking, not waiting for Stachel to get settled.

"I thought I was in charge of Pantel? You were looking into Holzer and I was looking into Pantel. That was your instructions. Now I hear from Sturmbannführer Gottlieb that you just saw him."

"Correct, I did. Plans changed. I wasn't aware that I needed to consult with you before I do anything."

Lakain looked down at the ground, upset over the reprimand. "You know I didn't mean it that way. I thought you approved of the way I was handling Pantel. Now it seems you don't."

"You were doing fine. But we're getting pressured to bring in a suspect. I decided that I needed to talk to him directly and decide once and for all if he was."

"And is he? Something's not right. He's not telling us something."

"And so you went and told Gottlieb that. Good work. Gottlieb told Holzer and Goebbels, and now I'm being ordered to bring Pantel in for interrogation. Immediately. It's a right mess you've created."

"But he came to me yesterday and demanded to know what was going on. I told him he should talk to you and he said he couldn't find you. What else could I do?"

Stachel let out a sigh, rubbing his eyes and wishing he could be done with Lakain. Have him reassigned. He was too junior, too inexperienced, Gottlieb would always be able to use him to get information and use it to force Stachel's hand. The less Lakain knew, the better. But then, the less he knew, the less useful he'd be in the investigation. Stachel was damned either way.

"To answer your question," Stachel said, "no, I don't think Pantel's the killer. He doesn't look like he could do much more than slap someone. He's spent, demoralized, like everyone else he wants to keep his head down and survive."

Lakain shifted in his seat and looked up at the picture of Hitler. "But in a rage, a killer can do just about anything, and this killer must have been in a rage. Why else would he stab an already dead victim so many times?"

"Remember, Uhl said the knife wounds didn't appear to be from someone in a rage." Stachel thought of telling Lakain about what Pantel had seen, about a shadow hovering over the body. But eventually Lakain would tell Gottlieb, who would assume Pantel was lying, and then he would have the mess he was trying to avoid.

"Look," Stachel said, running his hand across his desk as though he was wiping some debris to the floor. "You have to stop talking to people about the case. We have to keep control of the investigation and that means keeping prying eyes away."

"Even Gottlieb?"

"Especially Gottlieb. I will keep him informed of what he needs to know."

"But that puts me in an awkward spot. He keeps asking me what's going on. I have to say anything."

"Tell him to talk to me and then get away as fast as you can."

"What if he orders me?"

"Tell him you don't really know the details of the case and, again, he should talk to me. That you just do what I tell you."

"Makes me look like kind of an idiot."

Well spoken, Stachel thought.

"I don't want to look like an idiot to the boss," Lakain continued. "If he thinks I'm an idiot, I'll never get anywhere in the force."

"Get anywhere? Within a few weeks there won't be any police force."

Why did so many Germans refuse to accept reality when all around them was the evidence of their defeat? Yet the poison dwarf, Goebbels, kept feeding them lies and they kept lapping them up. Faith in the Führer was what Stachel kept hearing. Faith was just wishful thinking. Accepting something based on nothing because the reality was unacceptable. I want to believe because I want to believe. Like people who followed a religion because they couldn't accept their own mortality.

"The Führer has plans..." Lakain started to say, but Stachel cut him off.

"Forget the Führer. He's not going to help us solve this case and that's the only thing you should be thinking about right now."

It was getting late and Stachel was tired, and when he was tired, he knew he didn't make good decisions. Better to go home, hope he got some sleep tonight, pray that the British for one night would take pity on Germany.

"It's late. Get some sleep. Let's meet tomorrow morning. And stay away from Gottlieb." Stachel went to grab his coat, but Lakain stopped him.

"I forgot to mention. Your sister-in-law, Frau Traupe, was looking for you. She seemed upset but wouldn't tell me anything."

"That's another thing you can do," Stachel said as he put on his coat. "Keep her away from me. Tell her I've fled to the west, tell her I joined the Russian army, tell her I'm dead. I don't care, just get rid of her if she comes by again."

Lakain started to protest, but Stachel quickly left, ignoring him.

On his way home, Stachel stopped at a queue and walked away a half hour later with a few moldy potatoes and some turnips. They were out of the daily meat ration. A year ago, he would have thrown them in the garbage. Now they looked like a delicacy.

He had stopped locking his apartment door, since there was nothing to steal inside, so he just kicked it open, letting it bang against the wall. He was surprised to find that the lights were working and that he had running water. But alas, no hot water. He would have loved a hot shower. By the time he cooked the potatoes, the lights had gone out, so he ate in the dark, slowly chewing to prolong the moment, trying to decide what to do with Lakain. And what to do about Holzer.

Chapter Fourteen

Finally, after two days of steady drizzle, the rain let up and Stachel was able to walk to the Alex without pulling up his collar, or cursing the fact that he had forgotten his hat. The rain had helped to wash away some of the debris off the streets, but small pockets of fire still burned, giving off a trail of gray smoke that curled up to the sky, alerting the Allies that they didn't need to bomb that area again, it was already destroyed. That wouldn't stop the British. Too often, they dropped their bombs as soon as they got over the city, not caring where they landed, and then ran. With the clearing clouds, he knew the Allies would be back in force. The rain never let up, it just changed from water to bombs.

As Stachel took the stairs to the second floor, he could hear the murmur of excited voices. Something had undoubtedly happened. He prayed it was the death of Hitler.

One of the secretaries ran by, yelling down the hallway to Gottlieb, who was about to turn into his office. "They found him, they found him."

Stachel reached for the secretary's arm but she was already by him. He followed her into Gottlieb's office. Gottlieb was behind his desk, dialing the phone. He looked up at Stachel and grinned.

"Yes, it's true," Gottlieb said. "Finally, something has turned our way."

"What's true?"

There was a gleam in Gottlieb's eyes as he realized he knew something Stachel didn't. "Pantel. The Gestapo went to his apartment last night to arrest him and found him gone. They've been searching all night and have just found him. Hiding like a rat in one of the U-Bahn tunnels."

Finally, Gottlieb got through to whoever he was calling. "Hello, Sturmbannführer Ochs, please. Yes, this is Sturmbannführer Gottlieb. I understand you have the criminal Pantel. Is that true? Yes. Good work, excellent work. I have already sent one of my men to help in the interrogation. Again, excellent job. I commend you and your men."

Gottlieb put down the phone and turned to Stachel. The secretary had already left the room. "You see, I was right. Pantel is the killer. In these times, we must act, not sit and analyze. If you had brought him in when I told you to, we would be getting the credit for his arrest. Now the Gestapo has control, and we can only watch."

Stachel shook his head. "Pantel's no more a killer than you are. I take that back. He's less of a killer than you."

Gottlieb pursed his lips and drummed his fingers on the desk, trying to think of an adequate response to Stachel, then decided to ignore it.

"Then why did he run?" he asked, walking from behind his desk and standing in front of Stachel.

"Because he was scared."

"Why should he be scared unless he was guilty?"

"Because we've been a little free with justice recently…"

"As we should. There's a war on and the enemy is everywhere."

Stachel shook his head again. "Regardless, Pantel's not the killer."

"We will soon find out. The Gestapo will get the truth from him."

"The Gestapo will get a confession from him. Not the same thing."

"Innocent men don't confess. The Führer has said so."

Stachel wanted to respond that the Führer was an idiot but held himself back. It would do him no good. Talking to an idiot turned you into an idiot.

"The war's lost, despite what they say. And if the Führer stays in Berlin, he'll be arrested or dead within a few weeks."

"The war is not lost." Gottlieb turned back to the shelter of his desk. "The war is not lost. We will win. We must have faith in our Führer. His genius has made us rulers of Europe. He will find a way."

"Genius? His genius has destroyed everything we know. And blind faith in anything is just that, blind. From what I hear, your Führer sits in his bunker all day staring at pictures of Frederick the Great."

Gottlieb looked alarmed. He pushed Stachel aside and closed the office door. "You've gone to far. You're talking treason. You'll get yourself killed and me arrested for listening to you. If you continue, I will be forced to turn you in."

"Kill me now, kill me later. We're already dead. The Russians aren't going to be in a nice mood when they get here."

"They won't get here. We will stop them at the Seelow Heights. History will not allow us to fail."

"We have no history and God has deserted us."

"Leave God to the priests. God deserted us when we lost the Great War. The Führer is our God now."

Stachel didn't respond. The conversation had overheated, and he knew saying any more wouldn't change anything. Gottlieb would still be a fool and Germany would still lose the war. All that mattered now was to catch this killer and for that he needed Gottlieb out of the way.

"Anyway. I need to get over to Gestapo and watch the interrogation. Make sure the goons don't spoil my witness. Where are they?"

"A building near Prinz Albrecht Strasse HQ. You'll find it by the guards out front."

"Who did you send there to help them torture the prisoner?" Stachel spate the word torture out like he had just eaten something rotten.

"Lakain is there. He can handle it."

Stachel shook his head again and walked out of the office. "Lakain's a boy masquerading as a man."

Stachel headed over to Prinz Albrecht Strasse as quick as he could. With HQ destroyed by Allied bombs, the Gestapo either dealt with their prisoners in the open or found a building still standing to hide their deeds. They weren't about to let a few bombs stop their salon of death.

As Gottlieb had said, there were two guards in a building just down the street. He showed them his badge, then headed down the stairs to the basement. Though he had no idea what room in the basement Pantel was in, he figured he would find it from the screams. The Gestapo were always very quick and efficient at delivering the greatest pain in the least amount of time.

When he reached the basement, all was quiet. It was a long corridor, with steel doors to either side running off into the darkness. The lights were on, but there wasn't a sound coming from any of the cells. He could hear the slow dripping of water echoing in the darkness. The silence made Stachel nervous, like he had entered the land of the dead and was about to meet Lucifer.

Then he heard voices further down the corridor. He slowly started walking, conscious of each echoed step he took. The fourth door down on the right was open. He looked in and saw Pantel tied to a chair in the back, with two men silently standing to either side of him. A third man was near the door, leaning against an oak table. Lakain wasn't present. The man at the oak table turned when Stachel entered the room.

"Get out," he said, standing up and blocking Stachel. He was a short, stocky man with a small pencil-thin mustache and small round glasses. He looked like Himmler's twin. Another Nazi who had lost all sense of his self.

"I'm the investigative officer in this case. Pantel is my suspect." Stachel walked pass the man and started towards Pantel. The man grabbed him by the arm and pulled him back as the other two men closed ranks in front of Pantel.

"Was the officer. He's our prisoner now."

"The case is still open and until I hear differently, I'm still in charge. Where's Lakain? I was told he was here."

"You mean the boy who showed up an hour ago? Gone. We told him to leave, and he didn't argue. Just took off like a hare being chased by a wolf." The man laughed and pointed to a corner. "You're Stachel, aren't you? OK, I will be nice to the Kripo this once. In the corner, but don't say anything."

Stachel wanted to push the point that he was still in charge, but knew it was no use. The Gestapo were above the law and arguing would only get him thrown out of the room. He kept his overcoat on, thrust his hands in his pockets, and stood back in the corner, out of the light, leaning against the concrete wall.

The man turned back to Pantel. Pantel looked like a worm exposed to the sun.

"You killed Sophie Holzer. Confessing or not means nothing since we already know you did it. But we like things nice and tidy, you know, follow the letter of the law." And the man laughed at his joke. "So, admit to killing her and we will stop. It's simple. It's entirely up to you."

Pantel's head was down, his chin against his chest, sucking in air through his mouth, gasping as though he was drowning. Blood seeped from a wound on the side of his head. His nose had been smashed long ago and was now a large clot of dried blood. Stachel couldn't be sure but it looked like one of his ears was missing.

"Admitting to something I didn't do isn't going to change anything," Pantel said. "You're going to kill me regardless."

"I promise you that it will be less painful than what we'll do if you don't talk."

"The guillotine rather than hung by a wire?"

The man motioned to one of the men who had a knife in his hand. "You know, you don't look right. We really should take the other one off, so you don't look so lopsided."

The man to the side placed the knife on Pantel's ear, getting ready to slice.

"I tell you," Pantel sobbed, tears sliding down his face. "I didn't kill her. I've already told the Hauptsturmführer everything I know," and Pantel motioned his head towards Stachel.

Stachel was sickened by the whole thing. Since he'd lost his faith in the Führer, he now could see what a waste it all was. He pushed himself away from the wall and walked over to Pantel.

"Please, take the knife away." The man looked at his superior, who nodded. He stepped back, but held the knife out, ready if needed. Stachel bent over so he could look at Pantel's face. "Did you tell me everything yesterday? If you did, then why did you run?"

Pantel wouldn't look at Stachel. He shook his head violently to the side, then stopped and breathed heavily. "You'd run if you'd open your eyes and see what this country has become. As I told you, I did see something. I heard noise, I looked out the window and saw a figure hunched over someone on the ground. It was dark so I couldn't see who it was. That's it. I swear."

"Nothing more? Like maybe that you went out and searched the body afterwards?"

"No, I didn't. I was scared. I just wanted to forget what I'd seen."

"Now tell me. This man you saw. What was he doing?"

"He was standing over the body. I could hear him breathing hard, then I saw him pull something out of his pocket. At that point, I stepped away from the window. I didn't want to see anymore."

"What did he pull from his pocket?"

"I couldn't see. It was the middle of the night. It was dark. How could I see anything?"

The man at the table came over and grabbed Pantel by the hair and lifted his face up. "You didn't see anything because you were the murderer. You killed Sophie Holzer, you know it, we know it." The man slapped Pantel across the face, then let his head fall down against his chest. He turned to Stachel.

"Leave, now. I don't care about Gottlieb or you. He's ours now. We'll finish what you couldn't."

"But…"

"Now or would you like a little keepsake." He bent down and grabbed Pantel's bloody ear that had been severed earlier off the floor and held it out to Stachel. "A little souvenir. He won't be needing it anymore."

Stachel stared at the man and knew any argument was useless. "I'm sorry," he said, looking at Pantel, and then left the room. The goons were going to kill his only witness. And regardless of what anyone thought, he knew Pantel wasn't the killer, and knew that now, if anything just to spite the Nazi party, he had to find the real killer. If only to convince himself that the Nazis really were fools.

Chapter Fifteen

Stachel stared at the enclosing walls of his office, remembering the last time he had a Jägermeister schnapps or a pint of beer. A good drink was a thing of the past now. The only beer you could get was made from sugar beet. It had a nasty taste and Stachel refused to drink it.

Pantel. There was nothing he could do for him. The man was lost. Once the Gestapo had its claws sunk into someone, there was little hope. Maybe Pantel was the killer? Stachel didn't know for sure. It wouldn't be the first time he had cleared a suspect and then found out he was wrong. When in doubt, follow your instincts. That was what his partner Klein always said. If his instincts were right, then Pantel was not the killer. That left Holzer as his only suspect. If Holzer had ordered his wife killed, there was little Stachel could do about it. But the murder didn't look like an execution. Assassins shot you in the head or stuck a knife in your gut. They didn't strangle and then stab you.

He had to get to Stehen. Stehen had always come through for him. Stehen always found out something. Especially these days, the street knew more about what was going on than the government. The *Schwarzmarkt* would know if it was actually a robbery gone wrong.

He made a call to Stehen, leaving a message as before. Then he waited, drumming his fingers on the desk, without thinking tapping out the jazz drum rhythm from *Sing, Sing, Sing* by Benny Goodman. Forbidden by the Nazis.

He knew he should write up a status report for Plettner and Gottlieb. Of course, they would consider it his last report. The murderer was caught. All they needed was a confession to close the case. Stachel would be told to refocus on the Wicke case. Lakain would be back to catching defeatists and preparing for the defense of Berlin. A fool's errand. They would all be killed.

Stachel started jotting down some notes for the status report, then realized that he couldn't write it truthfully without mentioning that he didn't think Pantel was the murderer. Gottlieb would insist he change the report. Better to write nothing than help the Nazis with their lies.

The phone rang. He picked it up quickly, breathing heavily, hoping it was Stehen and not Gottlieb or Plettner. Fortunately, it was a message from Stehen, given by the same man who had answered before. Stehen could not meet, but he would phone this number later that night, between ten and midnight.

"Can't you give me an exact time?" Stachel asked. No, was the answer and then the man hung up.

It was seven in the evening. He would have to wait at least five hours. And he was hungry. Right now, he'd settle for a few potatoes and dream about a nice bit of pork. He grabbed his overcoat and left the office. Taking a haphazard route home, he wandered by a few stores, but everything was closed. There were people mingling in the streets. An older woman, wearing a long flowing skirt, was digging through some rubble, muttering to herself as she scraped at the debris with bloody hands, tumbling bricks into the pathway. He walked over, grabbed her by the shoulders, and asked her what she was looking for.

"Our house was hit earlier today," she said, tears streaming down her face, "and the phone, buried, is ringing. I need to answer it. It could be my husband."

"Where's your husband?"

"I don't know. He's in the army, in the east, but I haven't heard from him in months."

Stachel wanted to tell her not to bother, that her husband was probably dead, that he would never be coming back. If he was still alive and could get to a phone, he was probably a deserter. Which meant he would eventually be caught and shot. Dead either way, serving his country or not. But Stachel said nothing. He walked away, letting her continue trying to get to her phone.

At home, the water was out again, so he grabbed a bucket and walked down the street to a public water pump and stood in line for forty minutes until he got to the pump. Back at the apartment, he sat down on the sofa and drank a glass of water. There was a knock at the door. Looking at the clock next to his bed, he realized it was only nine. The Gestapo would not come this early. It was one of his neighbors, a short elderly woman who dyed her hair, for what reason Stachel didn't know. Maybe she was trying to look attractive for the Russians.

"Hauptsturmführer Stachel," she said, padding him on the chest as though she talked to him every day. "I had some sausage for you. A very nice sausage that the grocer, Kubisch, gave me today, saying it was meant for you. But an SS officer came by, looking for you. He knocked on my door and when he saw the sausage, he took it."

Stachel's first thought was about the sausage. Wouldn't that have been nice right now. But then he thought of the SS officer, grinning as he eyed the sausage. That did not bode well.

"Why was he looking for me? What did he look like?"

"Oh, about five ten, blond hair, I'd say around thirty. He had some metals pinned to this chest. Strutting his "heroism" as the SS like to do."

"That could be anybody. Is this the first time you've seen him?"

"Yes, and hopefully the last. He didn't look very nice."

"No one is these days." Then Stachel noticed that she was holding a brown bag in her other hand. When she saw that he was looking at it, she gave it to him. "I'm sorry about the sausage, it would have been good, but I saved you some bread. It's all I have, but please take it."

Stachel wanted to say no, felt guilty, but his stomach was growling, and bread would fill it up. Guilt was a luxury no one could afford anymore.

After finishing the bread, Stachel lay down to get some rest before heading back to the office at midnight. Three hours later he woke with a start, saw that it was already eleven-thirty, and had to run to get to the Alex before midnight.

Out of breath, wiping the sweat from his forehead and neck with a handkerchief, he tried to calm his beating heart. It would be just his luck to die of an heart attack.

The phone rang at twelve-thirty.

"I'm still looking, but I don't really have anything to tell you yet. Everyone knows about Sophie Holzer. I don't think anyone particularly liked her because of her radio broadcasts.

Despite what the poison dwarf said, her broadcasts made everyone realize that the government was desperate and we were going to lose the war."

"Tell me something I don't know."

"Well, I know that August Holzer isn't the strict, upright German everyone thinks he is. Like his boss, he's had his affairs over the years. And not only of the proper kind."

"What's that mean? The proper kind?"

"He was keeping a Jewish mistress in an apartment over in Potsdam. I heard that in so many words a few times, but no one would ever give me any details."

"So what are you saying? That Sophie Holzer was killed because she found out her husband was having an affair?"

"No, probably has nothing to do with it. Just an interesting bit of information. About her murder, no one seems to know anything. She definitely met someone from the black market and bought food, but no one would tell me who. Someone is being protected."

"Is that it? After two days, this is all you've found?"

"It's not easy right now. No one's talking, everyone's just waiting for the war to end." Stehen coughed. Stachel could hear the thin rasping scratch of lungs that had breathed in too much smoke and soot. "But I did hear another interesting bit. There's talk of a stranger living in the area. They call him the shadow man, a joke on Goebbels's poster of the silhouette of a man warning people to be quiet, that spies are everywhere. But no one knows who he is, no one's ever seen his face. It's weird that people are worried about this guy. With so many refugees in the city, so many strangers everywhere, I can't figure out why this shadow man causes concern. It's like they think the Jewish Golem has come back to life."

"Well, keep looking. Somebody must know something."

"No promises. It's getting more difficult every day. Everyone's gone into hiding and is waiting for the Russians."

Chapter Sixteen

When he woke the next morning, he could still remember the bread he had eaten for dinner last night, but his stomach had forgotten and wanted more. The Alex had a canteen on the first floor. A few years ago, fluorescent lights had been installed. Stachel never liked them. He felt they made the room to harsh, to sterile, like he was in an operating room and would be served a pint of blood for breakfast. These days the canteen was mostly empty. What was the point when you were lucky if all you could get were some moldy potatoes and ersatz coffee? But to his surprise they had one egg, hard-boiled. Warm, but not hot, Stachel rolled it around in his hands, examining it, worrying that it was somehow fake. But it looked fresh, though how do you know an egg is fresh? In the end, you go on faith. It wouldn't stop him from eating it anyway.

He purchased the egg and some potatoes. As he turned from the register to the empty room, he noticed Hugo Baer at a table in the corner.

"What are you doing here?" Stachel shouted as he walked over to Baer. His words echoed through the empty room, making it sound like he was holding a megaphone.

"Reinhardt, come and join me," Baer called out, motioning with his hand. "Here interviewing someone accused of sabotage. Caught last night by one of your zealous policemen."

"Where did you get the sausage?" Stachel asked, noticing the last pieces of a bratwurst on Baer's plate. "You must have bribed the staff to get that."

"Last one. I was lucky, and no you can't have any. It's probably the last one I'll see for a while."

Stachel smiled and shook his head, cracking the shell of his egg with the eagerness of a child unwrapping a piece of candy.

"I probably shouldn't tell you," Baer said, "and you didn't hear it from me, but we brought in a suspect in the Holzer case yesterday."

"I already know. Pantel. I was there for part of the interrogation."

"Well, he's dead. Apparently hanged himself last night."

Stachel stopped peeling his egg and placed it back on his plate. He stared across at Baer and then looked around to make sure no one was close by. "Dead? That was quick. The Gestapo didn't waste any time."

Baer shrugged his shoulders and finished eating his sausage, then leaned back and gave himself a satisfying pat on the stomach.

Stachel leaned over the table and whispered to Baer. "You know, he was innocent. Pantel didn't kill Holzer or anyone else."

"The men who brought him in think different. And he confessed apparently."

"Confessed? Since when did that mean anything. The Gestapo don't care about truth?" Stachel leaned back, exhaling in anguish. "Well, the Gestapo will close the case now. The killer was caught and carried out his own execution. Nice of Pantel to save the state the trouble."

Though Stachel wasn't surprised at Pantel's death, and he didn't believe for a minute that it was suicide, it still bothered him at the finality of it. Another innocent killed by the death machine. Justice ignored. Well, this time justice would not be swept under the table. This would not be another Memel incident. He would not walk away.

"Listen, I have to go. I'll talk to you later."

"Your food." Baer pointed at Stachel's plate.

"You have it. I'm not hungry."

"Suit yourself." Baer greedily slid the plate over and finished peeling the hard-boiled egg as Stachel left the canteen and headed back to his office.

On the second floor, walking down the hallway, he noticed Gottlieb at the end, talking to one of the secretaries. He quickly ducked into his office, hoping Gottlieb hadn't seen him. No such luck. Before he had sat down, Gottlieb was in his office and closing the door.

"Pantel's dead," Gottlieb said. "He confessed, signed a statement yesterday. Last night he hanged himself in his cell."

Stachel acted as though he didn't know.

"I'm not happy about this," Gottlieb continued. "We were supposed to catch the killer. It would have made us look good to Goebbels. Now, since the Gestapo had to do the dirty work and solve the case, we look stupid."

"Dirty work is right. Why are there always a lot of suicides at the Gestapo? This isn't over. Pantel is not the killer. I'm going to continue looking for the real killer."

"No, you're not. The case is closed. Go back to what you're supposed to be doing. Helping the war effort, looking for spies and saboteurs, defending Berlin. "

"What about the Wicke case?"

"Continue with that. And write up a final report and send it to Plettner and me. The bastard called me this morning to crow over his people catching the killer."

"Catching a killer is easy for him. All he has to do is look in the mirror."

This place is a madhouse, Stachel thought, as Gottlieb left. How could he have ever thought he was doing any good. The Nazis had made a mockery of his whole career. He had to get away, where he didn't know, but anywhere was better than here.

As he headed down the stairs, he heard the radio that the guard at the front door was playing. Goebbels was giving another one of his talks about Germany's ensuing victory. And he brought up that another enemy of the Fatherland had been captured and eliminated. He didn't mention Pantel's name, but Stachel knew that's who the dwarf was referring to. The idiot should stop with the lies and start preparing a eulogy for the country's funeral.

And his back hurt more than ever, a sharp pain that traveled up his spine to his head, leaving him confused and disoriented. He didn't know what to do next.

Chapter Seventeen

Before the war, Stachel and his wife liked to take a walk around the neighborhood after dinner. For both of them, it was the most enjoyable time of the day. There was no talk of work or money. Sometimes they talked about retirement, about opening a pastry shop back in their hometown of Merseburg. But usually they walked in silence, observing the colors and sounds of the city. The neon lights of a newly opened shop, the whispers of two embraced lovers. The glitter of a movie palace highlighting the latest film with Lil Dagover.

After leaving the office, Stachel roamed around the city for a good part of the day, thinking back to those earlier walks. When Hilda died, it was like a chasm had opened up and swallowed everything he believed and hoped. Now the colors and sounds of the city were the hollow grey of destroyed buildings, the blackness of soot dancing in the air, the roar of artillery fire to the east. The only bright lights were of pockets of fires that people struggled to put out. Better to die than continue living in what Germany had become. Maybe he would step in front of a Russian bullet and let it pierce his heart. A quick death was his only hope now.

When the air raid sirens went off at four in the morning, Stachel was asleep, having a recurring dream that took place at Tempelhof airport. He was heading to the gate but kept getting lost. He wandered around the airport in a circle, disoriented, trying to find the gate, asking people and getting contradictory information, go this way, no, go that way, until he was hopelessly lost. When he finally reached the gate, just as the plane was boarding, he realized that he had left his suitcase back at check-in. The nightmare would begin again, in reverse, with Stachel trying to find the check-in counter. Ironically, Stachel was happy to hear the air raid siren, since it pulled him out of his feverish dream.

Though his building had a cellar, Stachel preferred to go to the building next door. He just didn't like looking at his neighbors while the ground shook around them and dust fell from the ceiling. Besides, the building next door seemed better built, more solid. His building was built after Hitler took power, where the building next door was built before the Great War. That alone made it feel safer. Besides, he felt that God would not let him die among strangers.

Stachel had not bothered to undress the night before. He had collapsed in his bed when he got home and fallen asleep immediately. So, all he had to do was slip on his shoes and grab his overcoat. He was out the door and down the stairs in seconds, following one of his neighbors. It was Conrad, a short balding fellow, who looked over his shoulder and gave Stachel a quick hello.

"Still going next door?"

Stachel grumbled an affirmative and, disoriented because he had just woken up, asked Conrad what day it was.

"April twentieth. Hitler's birthday."

"Great, I'll bake him a cake." Stachel knew that Conrad had no love for the Nazis. He lived in an apartment on the second floor, by himself since his wife had left him a few years back. Now Conrad was always playing up to Stachel, as though being close to a policeman would protect him from the Allies.

"You should come downstairs," Conrad said. "It would make everyone feel more comfortable if you were there, lending your support. They find it odd that you go next door. And, of course, the gossiping women all think you must go there because you're sweet on someone."

"I make them feel safer. We're all in the same boat and it's sinking."

"But you're a policeman. Everyone would feel safer."

"Safer from what? The bombs? They'd probably target this building if they knew I was here. The Russians? I'll be the first one they'll arrest."

"Exactly," Conrad looked over his shoulder and smiled. "They'll take you and ignore us."

"Nice. I'll remember to give them your name."

"Don't bother."

When they got to the ground floor, Conrad continued down the hallway and down the stairs to the cellar. Stachel circled around the stairs and out the front door. The street was empty. The sirens, Meyer's trumpets, were still blaring away, but there was nothing from the anti-aircraft artillery yet. When he got to the cellar, the people were already huddled in small groups based on family and friends. There were three lit candles. One on the floor, one on a chair, and one on a shelve near the ceiling. It was a system they had devised to check for oxygen. If the candle on the floor went out, children were picked up and placed on laps. If the candle on the chair went out, people started thinking about evacuating the cellar. If the candle on the shelve went out, then everyone fled the cellar, regardless of the bombing above.

Stachel found a seat in the back corner, facing the group and the door. He nodded his hello, then pulled his coat collar up and waited for the air raid to begin. When he looked around the room, he saw the familiar faces that were always there; Mrs. Ochs with her two small children, husband long gone and probably dead. Annelie Rost, the eldest daughter of parents who had fled west a few months ago, leaving her behind. Stachel had heard she refused to go because she was waiting for her lover to return from the war. A fool's wait. And old Mr. Bunzek, sixty-four years old and already lost to the world, babbling that the Führer would save them. Everyone tried to ignore him, knowing that he was mad and worried that he'd turn pigeon if anyone said anything negative about Hitler.

Also, there was his neighbor Minna, who lived on the second floor, next to Conrad, and felt the same way about their building. Sitting next to her was someone Stachel had never seen before. Minna was in her thirties and a widow. Her husband had died on the Russian front a few years back and left her with three children. She struggled to exist, as did everyone. Sometimes Stachel took pity on her and gave her some of his ration coupons, which she was always grateful for.

The other woman, who was obviously a friend since she was bouncing one of Minna's children on her lap, looked older, maybe early forties. She had on a grey dress with a white lace collar, her black hair pulled back. All the women these days either cut their hair short or had it pulled back in a bund. Less chance for lice that way. She was thin, but then everyone was except for the Golden Pheasants. Originally, only Nazi party officials who were one of the first 100,000 to join were called Golden Pheasants, but now people called anyone who wasn't thin by that name. Everyone figured the party was hoarding food. And Stachel knew there was some truth to that, though he didn't think the party had as much as people thought. People often said that the war will be over when Goring looks like Goebbels.

Then the bombs started. Though they were far away, everyone could still hear the rumbling, a beast awaken. The noise kept getting louder and louder, like the beginning of Beethoven's fifth, a crescendo of hammering chords. They were lucky this time. The British must have been targeting one of the munitions plants on the other side of the city. Everyone remained tense and quiet. Particularly with the British, who bombed indiscriminately, a stray bomb could change everything.

This time the air raid only lasted about an hour, so they were soon working their way back upstairs to their rooms to try and get some sleep before the sun came up. Sitting in the back corner, Stachel waiting for everyone to leave before exiting.

To keep his mind off the bombs, Stachel thought about the case. Poor Pantel, another person in the wrong place at the wrong time, another victim of the Nazi horror. Everything pointed to August Holzer. He had the motivation, and he had the means. If it was an execution, it would explain why the food and the money weren't taken. But it wouldn't explain why she was stabbed after she was dead.

Maybe Pantel did kill Holzer? It would be easier to accept his confession and move on. But it gnawed on him, like that rat working its way through a loaf of bread.

He had also been told to concentrate on finding defeatist and saboteurs, that nothing was more important than helping to ensure that the Third Reich defeated its enemies. Stachel was sick of hearing the same thing repeatedly. The government, if he could still call the Nazis that, refused to believe that they would lose the war. Yet, in contradiction, they asked people to fight to the end, that a hero's death in war was better than a coward's death in peace. Old men who hadn't shot a gun since the Great War, boys no more than fourteen or fifteen, taking up weapons that they didn't know how to use. A slaughter, just so the Nazis could claim it wasn't the Great War all over again, that they hadn't surrendered.

It was dark and cold, and a light rain had begun to fall as Stachel came up to the street. As he opened the door to his apartment building, he saw Minna and her friend standing in the foyer. Minna was holding the hands of two of her children, and the youngest was in the other woman's arms, cradled on her hip. Minna turned to Stachel and gave him a quick smile, motioning for him to come over.

"Eliana, this is Hauptsturmführer Stachel," Minna said. "He's with the Kripo."

Eliana looked at Stachel as though she was looking at a snake about to strike. She apparently had no love for authority and wasn't afraid to show it. She extended her hand, but only gave a cursory handshake, then turned back to Minna.

"Please, you should take something for little Bruno. He is looking so thin and pale."

"I can't possibly take your ration card. What will you do then?"

"I can survive. Trust me. I wouldn't give you my rations unless I had something for myself."

Eliana put down the child she was holding and reached into her purse, which was hanging from her shoulder, pulling out yellow and green ration cards. One for milk and one for meat. She handed them to Minna, said she would visit again before the end of the week. As she left, she told Stachel how nice it was to meet him, though her eyes showed that she hoped to never see him again. Stachel watched her go.

"She is beautiful, no?" asked Minna.

Stachel turned to her, puckering his lips in embarrassment. "Yes, I suppose so."

"You need a woman to take care of you. Elaina's husband was a soldier in Russia but disappeared at Stalingrad. No one knows if he's dead or was captured. Every woman needs a man to protect her, and every man needs a woman to take care of him."

"Perhaps, but I really must be going. Thank you. Maybe I will meet your friend another time under better circumstances."

Minna's attempts at match making annoyed Stachel. She had started a few weeks after Hilda's death, running through a list of all the widows in the neighborhood.

"Time to stop mourning," she said.

Stachel always rebuffed her. The last thing he needed right now was someone to worry about. And besides, a part of him wanted to believe that Hilda would suddenly show up. Her body was never found, vaporized by the bomb, he was told, and that gave him hope that she hadn't been home that day. Maybe she had gone out right after him and was now lost somewhere in the city, trying to get back to him, but not knowing where he was? Hope, no matter how irrational, was all he had left. He was no better than the Nazis.

Chapter Eighteen

Saying good-bye to Minna on the second floor, Stachel slowly worked his way up the stairs to his third floor apartment, placing one foot at a time on each step like he had a ball and chain tied to them, the shuffling noise echoing through the stairwell. One inside his apartment, he kicked off his shoes and fell into bed, not bothering to pull up the covers. He fell instantly into a fretful sleep, dreaming that he was being chased by a man who he could only see in silhouette, a shadow with piercing eyes wearing a broad brimmed hat.

He was woken by a soft knock at the door. He glanced at the clock as he stood up. Seven o'clock. He had slept longer than he thought, and for once, he felt rested. He opened the door and immediately felt tired again. It was his sister-in-law, a white gloved hand raised to knock again. He didn't say anything, just opened the door wide and motioned her in. He was trapped.

"Good morning, Sommer."

"You look a mess," she said, pulling at a wrinkle in his coat and brushing a spot of dust from his shoulder. "You look like you slept in your clothes."

"I did."

She shook her head and walked further into the room and sat down on the edge of the bed. Stachel closed the door and sat down in the chair in the corner, rubbing his eyes, thinking about the shadow in the dream, wondering if he had been thinking of his sister-in-law. He tried to sit up straight, his lower back hurting again.

"Yes?"

She was wearing a beige overcoat that for these times looked very clean. Only a few spots of dirt. She took off her gloves as she looked at him, twisting them into a knot as she spoke. "Do you have my ration cards? For milk, for meat, for the children?"

Stachel stared at her with blinking eyes. Now he was in for it. He had completely forgotten about the ration cards. Not that it would have made a difference, but he should have at least tried. He wanted to lie to her, tell her he had asked, but was unsuccessful, but he couldn't do it. Too many lies already.

"No, I'm sorry, I forgot. I'll ask today."

"How could you forget? Didn't you get my message the other day? I went to your office at the Alex and left a message."

"Yes, I got it. I'm terribly busy with my present case."

"Sophie Holzer. Yes, I've heard. And you must catch the murderer. She was the wife of an important man. This murder goes against everything we're fighting for."

Stachel was taken back. The murder had never been made public.

"How did you hear of it?"

She waved her hand and looked the other way. "I have friends. Friends that do more for me than you do."

"Listen, as I've said, extra ration cards are not being handed out. I won't be able to get any, and if I try and steal some and I'm caught, I'll be shot."

"Don't lie to me. We all know that the government has all the food it needs. Only us civilians are suffering."

"That's not true. I don't know what Hitler or Goebbels or Goring and such are getting, but at my level, we get the same stuff as you, and it isn't much."

"No, it's not. My children are starving. Your niece and nephew are starving."

There she goes again, Stachel thought. Her problems are my problems. The opposite of her sister. Hilda never complained, never talked about herself, always kind, always ready to help someone in need. And Sommer had always taken advantage of her and now expected the same of him. Stachel only now realized that she was wearing perfume. Obviously trying to look and smell her best so she'd get what she wanted.

She continued. "It's horrible what the Allies are doing to us. We don't deserve this."

That's right, Stachel thought, we deserve worse.

"Anyway, Sommer, I need to get to work. I will ask today about extra rations, I promise."

Sommer stood up and walked over to the window that faced the street. "I saw that your neighbors have planted a small garden in back."

"Yes, one woman downstairs, who I barely know. It's a feeble effort but better than nothing."

"Can you ask her to give me a few vegetables? For the children."

"I'll ask, but not right now. Later today."

She turned back to him, her voice breaking. "With you, later today means never. Please, ask her now." She walked over and placed her hand on his shoulder, as though a human touch would change him.

"The vegetables aren't very good. Worn and pale, like us. They look like they've been grown in a cave. Food from a cave for cave dwellers."

"Well, they'll be better than what we get in our rations. Please ask." This time it sounded like a demand.

"I will, but again not now. I must get to work. Come back this evening."

Sommer bit at one of the fingers of her glove, looking like a little girl about to throw a temper tantrum. He started for the door to let her out.

"Wait," she said. "I have something else to ask." She sat back down on the bed, hands once again clutching her gloves and twisting them into a knot.

"I want to get the children out of Berlin. I went to the military office and tried to get documents, but they refused. Can you help me?"

Stachel stood there, hand on the doorknob, wanting to open the door and see her out. What she was asking was the impossible.

"You know that's hopeless," he said. "Your Führer has declared Berlin a fortress, to be defended to the death. No one can leave unless they have business that is deemed vital to the Third Reich. Even I can't get out."

"That's a lie. I've seen the military, officers, getting papers and heading west. They're abandoning us, betraying the Führer, leaving us to the Russians."

"I don't know about that, but it doesn't change anything. I can't possibly get you the necessary documents. Besides, why do you want to leave? I thought you still believed in Hitler."

"I do. But I must think of my children first. They are our future, so I want to get them away from the city, away from the Russians, to the Americans or British. I hear they have plenty of food and shelter."

Once again, she was using the excuse of her children to try and get what she wanted. Stachel knew she only thought of herself, that she'd do anything, say anything, to get what she wanted. The children were only a means to the end.

"I'm sorry," he said, opening the door. "I can't help you. I'll try and get you some extra ration cards, but I can't help you leave the city."

"Is there no other way?"

"I hear that one of the checkpoints in the Spandau district is letting people through. But it's only a rumor, and if Hitler hears about it, the people there will be shot."

She started to sob, shaking, thick tears that rolled down her face, which she wiped away with her gloves. She stood up and left, not looking at Stachel, muttering that she'll come back tonight for the ration cards. He closed the door behind her, knowing that he'd never be able to get them.

He stood at the door, listening to the sound of her steps down the stairs, then walked over and turned on the radio. These days he avoided the radio as much as possible, since it was full of Goebbels's rants, but he wanted the noise, the sound of voices other than his sister-in-law. He went into the bathroom and splashed some water on his face and started to brush his teeth.

The station was running a repeat of a broadcast from a few weeks ago, about the Werewolf organization, asking people to join up, to fight the enemy. The Werewolves were a guerilla organization created by Himmler to operate behind enemy lines to sabotage the Allied war effort and assassinate officers.

"Turn day into night, night into day! Hit the enemy wherever you meet him. Be sly! Steal weapons, ammunition and rations! Women helpers, support the battle of the Werewolf wherever you can."

There was a moment of silence, then it was announced that the next was a live broadcast. Goebbels annual speech on Hitler's birthday.

"I stand today as fate challenges him and his people with its last, most severe test. Fate will give the Führer a final victory. Germany still lives, Europe and the civilized world have not fallen into the abyss that looms from the east. Thanks to the Führer we will succeed."

The abyss? Germany was already in the abyss. With no hope of escaping. And how was the Werewolf broadcast any different than what Sophie Holzer had done back in February? Nothing. The military prowess of the Third Reich had come down to this. All the young men were dead. It was up to women and children and old men to defend the city. Cattle being sent to the slaughtering pen.

Chapter Nineteen

The daily bombings from the Allies had not disturbed the sense of normalcy in Berlin. People acted as though the city would go on. Shops opened, trams ran, when they could, libraries stayed open, until March the Philharmonic continued to play concerts. But now that the shelling of the city by the Russians had started early that morning, everything had changed. The city was under siege.

Standing in the center of the Tiergarten is the monument to commemorate the Prussian victory over Denmark in 1864. Designed by Heinrich Strack, the Victory Column is a symbol to war. Around the base are gilded reliefs of battles from Germany's subsequent wars with Austria and France. It had originally stood in the Konigsplatz, in front of the Reichstag, but was moved by the Nazis in 1939 because it didn't fit with Hitler's grand reconstruction of Berlin, the Welthauptstadt Germania.

It was probably too bad it had been moved, Stachel thought, because if it had still been near the Reichstag, it would have been bombed into oblivion by now. He always thought it was a symbol for everything that was wrong with Germany. The year of the move Germany invaded Poland, the official war began, and to Stachel the country started its long road to destruction. Had the killer chosen this spot for his latest victim to send a message? The victim, Heinz Mintert, was the head judge of the People's Court, a special court created by Hitler to deal with people accused of political crimes. It operated outside the normal law and had wide latitude to prosecute anyone. After Roland Freisler's death from allied bombings back in February, Mintert had taken over and if anything had been more brutal than Freisler.

It was eight in the morning and the city was as silent as a morgue. A light rain was falling and, once again, as he walked down the Charlottenburger Chaussee, he cursed the fact that he had forgotten his hat.

As he approached the center of the Tiergarten, he heard an explosion behind him, around the Brandenburg Gate. He turned around and saw a spear of fire spitting up into the sky, about where the Adlon Hotel stood. But there were no airplanes, no air raid siren. That meant only one thing. The heavy artillery was definitely within range. The Russians were sending Hitler a birthday present.

At the Victory Column, Matthaeus Uhl, was already examining the body. There were also two policeman present, standing off to the side, protecting the murder scene from sightseers who didn't exist. Uhl looked up, saw Stachel, and motioned him over.

Mintert was tied to one of the columns, dressed in his judge's robes, holding his gravel as though he was about to pass judgment on some helpless victim. He had lacerations around his throat. There were dark bruises on his left cheek and his forehead, his face buffed up such that without the judge's robes, Stachel doubted he would have recognized him. His robe was soaked in blood, and there was a pool of blood on the ground, trickling down the red granite steps of the monument.

"I kept him strung up until you got here," Uhl said. "Let me know when you want him cut down. Probably killed about four to six hours ago, but I can be more exact after the autopsy."

"He was strangled, correct?"

"Yes, and it looks like that's what killed him. The stabbings appear to have been done after he was dead."

"Like the Holzer killing."

"Maybe," Uhl said, shaking his head. "I don't want to say before I thoroughly examine the body."

Stachel knew Uhl was just playing for time. Once word got out that Mintert's death followed the same method as Holzer's, the Gestapo would be looking for reasons that Mintert's murder was different. Uhl would be second-guessed about every point of his assessment.

"Once again," Uhl continued, "the stabbings seem to be methodical. Not the random stabbings of someone in a rage, but who calmly stabbed his victim multiple times, almost painstakingly, like he was counting. The wounds don't have the savage thrust, the strength that you'd expect if the person had been out of control. "

"How many wounds?"

"Twelve."

"Why twelve? Why not twenty, or thirty?"

Uhl shrugged. "Who knows."

"You know what this means."

Uhl looked down the boulevard, at the blacken and stunted trees. "Yes, but I won't put it my report. Officially, I'll say it could be a copycat killing."

"A copycat killing? We've never mentioned these killing publicly. No one will believe you."

"You'll be surprised what people will believe these days."

As soon as Stachel had said "most," his mind started racing. Here was something he hadn't considered. Who in the Kripo, other than Lakain, Gottlieb and him, knew the details of Holzer's murder? Or was it the Gestapo? Plettner had to be talking to someone about Holzer. Or August Holzer, or even Goebbels. None of them seemed likely to want to kill Mintert. Sommer knew of Holzer's death, but she didn't know the details.

Uhl turned away from Stachel and walked off to the side, leaning against a column. He lit a cigarette and looked east towards the Brandenburg Gate. The fire from earlier had already burned down to a steady glow.

"Is that a real cigarette?" Stachel said as he leaned over the body. Uhl said that the cigarette was ersatz as Stachel checked under Mintert's fingernails for skin and felt inside Mintert's mouth. He didn't have any rubber gloves and the touch of Mintert's clammy saliva sickened him. "There's a piece of skin between his front teeth," he said.

"I didn't see that." Uhl came over and peered over Stachel's shoulder. He reached in his pocket and handed Stachel a tweezers. Stachel grabbed the piece of skin with the tweezers and put it in a plastic bag.

"Looks like he bit the arm of the killer while he was being strangled," Stachel said.

"Possible. We'll take a cast of his teeth."

"Check for other bruises when you get him back to the morgue. Maybe he fought with the killer. That would account for the facial bruises."

He examined the body again and found a paperclip on the coat lapel. Just like Sophie Holzer.

Stachel heard a car coming and looked up as a police car stopped at the base of the column. Wandel, the photographer, got out, holding a Zeiss Ikonta camera. The passenger door opened and Gottlieb got out, wearing a wide brimmed hat and a tan overcoat. Wandel ran up the steps and started setting up his camera and flash.

"Sorry I'm late," he said to Stachel, motioning his head towards Gottlieb as the reason.

Gottlieb, hands in the pockets of his coat, walked slowly towards Stachel, looking at him as he walked up the steps.

"Hi boss," Stachel said and positioned himself so he was between Gottlieb and the body.

"What do we have?" Gottlieb said to Uhl, ignoring Stachel. He looked scared, like a twitching deer in the forest that had just heard a sound.

"Heinz Mintert…"

"Yes, yes, I know already who's been killed. What have you found?"

Uhl looked over at Stachel, wanting him to step in.

"Strangled," Stachel said. "Knife wounds to the chest, probably done after he was dead. It looks…"

"Like Holzer? I don't want theories. Uhl, what do you think?"

"I need to examine the body further, so I can't say, but it is similar. There are bruises around the face, though I can't tell if they were done before or after death."

Gottlieb's eyes lit up as he saw a possible way out of the problem. "So, this might not be the same killer. Sophie Holzer wasn't beaten. This must be a copycat killing. Someone who knew Pantel's method."

"Yes, sir," Uhl said "I'll put whatever you want in the report."

"You can't hide it for long," Stachel said. He was angry at Gottlieb, trying to hide the facts. Bruises or not, it was the same killer. "Even the Gestapo will realize that they got the wrong man."

"The Holzer death is closed. The murderer was caught and got his just punishment. No reason to get anyone excited."

"You no more believe that than I do." Stachel couldn't look Gottlieb in the eye. The man had lost all self-respect, if he ever had it.

"I believe what I'm told to believe. It's safer. Keeps me alive. For once in your life, you might want to follow along."

Stachel didn't answer, just looked at the man for a minute, then walked over to Uhl, who was back at his column smoking a cigarette and staring to the east.

"How quickly can you get me a detailed report?"

"Maybe end of day. I'd like to do it quicker but there's only me at the morgue right now."

"Well, try for sooner. We need to find this guy before he strikes again."

Uhl just shrugged his shoulders. "Whatever. Does it matter anymore? We'll all be dead within the month."

Gottlieb had slipped over and shouldered Stachel away, talking to Uhl. "I want a report by noon. This should be top priority. And don't show it to anyone else."

"Even Stachel?"

Gottlieb didn't answer. He turned to Wandel, who had been taking pictures the whole time. "Are you done?" Wandel shook his head and said he wanted to take a few more pictures. "I correct myself. You're done. Let's go, or you'll be walking."

Wandel hurriedly folded his tripod and flash and ran after Gottlieb, who was already walking towards the car.

Stachel waited until they had gone, then turned to Uhl. "I expect a copy. It will get buried if you only give it to him."

"I'll give it to you, but you didn't get it from me. If it comes out, I'll say you stole it."

"Thanks for the support. You can cut him down." Stachel headed towards the Brandenburg Gate and the office. He knew there would be a frenzy now. Himmler and Goebbels would now be even more worried that this was the beginning of an uprising. And like the aftermath of July Twentieth, the attempted assassination of Hitler in 1944, things would get very bloody.

The killer must still be at large. But what was the connection? Then he remembered. Of course. Two days ago, Mintert had made a public announcement that the black market was subverting the war effort. There would be a crackdown and he would make sure that anyone convicted received the most severe sentence, meaning death. That had to be the connection. But that didn't make sense. Anyone in the black market would know that killing Mintert would start a feeding frenzy. Better to go into hiding and wait out the end of the war.

What if it was a copycat? What if the murderer was a member of the Kripo or Gestapo? It was as good an angle as anything else he had at the moment. He could rule out Holzer now. Maybe Holzer did have a motive for eliminating his wife, but Stachel doubted he would be involved in Mintert's death. The Gestapo was the obvious answer. There was a reason to eliminate Sophie Holzer if the rumor was true that she was planning to flee west. But Mintert? He was a good Nazi. He reveled in killing. He was known for handing out harsher sentences than Freisler. The Gestapo had to love him. He could understand someone wanting to kill Mintert, but he couldn't see why the same person would want to kill Holzer. The husband yes, he could see a connection between Mintert and August Holzer, if August Holzer had been the one killed. But not the wife.

Could a patrolman have done it? That made him stop walking. A chill ran over him as he considered Lakain as the killer. He was a patrolman, first to the Holzer murder scene, in the area at the time. But Mintert? Stachel couldn't see it. Lakain was to naïve to be a killer. He knew evil when he saw it and Lakain wasn't evil. There was another patrolman there, an older man. He would have to check on him but didn't see that he would have the physical strength to strangle someone.

He felt more confused than ever. He needed Klein back to help sort out this mess. All he had now was a boy who took everything as a great adventure. The two murders were connected. That was the only truth he had. And it probably was black market. He needed to talk to Stehen again. And find out who was on patrol the nights of both murders.

If he played by their rules, if he went along with the copycat killing story, it would be Memel all over again. And he could not let that happen.

And the back pain that had subsided after his sister-in-law had left earlier was back with a vengeance.

Chapter Twenty

The Memel Incident

Stachel knew it was going to be a bad day when he woke up and noticed that Hilda was not sleeping next to him. They were on holiday, staying at an inn in Memel, a small town on the Baltic in the country of Lithuania. It was March Twenty-Third, 1939. It was Stachel's first holiday in three years and he was determined to make the most of it, to relax, to see the sights, and most importantly to try and forget about his last murder case. So far, the holiday had gone well. They had arrived two days before and had spent yesterday walking around the town, holding hands, kissing discretely, like two teenagers guilty over forbidden love.

Until last night, when walking back to the inn from dinner, Stachel had picked up an evening newspaper and read the headline. Hitler had demanded the return of Danzig to Germany. And the Memel territory was somehow mixed up in the demand. Though part of Lithuania, the city was predominantly German. The Lithuanians lived in the rural areas. The territory had been part of Prussia before the Great War, when it was ceded to Lithuania as part of the Paris peace treaty. Now Hitler wanted it back.

Stachel always woke a good two hours before Hilda. Holidays didn't matter. In Berlin, he was always up by six and on his way to the Alex by seven, determined to get there while the office was still quiet. And on holiday, he had continued to wake at six, silently dress, and go downstairs and sit in the dining room of the hotel, drinking a cup of coffee.

It was now six and his wife was already up and about. That meant that she was worried, and Stachel guessed it was about Hitler's demands. They had talked about it last night before retiring and considered heading back to Berlin, but finally decided that they would enjoy their holiday no matter what, and pretend that strutting peacock didn't exist.

He sat up and eyes still shut, shuffled around with his feet, looking for his slippers. The room was cold, the temperature outside below freezing for the last two weeks. Apparently, the inn turned off the heat at night. He decided he would complain at the front desk, after he found his wife. On his feet, he put on his robe and headed down the corridor to the bathroom, hoping that his wife was there. But the bathroom was empty. She must be downstairs in the common area. He relieved himself and started back to his room to get dressed, then decided not to bother. He was on holiday. He'd dress how he liked. Still in his slippers and robe, he went down the stairs and walked into the common area. It had two couches facing each other, with a coffee table in the middle, centered around a cold fireplace. There were upright chairs in each corner of the room. But his wife wasn't there. The room was empty. The dining room was down to the left. It was also empty.

Now that's odd, he thought. There's nowhere else for her to go in the inn. Unless she snuck into the kitchen, which he doubted the ownership would allow. The entrance to the kitchen was in the back of the dining room. He stuck his head in, looking for his wife, but saw only the proprietor busy at the stove. A short, balding man, he sensed Stachel's presence and looked up.

"Yes, sir."

"I'm Herr Stachel. Have a room upstairs," and Stachel pointed at the ceiling.

"Yes, I know sir. Can I help you?"

"My wife. Have you seen her?"

"Yes sir. She left about thirty minutes ago. Said she was going to the Church of Saint Casimir."

"A church?" Now Stachel was definitely worried. They were not particularly religious. She only went to church when someone close was ill or had recently died. Where's that?"

"Just down the road. Go right out of the inn, two blocks, then turn left and you'll see it on your left. But be careful. It sounds like there's a fire in the area. Saw a fire truck come racing pass here just a few minutes ago."

"I didn't hear them."

"Siren wasn't on, but they were definitely in a hurry."

Stachel went back to his room and got dressed. A few minutes later he turned down the street to the church and stopped.

There was a fire truck in front of the church and four firemen busy connecting hoses to the one fire hydrant nearby. A furious cloud of smoke was billowing from the roof. Standing on the other side of the street were on-lookers. Stachel saw his wife huddled against a building, watching the firemen trip over themselves. Seeing her from a distance, Stachel thought she looked older than her forty-five years. She had always seemed frail, almost emaciated, but now she looked worn and worried, as though everything she cared about had finally come crashing down on her. Despite the cold, she was only wearing a flowered cotton dress, one she usually only wore around the house. She noticed him staring at her and came over.

"Are you alright?" Stachel said.

"Yes. I woke early for some reason. I didn't want to wake you and the owner didn't seem happy to see me up so early, so I went for a walk and ended up here. I had no sooner sat down in the church when the fire started."

"You look cold." Stachel took off his coat and draped it over his wife's shoulders. "What happened?"

She pulled the coat around her like she was climbing into a cocoon.

"I don't know. A priest ran out from a door behind the chancel and told us all to leave immediately."

The firemen were yelling to each other in German, running frantically back and forth. It looked like something was wrong with the fire hydrant, since the hoses were connected but no water was coming out.

The smoke was now blooming out of the top windows like an angry god taking revenge on sinners. Unless they fixed the fire hydrant, the church would be gutted.

It was a shame. The church was a good example of baroque architecture, with windows facing the street and putti decorating the façade. The central projection was framed by two statues praying to a symbol at the peak. Stachel had no idea what the symbol represented.

The dome in the center had collapsed and it looked like the rest of the roof, what Stachel could see, was about to follow.

He was about to tell his wife they should leave, that there was nothing they could do, when a man wearing a cassock ran out the front door and started yelling and pointing back into the church. Stachel could only hear a few words. It sounded like the priest was saying something about a dead body.

The firemen had finally got the hydrant working. One of them pushed the priest back from the church and started spraying the top windows with water.

Stachel asked his wife to stay where she was and drifted over to the priest, who was dressed in a black cassock and cap, his hands hidden in the flowing cuffs.

"Excuse me, father," Stachel said. "But I couldn't help but overhear some of what you said to the fireman."

The priest looked at Stachel as though he was peering out from another world. "Who are you?"

"I'm a policeman, a detective from Berlin, here on holiday with my wife," and Stachel pointed back to where his wife should have been standing. But she had ignored him and was now standing next to him, looking at the priest.

"Hello, father," she said and held out her hand.

The priest coiled back from her and didn't offer his hand. He looked over at Stachel. "A policeman. That's good. In the church, lying on the floor between two pews, I saw the body of a man. He looked dead."

"Why do you think that?"

"I thought at first that he was asleep, then thought he must have passed out and fallen to the floor. I shook his shoulder and then saw the blood. It was everywhere, on the floor and on him. I guess I panicked."

"Did he look like he'd been dead long?" his wife asked. Stachel wanted to tell her to be quiet, that he would handle this, but knew that she would ignore him.

"I don't know," the priest said, addressing Stachel. "It was all so sudden."

"I'll take you to the police, if you want."

The priest looked at Stachel with horror in his eyes. "No, no, you don't understand. I can't go to the police. This church is Lithuanian, and right now, pardon me, but with your current leader, the city has turned hostile to anyone who isn't German. You can go to the police alone. Leave out that I discovered the body."

Stachel shook his head. "I can't do that. What would I tell them?"

"That you saw the body. Just what I described to you."

"They'll see through that in a minute. I'm an detective. They'd become suspicious when I couldn't give them anything but general impressions."

"But you must. Please."

"Reinhardt," his wife said, grabbing his arm. "You can help him. The fire is almost out. You can examine the body and then go to the police."

Stachel looked over at the church and could see that his wife was correct. The firemen had finally gotten the fire under control. It looked like within the hour they would have the fire extinguished. But he was annoyed that she had volunteered him. She knew that he needed a rest, that the last thing he wanted to do on his holiday was get involved with a murder. That's all he ever did, and for once he wanted to be away from all that and pretend that people were actually nice to each other.

Besides, it was a local affair and no good would come of him getting involved.

His wife and the priest continued to plead with him, though he kept shaking his head no. Finally, to shut them up, he agreed that he would look at the body and then report it to the police. Then he would let them take over the investigation. He would not get involved any further.

The roof of the church had been made of wood and was completely destroyed, the church open to the clear blue morning sky. The frame of the glass dome in the center still stood, though the glass had all broken and fallen to the floor. Though the fire had not reached the nave, the smoke and water from the hoses had damaged the pews and stained-glass windows.

With the priest at his side, Stachel walked slowly down the middle aisle, hearing the crackle of broken glass as he took each step. Water dripped from the ceiling and echoed as it hit the floor, making the church feel like a cave. The pews had not been anchored to the floor, so many of them had been pushed aside or tipped over by the firemen when they entered the church after the fire had been put out. They had seen the body and had stayed clear of that area. The fire chief had told Stachel that he would have to contact the police. Stachel agreed, though he knew the priest would be unhappy.

Even though the man was lying face down, Stachel could tell immediately that he was dead. He never understood why, but he had always been able to tell without getting close if a body was asleep, unconscious or dead. There was something final about death, like the hand of God had waved over it and extinguished the spark. The blood the priest had mentioned had been washed away by the water. Turning the body to the side, Stachel could see the bullet wound in the middle of the chest, a gapping maw of torn flesh and congealed blood. The man's face was fixed in a grimace of horror. By the charring of the skin, he could tell that the shot had been fired at point blank range.

"Do you know who this is?" Stachel asked.

"No, I've never seen this man before. And I don't know when he got here. The doors are never locked. I keep the church open so anyone can come in and pray whenever they want."

"So, the body could have been here for hours?"

"Yes, though I had a small service last evening. The body would have been discovered if it was here then." The priest was walking back and forth in the aisle, full of nervous energy. "Perhaps you should leave. I shouldn't have asked you to get involved. I heard the fire chief tell you he would be contacting the police."

"Yes, they should be here shortly. Thank you for offering, but I'll wait for them."

Not wanting to touch the body anymore and risk corrupting evidence, Stachel went back outside, where Hilda was waiting.

"I'm sorry. I shouldn't have said anything," Hilda said, looking guilty.

"It's alright. There's not much I can do anyway. The police are coming."

"Then let's go back to the inn. I know you. If you're here when they arrive, you'll get involved."

"No, not this time," and Stachel firmly believed that statement, though he knew his wife was probably correct. He always got involved. He could never let something go. "You go back to the inn. I'll talk to the police and then meet you there."

"How long?"

"No more than an hour. If they're not here in thirty minutes, I'll leave anyway."

"OK but promise me you'll do that. I don't want this to ruin our holiday."

Stachel didn't say anything. Hilda looked at him in frustration, then shook her head and left. The holiday was already ruined.

Stachel went back inside and sat down in one of the pews that wasn't wet. Fifteen minutes later a man walked into the church. Stachel could tell immediately that he was a detective by the trench coat, black hat and black shoes. Trying to mime the Gestapo. He was young, probably hadn't seen his thirtieth birthday yet. He looked out of sorts, like he didn't want to be bothered by anything so mundane as a murder. Stachel got up and walked over and introduced himself. The man stared at his outstretched hand before reluctantly extending his.

"Who are you?" the man asked.

"Obersturmführer Stachel, from Berlin. Here on holiday. I happened to be here at the church when the body was found."

"Hauptsturmführer Armin Strippel. Now please stay out of my way."

So, the local police had already started using Nazi military ranks, Stachel thought. The Nazi moved fast.

Strippel nodded to the priest, then bent down over the body. He asked the priest the same questions Stachel already had and got the same answers.

"Well, I can tell you who this man is," he said to the priest, ignoring Stachel. "It's Tomas Vytautas, a minister in Mironas's cabinet."

"Who's Mironas?" Stachel asked.

Strippel looked over at him, clearly annoyed that he was still there.

"Prime Minister of Lithuania. Though not here anymore. He ceded the territory over to Germany last night. Memel is now part of the Third Reich."

The man said it with pride, staring at the priest, as though he was telling him he was no longer wanted in the city.

"It's still Klaipeda," the priest said. "No matter what Germany might think."

"Be careful Father," Strippel said, "you're not in Lithuania anymore." He looked back at the body. "I will call the coroner and have them pick up the body. I suggest you find other things to do in the meantime." He then turned to Stachel. "Though this is now Germany, you have no authority here. I ask you respectfully to leave and continue your holiday."

"Aren't you going to photograph the murder scene? It looks like the man was killed here and I wouldn't be surprised if the fire was started to try and destroy evidence."

"No, we can't be bothered. If alive this man would have been arrested as an agitator. Someone has nicely done our work for us."

The priest shook his head and started walking away. Stachel followed him with his eyes for a minute, then looked back at Strippel.

"Regardless of what the man was, or did, you can't let a murderer go free."

"I thought you were German? Wouldn't you have put him in a concentration camp?"

"I wouldn't. I arrest people. It's up to the courts to decide what to do with them."

"Well, here we don't have concentration camps..."

"So, you have other means?"

Strippel looked nervous now. Probably too low level, Stachel thought. A junior detective who's use to people doing what he says. A bureaucrat who can't think.

"I believe our conversation is at an end, Herr Stachel," making sure Stachel noticed that he did not use his title. "Please continue with your holiday while we deal with the legitimate business of the Third Reich." He spat out the last words as though they gave him an authority he'd never had.

Stachel thought better of continuing to protest. After all, hadn't he told his wife he didn't want to get involved? Trouble could only come of pressing Strippel. So, he quietly left, trying to put his hands in the pockets of his overcoat when he realized that he had given it to his wife. Huddled against the cold wind coming off the harbor, he headed back to the warmth of the inn.

"Can you believe they will do nothing?" Stachel said to his wife. "A man's been murdered, a politician, and they wipe their hands and say he had it coming."

"Is it any different in Germany?" Hilda said. She was sitting on the bed, pillow against her back, legs up, holding the local German language newspaper. Stachel was sitting in the one guest chair, wedged back in the corner, acting as though he had found the perfect place to hide from the world.

"It's not the same. I always investigate a murder, always."

"And sometimes it leads to people you can't touch, and you have to drop the case."

Stachel didn't want to hear about the compromises he was forced to make in his job. It had been different before Hitler came to power. Then the law mattered. Now it was the law of Hitler and no one dare stand in his way. He'd been wrong to vote for Hitler in '33. He had hoped that Hitler would correct the wrongs of the peace treaty, but instead the man had committed new wrongs. And they were worse than anything the peace treaty had subjected to Germany.

"Please don't remind me. I'm afraid of what Germany is turning into. I believed in Hitler. I voted for him. So did you. And now I fear he's leading us to war."

"He's uniting the German people. At least, that's what everyone says. That's what he says to justify his means. Look here," and Hilda tapped her finger on the front page headline. "It says that Memel is free at last. Liberated they say, completely ignoring that half the population has no interest in being part of Germany."

"That's my point." Stachel stood up and started pacing around the room, waving his hands and pointing his finger out the window as he made his argument.

"He's uniting the German people, yes, based on common language, but what about everyone else? Into the concentration camps they go as enemies of the state. I fear things can only get worse."

"Hopefully Hitler is finished now that he's achieved his goals."

"What are his goals? I fear he won't be happy until he's at war with someone. Doesn't he keep parading around like a popinjay in that military uniform." Stachel sat down on the bed. He reached behind him and clasped one of her slippered feet, shaking it as he spoke. "So, what do we do? Should we leave? Go back home to Berlin?"

"And cut our holiday short?" Hilda shook her foot out of Stachel's hand, got out of bed, and walked over to the window. "You're not going to be happy unless you do something about this murder. If we leave now, you'll just keep thinking about it and driving me crazy."

"No, I won't. I've already forgotten about it."

Hilda turned back into the room, shaking her head and laughing. "You know I'm right."

Stachel knew she was and that's what perturbed him the most. She knew him better than he did himself. If he did nothing, it would gnaw at his brain like a cancer. He would lay awake at night thinking that he had allowed nothing to be done about a murder. What was the point of being a policeman if you ignored crimes, if you let the criminals go free?

"Why don't you at least go back and talk to the priest," Hilda said, sitting down next to him on the bed. "Maybe he knows something. There must be a reason the body was left in that church instead of somewhere else."

"Or he was in the wrong place at the wrong time. It happens. The priest said the church is always open. That doesn't help narrow down the list of suspects."

"Well, your list is empty so it can't get worse. Go, talk to the priest, now, I'll wait here. Be back by lunch. The morning's ruined anyway." Hilda grabbed Stachel by the arm and started pushing him towards the door. She was right. It was half past ten already. Spending an hour looking into the case wouldn't hurt and would placate him that at least he'd done something. And then they'd enjoy what was left of their holiday.

She grabbed his hat and plopped it on his head as he opened the door, giving a quick pat to the top to push it down firmly. The hat slipped down and covered his eyes. Partly blind, Stachel walked down the corridor to the stairs, bumping into the wall, adjusting the hat before he headed down the stairs.

Stachel found the priest in the nave of the church, leading a group of people who were there to help clean up the mess made by the fire. When he saw Stachel, the priest glanced around him, as though looking for a place to hide. When he realized that Stachel had seen him, he sighed and waited for Stachel to walk over.

"Father, I'm sorry to bother you. It looks like you're very busy right now. But I can't help thinking about Vytautas and the fact that the police apparently will do nothing."

The priest grasped Stachel's arm and led him towards the back of the church, away from the people cleaning. They went up three steps and stopped in the back of the high altar, which was relatively undamaged by the fire. There was a table next to them, covered in a red cloth that was dotted with soot. Behind them was a large carved triptych illustrating the crucifixion and resurrection of Christ, a portrait of Saint Casimir in the bottom right corner, halo circling his head, looking up in prayer.

The priest was clasping his hands inside the sleeves of his robe, then pulling them out, then not knowing what to do and thrusting them inside his robe again.

"My name is Father Miskinis. It would be better if you didn't get involved in this."

"But earlier you asked me to get involved." Stachel was at a lost to understand what was going on. A man, a local politician according to the detective, had been killed, and everyone wanted to ignore it. Even in fear-ridden Berlin, people expected murders to be investigated, especially when they were officials of the government.

"I've changed my mind. Things are not always what they seem in Klaipeda…"

"You mean Memel."

"Klaipeda! Memel is the German name for the area, and I refuse to use it. As do all Lithuanians. And we are no longer welcome here. We hear rumors that Hitler has already announced that all Lithuanians who moved here after the Great War must leave the city immediately."

"Does that include you?"

"No. I was born and have lived my whole life in the city. But many of my parishioners are from the countryside and must leave. It is not good. We fear that Hitler will treat us like he treats the Jews in your country."

Stachel wished the priest had not used that comparison. The treatment of the Jews had always bothered him, but he had chosen to look the other way, to pretend as much as possible that it was temporary and that eventually Hitler would stop his insanity and see reason. As a policeman who was supposed to uphold the law, he knew he was wrong. He had spoken out once a few years ago and for a few days after that had lived in constant fear that he would be sent to a concentration camp. He knew he should do something but was at a lost as to what that something would be. So, he had kept his mouth shut, head down, focused on the work at hand, pursuing murderers while a murderous government went free.

"Father, earlier you said you didn't know the man. Was that true? Did you know him?"

"Yes," the priest said, reluctantly shaking his head. "I knew him, though I had never spoken to him. He came to the church occasionally, never during a service though, and sat in the back and prayed. A few times I was going to introduce myself, but he always looked so serious about his prayers that I never did."

"Did he ever look frightened?"

The priest thought for a moment. "He always looked frightened. As though he was being followed. But I never saw anything that would make me believe he was followed into the church, or that he was in any actual danger." The priest reached across and shook Stachel's arm. "He was a patriot, defending our country against Germany and Russia. Not a coward like that pig Mironas."

"The prime minister."

"Was, I believe. After today, I don't think his government will survive." The priest paused, head down, lost in thought for a moment. "Earlier today, I believed that the Germans killed Vytautas, but now I'm not so sure."

"Who will take over?"

"I don't know. I try and stay out of politics. But I know a man who might know. He seems to know everything that is going on in the city. How he knows I've never understood, but he knows, he knows. He has a gift," and the priest tapped the left side of his nose as he spoke. "He can help you. Go to him. His name is Raimondas Zydras. Tell him I sent you. If you don't, he won't talk to you. He has a shop, a grocery store, on Darzu, near the Lithuanian History Museum."

"Father, I will do what I can, but I doubt I can find Vytautas's murderer."

"But you are German. The police will not hurt you."

"Probably not, but they can throw me out of the country. And say something back in Berlin. I don't need that kind of attention right now."

The priest padded Stachel on the shoulder. "Do what you can. But please, go safe and let me know what you find."

"I will, if I can."

The shop on Darzu Street was old and showed signs of neglect. The building foundation had many cracks spiraling up the side. It would eventually collapse if it wasn't repaired. It was obvious that the shopkeeper didn't invest much time in cleaning the outside of the shop since there was a layer of dirt on the sidewalk. The blue striped awning was torn in three places and strands of thread hung down such that you had to wipe them away with your hand as you entered the shop. There were two wooden bins out front where fruit or vegetables would usually be on display, but both were empty.

Inside the shop, the shelves were stocked, but there were holes where product was missing. Cans of vegetables were stacked neatly in an aisle, but some of the labels were torn and there was a thin layer of dust on top of the cans. A counter lined the back of the store, with an old cash register in the center. Anything expensive was on shelves behind the counter. A gray haired man with a protruding belly and a ruddy complexion was standing behind the counter. He was wiping the counter with an old dirty rag. Apparently, he had a cold, as he would wipe the counter and then wipe his nose and then continue wiping the counter, all with the same rag, coughing without covering his mouth and constantly sniffling.

At first, Stachel backed away from the man, afraid he'd end up catching his cold, but then decided he really had no choice if he wanted to find out what was going on in Memel.

"Excuse me," Stachel said, "are you Raimondas Zydras?"

"Yes," the man said through wary eyes. The man's German was good, but he spoke with a distinct accent. "What of it? If you're a salesman, I don't need anything. If you're a policeman, and you look like a policeman, then I definitely don't need anything."

"Father Miskinis from the Church of Saint Casimir gave me your name."

"You haven't answered my question."

Stachel shook his head. "I didn't realize you asked a question."

"Are you a salesman or a policeman? You look German, and you smell German."

"Yes, I am German," Stachel admitted. "Let's just say I'm concerned about what is going on these days."

"So am I, but probably different from you."

"Maybe not. I don't approve of what Hitler has done."

"That makes two of us. I don't approve of what your Führer has done either." He said Führer as though he was spitting at a snake. "Father Miskinis picks some strange friends."

Stachel didn't know how to respond to that, so stood quietly, waiting for Zydras to continue.

"Well, the Father sent you here for a reason. What is it?"

"You've heard of Tomas Vytautas?"

"Yes."

"He's dead."

Zydras bumped against the shelves behind the counter. A few items fell to the floor, but he didn't take notice. His lips were shaking as though he was fighting with himself to not break out in tears.

"Dead? He can't be. I just saw him yesterday."

"Killed. In Father Miskinis's church. I'm trying to find out who did it."

"Why, the Germans did, of course. Who else?"

"Your government perhaps?"

Zydras looked down at the floor, then grabbed the rag and started wiping the counter again. He was clearly lost in thought, so Stachel waited quietly.

"It's possible," he finally said, reluctantly shaking his head. "Vytautas and Mironas did not get along. And the latest from your country has not made their love any better."

Stachel again didn't know what to say. He wanted to apologize for the actions of his country, but felt the words had no meaning since he had no power to do anything about it. He was a man who believed in results, not words.

"But our prime minister would not kill anyone," Zydras continued, "he is a priest, a man of God. But let me call someone. Someone else who was with Vytautas last night." Zydras was tapping the side of his nose, like Father Miskinis. Stachel wondered if it was a local affection of Lithuanians.

Zydras excused himself and went into a back room of the shop, behind a green colored curtain. Stachel could hear him dialing a phone and then talking to someone in Lithuanian. He was only on for a minute, then hung up and came back to the counter.

"Yes, he will see you. But his German is not too good. Do you speak Lithuanian?"

"No, I'm afraid not. Will you come with me and translate?"

"No, definitely not. Liepa, that is his name, and I cannot be seen together. Liepa, Steponas Liepa, will meet you at Teatro Square at noon. Do you know the square? It is the main square in town, only a few blocks from here."

"Yes, I know where it is."

"It is a good place to talk. At noon, many people will be there, so it will be easy to hide. And the rumors are that your Führer is in town and will give a speech later today. If true, it will probably be at the square." Again, Stachel's arm was grabbed and shaken, like it was an extension of the rag Zydras held in his other hand. "You must find out who killed Vytautas."

"What's he look like?"

"Don't worry, he will find you. Go, show our people that all Germans are not bad."

"I will do my best," though Stachel doubted his best would be good enough.

Teatro Square was in the center of old Memel, or Klaipeda, as Stachel kept telling himself he needed to call the city when he was around Lithuanians. The square was dominated by the Drama Theatre, with its balcony in the center overlooking the square. In front of the theatre was a fountain and statue dedicated to the poet Simon Dach. The statue was not of Dach, who was born in Klaipeda of German parents, but of a popular poem Dach wrote to the love of his life, Ann of Tharau.

Because of the German occupation, some of the shops were closed, but there were still many people in the square. There were also a lot of German soldiers, looking very serious in their crisp uniforms, with Beretta submachine guns at the ready.

The cobblestone square was still wet from a recent cleaning. The reflections of the people milling about made the square look like a giant cubist painting. The water also made it slippery, so Stachel found himself having to walk next to the shops, holding one hand against the side for support. He didn't know how he was going to find Liepa. Zydras had never described him but had only said that Liepa would know who he was.

He stopped, hands in the pockets of his overcoat, under an awning next to a restaurant, and looked out at the people, trying to spot Liepa.

Then suddenly there was a man standing next to him, wearing a black coat, brown collared shirt and tan derby hat. And he was tall, over six feet, and looked down at Stachel like a reptilian gargoyle about to pounce.

"Come with me," the man said in stuttered German. Without waiting for a response from Stachel, the man walked across the square, ignoring the German soldiers, and into a small café next to the Drama Theatre. He waved quickly to one of the waiters and sat down at a round wooden table in the back corner, facing the street, a door to his right led into the kitchen. Stachel took the seat across from him.

"You are Steponas Liepa?" Stachel asked. The man nodded yes but didn't say anything. He lit a cigarette but didn't offer one to Stachel. Stachel noticed that there was no ashtray on the table.

"And you talked to Zydras? You know who I am?"

Again, the man nodded yes. The smoke from his cigarette was forming a cloud in the middle of the table, obscuring Stachel's view. Finally, the man spoke.

"I know who you are. A German. I don't need to know anything else." He spoke slowly, translating each word before speaking. But his German was better than Zydras had said.

"All Germans are not bad."

"Right now, they are. You have invaded my country."

"I am not invading," Stachel said, thumping his finger against his chest.

"Then why are you here?"

"I'm on holiday." As he said it, given what was happening, Stachel wanted to laugh. Was a lamer excuse ever said? Great place to pick for a holiday.

"And you just happened to be on holiday when your beloved Führer gave us his ultimatum? Coincidence? I don't like coincidences. There's usually a lie behind them."

"Nevertheless. I am here on holiday, with my wife, who is back at the inn and is not enjoying herself, because I am here trying to find the man who murdered a Lithuanian."

Liepa flicked ash on the floor as he blew smoke across the table, obscuring Stachel's view.

"I do not know who killed Vytautas. At this point, I'm not sure it matters. He is dead, and another patriot is gone."

"Zydras said you saw Vytautas last night."

"Zydras talks to much."

"Is it true?"

Liepa looked over Stachel's shoulder, out into the street. His cigarette was about to burn his fingers. He got up and walked over to an empty table and put the cigarette out in an ashtray. Carrying the ashtray back to their table, he sat down and lit another cigarette. Stachel could sense that the man had finally made up his mind to talk to him, to tell him what he knew.

"It is true. Vytautas and I were at a meeting last night, though I did not talk to him. I was there to observe, not to participate."

"Who was the meeting with?"

"General Cernius. You know who Cernius is?"

"No."

"Leader of the opposition to Mironas. I believe Vytautas called the meeting. He wanted to fight the Germans, to resist the occupation. Cernius said it was impossible. They would accomplish nothing other than to kill a lot of Lithuanians. They argued back and forth for a while, the details are not important. The conversation became heated and Vytautas called Cernius a traitor. Cernius said that he would regret saying those words. The meeting then broke up, with Vytautas saying that he would fight the Germans himself, alone if need be."

"Then what happened?"

"That's all I know. Vytautas left very much alive. I stayed at the meeting, but Cernius left shortly afterwards. He looked clearly agitated but didn't say anything."

"Zydras thinks the Germans killed Vytautas, but he admitted that Mironas could have ordered it."

"No, Mironas wouldn't have done it. He's out. His government has been dissolved as of today. The rumors are that Cernius will form a new government."

Stachel reached out and tried to wave the cloud of smoke away, trying to get a better view of Liepa.

"Did Cernius kill Vytautas?"

"It is possible, though I believe it is the Germans. They have more reason to want to eliminate him."

"But then why leave the body in a church? Why have him assassinated? The Germans, the Gestapo, would just arrest him and you'd never see him again."

"That is what bothers me. I don't want to believe that one of my countrymen would kill Vytautas. But you should leave. Go back to your country. Things will not be easy here. Especially for someone on a holiday." Liepa said holiday as though it was the punch line of a joke, a joke too painful for laughter.

"Thank you," Stachel said, not having any other questions to ask.

"You still want to find Vytautas's murderer? As I said earlier, it is better to let it go."

"I can't. I told Father Miskinis I would try."

Liepa let out a deep sigh. "That is all we do these days, try. And look what it's gotten us. If Hitler doesn't take over Lithuania, Stalin will. Two hungry beasts staring at each other, with Lithuania as the meal."

"What time is it?"

Liepa pointed to a clock on the wall. Ten minutes to one. He had told Hilda he would be back by noon.

"I must leave," Stachel said, rising from the table. "But I haven't given up. Not yet."

"What will you do?"

"I don't know. But I will try to find this killer before I leave."

Liepa said nothing more. He stubbed out his cigarette and left through the door into the kitchen.

Stachel headed back to the inn as quickly as he could. There were more people gathering in the square and on the streets. He had to push his way past them.

Hilda told him immediately that he should drop the case, that it was to dangerous, that the killer could be from either side and that both sides were desperate right now. A good way to get arrested, if not killed.

The curtains were drawn, making the room dark and morose.

"This is none of your business," Hilda said. "In Berlin you might have some authority, but here you are just a tourist, a tourist sticking his nose in things better left unknown."

Though Hilda sounded angry, Stachel could tell from the look in her eyes that she was actually scared. When she was angry, her whole body shook with emotion. When she was scared, her body was quiet, soft, as though she was struggling to not break down into tears.

"I know you're right," Stachel said, "but I can't just walk away. This man seemed to be highly respected. Either the Germans or the Lithuanians killed him, and the guilty party should be known. Even if they will never be prosecuted, just knowing who did it will make me feel better."

"Why? And what would you do now? You don't know anyone here."

"I'm a policeman. It's my job. I'd be no better than the killer if I look the other way. And I don't know what I'll do next. I suppose talk to the priest again and find out if anyone else was in the church last night and saw something."

Hilda had been sitting on the end of the bed. She grabbed a pillow and started puffing it up, acting as though it was a punching bag. "The innkeeper said that Hitler is in town and will give a public speech later today announcing that Memel is now part of Germany. I don't want to be here when that happens."

Stachel walked over and put his arms around his wife. "Then you should go back to Berlin. I'll stay here for a few more days and poke around."

She pushed his arms away. "No, if we leave, we leave together. I'm not going back to Berlin so I can find out that you've disappeared."

Stachel walked back to the chair he had been sitting in and sat back down, hands clasped in front of him as though in prayer. "So, the only way to keep you safe is for us both to leave?"

"The only way to keep both of us safe is for both of us to leave. And I've already checked. There's a train leaving for Berlin at four today. And it's pretty empty. No one wants to go to Berlin these days."

They didn't say anything for a minute. The room was so quiet that the rumbling of Stachel's empty stomach sounded like a truck was passing by on the street below.

"You haven't eaten," Hilda said. "Let me see if the innkeeper can make a sandwich."

"Don't bother. I don't feel much like eating…"

There was a knock on the door, three solid knocks as though someone was trying to break the door down with his fist. Hilda started for the door, then sat down on the bed when Stachel yelled out who it was. Police came the roar from the closed door. Stachel whispered to her to go into the bathroom. She shook her head no, so he took her by the arm and forced her into the bathroom, closing the door and asking her to please keep quiet.

Not to his surprise, it was the detective from the church standing in the corridor, Armin Strippel. Strippel walked past Stachel and into the room without waiting for an invite. The nervousness from earlier that day was gone. He looked confident, a man who felt he was in control, a man who expected people to do what he said. He stood by the window, pulling the curtain back and tapping on the glass. His other hand was in his overcoat and looked like it was clasping a gun. Stachel noticed now that the man was wearing a Nazi swastika armband, which he had not had on earlier that day.

"You have been talking to people, people it is better not to be seen with."

"I have talked to some people, yes."

"You should not have done that. These people are dangerous. They are suspects in the killing."

"Suspects? I thought you weren't going to investigate the killing?"

"That's not your concern. I'm here to give you a message. You should leave immediately, today. If you stay, we cannot be responsible for what might happen to you."

"And what is that?"

"I told you these people are dangerous. They will do anything to get back at Germany, including killing a German policeman."

Stachel sat down on the bed and motioned for Strippel to sit in the chair. Strippel ignored him.

"I doubt that."

"Whether you doubt it or not is not important. You will leave immediately."

"I'm on holiday."

"Not anymore. As of now, your holiday is over. Leave. Let us deal with the Lithuanians."

"When's enough enough? When will Hitler stop?"

"When Germans are all united under the Third Reich and we are once again seen as a force in Europe. A powerful nation who will be respected."

"And feared?"

Strippel was obviously done talking. "Leave," he said again, and left the room. As soon as the door closed, Hilda came out of the bathroom and started packing, not saying anything to Stachel. He started to say something, but she cut him off and told him there would be no more discussion. They were leaving.

Stachel gave in. What else was he going to do?

They checked out of the inn, paying for a week's stay even though they had only been there a few days. The train station was crowded, full of Lithuanians trying to get on any train going east, away from Germany. The clerk at the ticket office was surprised that they wanted to go to Berlin, until he realized that they were German. Then he gave them their tickets without saying another word.

There were only a handful of people on the train, so they were able to get good seats, with plenty of room to spread out, though neither did, preferring to sit close to each other. As the train pulled away and started west, Stachel overheard a couple sitting a few seats in front of them talking about the speech Hitler had just given from the balcony of the Drama Theatre in Teatro Square.

"Germany is at last united," the man said to his wife. "Hitler now has what he wants and will start mending fences with Britain and France."

Stachel knew that Hitler would never stop. Madmen never do. And no one would try and stop him until it was too late. Like Stachel with Vytautas's murder, everyone would look the other way. For how long would he continue to do the same?

Chapter Twenty-One

At the office he immediately ran into Lakain, who had heard about Mintert and was upset that he hadn't been called.

"There wasn't time," Stachel said with a curt aside that the matter was closed.

Lakain sat down and started asking for details about the new murder.

"Haven't you been reassigned?" Stachel asked.

"No, should I have been? No one has talked to me." Lakain looked disappointed. He wanted to stay in homicide. Found it exciting. Better than being a patrolman, dodging bombs and chasing people who had stolen ration cards.

"The Holzer case is closed. Someone should have talked to you about returning to whatever you were doing beforehand. Besides, don't you have a family to go to? It's almost the end. You should be with them?"

"Well, no one has." Lakain leaned over the desk and whispered. "And until they do, I'd like to continue working with you. And my Mom and Dad are both in the countryside near Munich. They don't need me."

Stachel also leaned over the desk so that their noses were almost touching. "You don't need to whisper. No one's listening. Not even him." He pointed at the portrait of Hitler.

Lakain looked at Hitler's icy stare and shuddered. "I heard Mintert was strangled and then stabbed. That sounds like our killer's still loose." Lakain's eyes lit up at the thought.

"*Our* killer? What are you going to do? Adopt him? Besides, the official word is that Mintert is a copycat killing. So, we need to focus our efforts on people who knew the details of the Holzer murder."

"But only a few of us knew," Lakain said, throwing up his hands in exasperation, "and none of us is the killer. And no one in the public knew."

"What about the other patrolman who was at the Holzer crime scene?"

"Gert? He's harmless," Lakain said with a small chuckle. "The man doesn't do anything on his own. Just waits there for someone to make a decision for him. Drives me crazy when I've got the same shift as him. He looks at me like I'm his supervisor, even though he's probably thirty years older than me. Who else?"

"August Holzer and Goebbels knew, and whoever they might have told."

"Oh good, let's investigate Goebbels. That will lead to a long and happy life."

Sarcasm? From Lakain? Maybe the lad had something in him after all.

"Not Holzer or Goebbels. But who did they tell? That's what we need to know. Look into that."

"How? I can't just call them up and ask them."

"I don't know. Figure it out. You want to be a detective, start detecting. Now go." Lakain ran out the door, heading

God knew where. Stachel didn't care, as long as he was left alone.

He knew he had to be quiet and not arouse any suspicions, particularly from Gottlieb, that he was still investigating the Holzer murder. In case he was found out, he had to have a prepared story about what he was doing. Rounding up witnesses was what he usually said, but he doubted there were any witnesses since the Mintert killing had happened at night in the middle of the park. He could say he heard a pedestrian had been wandering through the Tiergarten and could have seen something. It was a story that maybe would keep Gottlieb at bay for a while.

Was a serial killer on the loose? Or was this the beginning of an uprising?

The connection with the black market looked better the more he thought. Or was it because they were both Nazis? That narrowed down the list of suspects to ninety percent of the people in the country. No, start with the patrolmen. That was the only thing that made sense right now. Look for a patrolman who either was anti-Nazi or had a suspected involvement in the black market.

Every patrolman punched a time clock and those records were all kept under file. In the past, the file room was always open during the day, with a clerk who would retrieve files for you. But the clerks had all joined the military long ago, so now the room was under lock and key and usually guarded by a patrolman. The key was with the staff sergeant, and one had to sign a form when requesting the key, stating the reason why they wanted to access the files. Stachel didn't want to create a paper trail that Gottlieb could find. The staff sergeant right now was a man named Neuling, who Stachel barely knew, so he didn't see him doing Stachel a favor. Besides,

Neuling was known for being a stickler for following the rules, as long as they were Nazi rules. He needed to figure out a way to get the key without signing any forms and without Neuling knowing. Maybe he could get Lakain to create a distraction while Stachel lifted the key from the staff sergeant's desk? Of course, without telling Lakain why.

He found Lakain at his desk, looking at photos of the Mintert killing, and motioned him into his office. How the hell did he get those photos? Now the lad was talking to Wandel to.

"I need you to talk to Sergeant Neuling. I've heard that he might know something pertinent to the Mintert case. Take him to one of the interrogation rooms and find out what he knows." Stachel couldn't look Lakain in the eye as he talked. He hated lying, but he had no choice.

"Isn't he the staff sergeant? He can't just leave the desk."

"With the way things are right now, who's going to care? Tell him it's important. Don't give him a chance to argue. Insist that he come with you."

"Alright, but he's not going to be happy."

"Who is these days? Just do it."

Lakain scampered out to follow his orders. The coffee room was near the front desk and there was a window looking out on the main foyer where the staff sergeant sat. Stachel went to get a cup of coffee. He saw Lakain talking to Neuling though he couldn't hear what he was saying. Neuling was shaking his head no and tapping his finger on the desk, presumably saying that he needed to stay there. Lakain banged his fist on the desk, pointed to a room down the hall and grabbed Neuling by the arm. Neuling tried to shrug him off but Lakain pulled him along and into the room and closed the door.

Lakain is looking better and better. At least he does what he's told.

As soon as the door closed, Stachel dropped his full cup of coffee in the sink and headed out to the desk. The keys were on a peg board behind the desk, all nicely labeled. Stachel took the file room key and put a key for one of the interrogation rooms which looked similar in its place. Putting the key in his pocket, Stachel then opened the door to the interrogation room and told Lakain and Neuling, who were sitting at opposite ends of a desk, that he had been told incorrect information and that Neuling could go back to his desk. Neuling quickly jumped up, relieved that he was let go, while Lakain sat stunned.

"You made me look like a fool," he said.

"Sorry. The fool's the one who told me Neuling knew something. Go back to your desk. I'll explain to Neuling that it was my fault." The man's like a rabbit, Stachel thought, as Lakain scampered off again. After explaining to Neuling what had happened, and getting cussed out, Stachel headed to the basement.

As he descended the stairs, Stachel tried to think of a good story to tell the guard. He couldn't come up with anything very plausible other than that he was checking to see who was on patrol the night of Mintert's murder so he could find out if they had seen anything suspicious.

But when he got to the door, he was surprised to find that there was no guard. Had they given up guarding the room or was the guard just absent for a short time? Stachel didn't want to find out, so he quickly unlocked the door, and then locked it from within. He had brought a flashlight, in case he had to work in the dark, but luckily the lights were on, and only in a few places were the bulbs burned out.

The file room was not very big and only held the last three months documentation. After three months, everything was moved to an offsite location. If you wanted something from there, you needed to fill out a written request and wait one day for the file to be delivered to HQ. Since Stachel didn't need to go back that far, everything he wanted should be in the file room. The left side of the room had the files for each patrolman, organized by date. The right side was documents for past investigations. And for once, Stachel could praise good German efficiency. Even though the city was in chaos, the patrolmen still seemed to follow their routes, still on patrol, punching the time clock, documenting what they had seen. He quickly found the files for April Fourteenth, the date Holzer was killed.

There were only three patrolmen walking the Mitte district from midnight to eight in the morning: Michael Schlueter, Alfred Ammer and Curt Banze.

Schlueter had been with the force for eleven years but had never risen above the rank of patrolman. He had been disciplined twice. Once for being overly zealous with a civilian and another time for not showing the proper respect to his supervisor. Neither were serious infractions but seemed to be enough to keep him from ever being promoted. Or maybe he just liked being out on the street, away from the office politics.

Both Ammer and Banze were new to the force and had joined within the last year. Both were young, in their early twenties, and both had a handicap that had kept them out of the military; Ammer had an arm that was shorter than the other and Banze's left leg was shorter than his right, so he walked with a pronounced limp. Maybe he's Goebbels illegitimate son, Stachel thought. Ammer was from a small village in Bavaria and had moved to Berlin in 1944, joining the force a few months after arriving in the city. He had no marks against his record and one commendation for saving civilian lives when a bomb had destroyed an apartment building. Banze was another matter. He was from a small village near the Danish border. His parents were Danish and had migrated to Germany before the Great War. Banze had been born in Germany and was a German citizen. He had also moved to Berlin in '44 and joined the force immediately. And he had three marks against his record already. Once for helping a Jew who was being beaten, once for not giving the Hitler salute when Himmler had visited the office, and once for telling his supervisor he wouldn't arrest someone just because he was an undesirable. The only reason Banze still had a job was because all abled-bodied men were in the military.

Stachel ruled out Ammer immediately. No signs of insubordination, and coming from Bavaria, the birthplace and still a hothouse for all things Nazi meant he probably supported the current regime. Maybe Schlueter, though because he had been in the Kripo for so long, Stachel doubted that he would suddenly turn against the Nazis. He looked like the kind that liked to stay under the radar, not make any fuss, just do his job and go home without any worries.

That left Banze. From the North, which had always been less supportive of the Nazis, and a record of insubordination for refusing to follow Nazi policy. Had he suddenly grown desperate, knowing the end was near and wanting to look good with the Allies by proving that he was against the Nazis?

He put the files back and was surprised to find the files for last night, April Twentieth. Someone was still overly diligent. Though assigned to the eastern side of the district, Banze had been on patrol that night. Three others had also been on patrol, but they all looked like Schlueter clones, quiet people just doing their job. Banze looked promising. And he was a large man, according to his personnel file. 6' 3", 220 pounds and a wrestler in his school days.

He would have to bring Banze in for questioning, but keep the questions focused on the Mintert murder and try to weave in the other murder without raising suspicions. Stachel wasn't worried about what Banze thought but wanted to make sure that his inquiries didn't get back to Gottlieb.

If it was a Gestapo agent, he wasn't sure what he should do. He doubted they checked in and out every day. Talk to Hugo Baer? That was the only thing he could think of, though he doubted it would get him anywhere. But where else could he turn?

He needed to put a twenty-four hour tail on Banze. But he didn't have the manpower to do it right. Lakain was out. He didn't trust him. Maybe he could get Stehen to agree? But until he could reach him, that left only Stachel, and he couldn't follow Banze all day and night. It seemed that the best place to start was during his patrol. See who he talked to, see if he diverged from his route at all. If that didn't turn up anything, then he'd have to watch him after work. Either way, it meant Stachel wasn't going to get much sleep. Didn't matter much. Lay in bed, staring at the ceiling, waiting for the sprint to the air raid shelter, or be productive and hope something would turn up quickly with Banze, or through Baer, with the Gestapo.

He left the filing room key in the door. Let Neuling puzzle over how it got there.

For once Stehen answered the phone when Stachel called. At first Stachel paused, surprised that he was hearing Stehen's voice, then asked that they meet later tonight.

"At the intersection of Potsdamerstrasse and Scharounstrasse," Stachel said.

"It's in ruins."

"Exactly. No one will be there. At ten." And Stachel hung up.

He called Baer at his apartment at seven, hoping he would be home. He was, though he didn't want to talk to Stachel. In a whisper, Baer told Stachel that things were getting crazy at Prinz Albrechtstrasse. They were starting to burn files, and people in the cells were being taken out back and shot. No one could be trusted anymore. When Stachel mentioned his suspicion that a Gestapo agent might have killed Holzer and Mintert, Baer laughed.

"Those two and everyone else. What else is the Gestapo doing these days. Look, I can't get involved. I'm sorry, but I have to think of my family first, and a dead husband and father isn't going to help them."

"Isn't there anyone you can think of who is ambivalent about the government and has shown violent tendencies?"

Baer laughed again. "Reinhardt, you're absurd. Everyone is ambivalent about the government now, and everyone in the Gestapo, except me of course, is violent. That's like asking if any newborn babies cry. They all do."

"OK, dead end."

"Good word. Death is an ending that we're all about to experience."

Stachel hung up. If a Gestapo agent was the killer, Stachel had little hope that he would be able to catch him. It was Banze or nothing.

Banze reported to Hauptsturmführer Albert Lederer. Stachel knew that if he contacted Banze directly and asked to speak with him, Banze would get suspicious. He knew Lederer had a reputation for protecting his men and would get all riled up and potentially cause a scene, even to saying something to Gottlieb, if Stachel talked to Banze directly. Stachel needed to do this properly, follow the chain of command he would usually ignore, and talk to Lederer first.

Lederer was in his office. Unlike Stachel's desk, Lederer's was neat and organized. It looked like he spent his whole day pushing paper from one side of his desk to the other and reminding people how important he was. He was a short, gruff man with a bushy mustache and a belly that looked like he spent more time eating sausage than walking.

When Stachel sat down in the guest chair and asked if he could talk to Banze, Lederer immediately went on the defensive. Stachel deflected his questions as best he could by saying he only wanted to ask Banze if he had seen anything on the night of the Mintert murder.

"Don't you think he'd say something if he had?" Lederer said. "He's one of my best patrolmen."

"I'm sure he would," Stachel replied, "but he might have seen something that at the time he didn't think was relevant. I'm just following up on the investigation and need to look at all angles. Besides, you know this investigation is given top priority by our superiors."

Lederer stroked his mustache, swore a few times and shook his head no, but eventually sighed and agreed once he realized it was in his best interest to help.

"Alright, bring him in, but only before his patrol begins. And I want his overtime charged to your department."

Stachel had one of the secretaries call Banze at home and tell him to come to work at eleven that night, one hour earlier then when he started his patrol. That should give him plenty of time to talk to Stehen at ten and get back to the Alex before Banze.

Knowing he had a few hours to kill, Stachel went out for a walk. Up until now he could go out in the evening and know that there was little risk of being killed in an air raid. But now, everything had changed. The artillery was constantly pounding the city. The whine of an incoming shell was like the beginning of Beethoven's Third. Two E flat major chords played by the Russians. There were pockets of fire everywhere. And the people had stopped caring. Where just a few days ago, the neighborhood would have rallied to try and put out a fire before it spread, now they left it burning. When not getting water or food, everyone was hunkered underground waiting for the end. Stachel knew he should do the same but hiding in a shelter would never solve the case. Besides, he was finished anyway. When your time comes, it will come. Today or in a few weeks didn't really matter.

As he strolled down Unter den Linden, his luck was with him. He found a restaurant just off the boulevard that was serving some blood sausage with potatoes. He ate until full and now in a good mood, ordered some schnapps, and then another, so by nine o'clock he was full and a little tipsy and in no mood to talk to Stehen or Banze. He derided himself for being so stupid and overindulging himself. And he hadn't even thought yet about how he was going to approach Banze without arousing suspicions. It looked like the night was turning into a disaster, and of his own making.

He left the restaurant and knew he needed to walk around for a bit and clear his head before meeting Stehen. Though it was cold out, there were people out on the streets, meandering among the rubble: lovers holding hands, old men huddled against the sides of buildings, wrapped in alcohol and misery, women at the neighborhood water pump, filling up a bucket to last the night. All, even the old men, seemed to be in a better mood than Stachel. Maybe he should chuck the whole thing, give up on the investigation and just do his best to stay alive? Leave Mintert to the Gestapo; that's where his corpse belonged. Why did he keep doing this? Why did he keep asking himself the same question every time? He must be going mad. The answer was always the same. Because he must, because he had nothing else to do, because it kept him from going mad, because it kept the thought of suicide at bay. Pulling up his coat collar and shoving his hands deep in his pockets, Stachel headed for Potsdamer.

Potsdamer Platz had once been the center of entertainment in Berlin but now it had been bombed into ruins. The hotels and the cafes were all empty shells, deserted or littered with people who had lost their apartments to bombs or fire. Stachel waited at the intersection of Potsdamerstrasse and Scharounstrasse for about twenty minutes. Then Stehen came out of the shadows and motioned for Stachel to follow him into the Tiergarten. The Tiergarten looked like a battlefield from the Great War. The trees were blackened silhouettes, all the leaves burned off. The bushes were stunted, struggling to stay alive in a wasteland. Bomb craters pocketed the area.

Where bombs hadn't hit, the grass had grown long and wild, not having been mowed in months.

They walked for a few minutes in silence, both lost in their thoughts, Stachel thinking about the wreck that was Berlin and if the Allies would ever stop bombing long enough to take the city. Eventually, Stehen started talking, mentioning that he had little new information. Everyone was suspicious, everyone was in hiding and keeping their heads down, afraid of both the Nazis and the Allies. "One rumor is that Holzer was a robbery gone bad. Another rumor thinks Holzer was an execution. Of course, no one has any details to explain why they think any rumor is true. Both make sense but can't be proven. Besides, a lot of people want to kill the Nazis, or anyone associated with them."

"But how many are willing to take up arms? Germans do what they're told, no matter how ridiculous."

Stachel asked for names. He needed to talk to whoever Stehen got the rumors from. Stehen refused.

"They'd kill me immediately and disappear."

"Black market?"

"Worse. These people are part of a criminal gang that's as bad as anyone in the Gestapo. But why do you care? I heard that the killer was found."

"A convenient suspect was found and executed. But I don't believe he was the killer. Another thing. Do you know a policeman named Banze? He patrols the Mitte district."

"I've heard of him, but only that he's relatively honest for a policeman these days. I hear he's on the take and has dealings with the black market. Random beatings now and then which is what everyone expects from the police."

"Random beatings?"

"Don't play naïve. The Kripo isn't full of choir boys. They'll beat up and arrest anyone just for looking cross eyed."

"Maybe I am naïve, but sometimes that's the only way to survive. Can you follow him, check Banze out, find out who he's working with?"

"You think he killed Holzer?"

"Banze is a suspect, that's all." Stachel stopped and looked around. They were near the Victory Column now and he was replaying the murder scene. "Did you hear about Mintert? He was murdered over there earlier today, tied to one of the columns."

Stehen looked perplexed. "Heinz Mintert? The Judge? No, I hadn't heard but I'll staying away from that one. That's got Gestapo bloodbath written all over it. They'll be out for revenge and won't care who they kill in the process."

Stachel ignored Stehen's comment. It seemed everyone was in a panic these days and they were all staring straight at him. Gottlieb would probably love to nail him to a wall. It would make him look good with Goebbels.

"You didn't answer my question. Can you follow Banze?"

Stehen shook his head. "I'd rather not. Get someone else. Besides, I think it's a waste of time. And if he sees me, at the best I'll escape with a good beating. I've been told the man always carries a riot bat and loves to use it when he's not happy."

"Come on. You should live for this. Your big chance to get back at us. And I need your help. You'll be well paid."

"Let me think about it."

"I need an answer now. I need to get answers quickly."

"Look, who cares," Stehen said, his right eye twitching slightly, which Stachel knew was a sign that he was nervous.

"Mintert and Holzer got what they deserved. We should be thanking this killer, not trying to catch him. If it is Banze, it's the first good thing he's ever done."

"I care. I'll pay you double."

"How?"

"Reich marks."

"Keep them. They're worthless these days. I want U.S. dollars, or schnapps and cigarettes. Good cigarettes. And a lot of them."

Stachel shook his head. "You know I can't get those."

"Well, if that changes let me know. Otherwise, no deal." Stehen looked around the Tiergarten with a worried look on his face, shook his head, then disappeared into the misery of the park.

Stachel wondered if he's ever seen him again. And his problem wasn't solved. He needed someone to watch Banze, and if Stehen wasn't going to do it, that meant he had to turn to Lakain. A problem unto himself.

He headed straight to the office now. He needed some coffee and he needed to prepare for Banze. It was already quarter to eleven.

"Heinz Mintert," Stachel said.

They were sitting in Stachel's office. Stachel behind his metal desk, second cup of coffee in front of him, still trying to shake off the effects of the schnapps. Banze sat across from him, leaning in, his elbows resting on his knees, hands clasped, looking the picture of a guilty person. He had the broad shoulders and the large hands of someone who worked in construction. He had limped into the office, holding his right leg as though he was in pain. Clearly, he was looking for sympathy. He had the wary look of a hunted animal.

"You heard about the murder the other day?" Stachel continued. Banze shook his head yes. "You were on patrol that night. I want to know if you heard or saw anything."

Banze leaned back, looking more comfortable now that he understood what the conversation was about. "I didn't see anything, but why would I? Mintert was killed at the Victory Column and my beat that night was the eastern side of the district. Nowhere near the Tiergarten. "

"I'm not asking if you saw the murder. I'm asking if you saw anyone on the street, anyone that looked suspicious, anyone that looked like they had something to hide."

"Everyone has something to hide these days. But I didn't see anything. There aren't many people out at night because of the blackout."

"How about the Holzer killing? That was in your patrol area."

"I thought this was about Mintert? I heard Holzer's killer was caught and confessed."

"Yes, he was caught, but there was no confession," Stachel lied. "He supposedly killed himself beforehand. I'm just tying up some loose ends on that case."

"What loose ends? The killer was caught, he died, case closed. Why do you care?"

Stachel was perturbed now. Who was this low level patrolman that he presumed to ask him questions?

"I will ask the questions here, Herr Banze. And you will answer them. Is that understood?"

Banze shrugged his shoulders. "No, I saw nothing the night of Holzer's murder. All quiet, just the way I like it."

"Well, obviously it wasn't quiet that night. You're on patrol to stop things like murders from happening."

Banze glared at Stachel and made ready to stand up.

"Sit down," Stachel ordered. "You'll leave when I tell you to leave."

"Then don't insult me by insinuating that I wasn't doing my job."

"What is your real job, Herr Banze?"

Banze stood up. "I don't need this. If you have any more questions, talk to Lederer." As Banze left the office, he stomped his left foot on the floor, as though making as much noise as possible gave him courage. Stachel couldn't be sure, but he thought that for a moment Banze was going to do the same with his supposedly injured left leg.

Well, that didn't go well, he thought. He's pissed off and I got nothing from him. He looked more worried at the beginning, before he realized what the meeting was about. Maybe Stehen's information was correct that Banze was involved in the black market. And that gives him a possible motive.

Banze changed into his black Kripo uniform, wearing the black crowned hat with the silver Swastika and Eagle. His uniform was clean and his shoes brightly polished. From the coffee room Stachel watched him walk out of the station, a holstered pistol on his right side, swinging a small riot bat by its leather strap with his left.

Stachel waited a few minutes and then followed him out the door, hugging to the shadows as much as possible and trying to stay about a hundred feet behind him. It was in the low forties, but the rain that had fallen earlier that day made it feel colder. And, of course, he hadn't dressed for the cold weather. He cursed himself for not thinking ahead and putting on some long johns.

Stachel had found Banze's normal route in the files. Banze started down Leipzigerstrasse, turned North onto Friedrichstrasse and worked his way towards Unter Den Linden, wandering up and down the side streets. At Unter Den Linden, he turned right and then south at Opernplatz and down Markgrafenstrasse towards the Gendarmenmarket, where Sophie Holzer had been murdered. Back on Leipzigerstrasse, he would continue east to the Spittelmarket, where he would turn south down Lindenstrasse and start working his way back to the station, where he would take a fifteen minute break and then start all over again.

The streets were relatively empty, though there were a few civilians about. When they saw Banze, they would quicken their pace, clutching anything they carried close to their chest. Often, Banze would raise his hat in greeting, and a few times, he would swing his bat lazily at a rushing passerby, telling them to hurry home, didn't they know there was a war on. Near the Gendarmenmarket, Banze stopped for a minute, looked around and then ducked into an alleyway.

Stachel stopped, leaned against the side of a building, while he decided what to do. Should he try and sneak up on the alley entrance? The risk was high that he'd be seen. But he couldn't just stay where he was. What was the point of trailing Banze if every time he disappeared, Stachel didn't follow?

But just as he decided to head into the alley, Banze came out and continued his route. Stachel waited a few minutes and then continued walking after him. When he was about ten feet from the alleyway, a short, hunched over man came out, stopped for a minute in surprise at seeing Stachel, and then headed pass him, going the opposite way. He made a quick decision and turned around and followed the man. He could pick up trailing Banze later.

The man continued down to the end of the street and then ducked into an apartment building. By the time Stachel got to the door, it was locked. Judging from the mailboxes there were only six apartments. There was enough light bleeding through the blackout curtains for Stachel to see the names on each box. He wrote the names down, then retraced his steps and continued after Banze. Banze talked to a few people on his route, berated one drunken man who was clutching a bottle and laying in the debris of a bombed out building. Banze poked the man in the side with his riot bat, told him to get up and go home, and took the bottle from him. The man tried to grab it back and Banze pushed him down, warning him that he'd beat him senseless if he moved again.

By three in the morning, Stachel couldn't stand the cold anymore and headed back to his apartment, jumping under the bed covers with his suit still on. The British bombing would start soon, but he didn't care.

The next day, Stachel checked the names he had written down at the apartment last night against the files of known criminals and got two hits. Jan Mielke, arrested five years ago for assault, nothing since then. And Thomas Munzel, who had been arrested three times recently for petty theft and spent six months in a concentration camp, released only a few months ago. Munzel seemed the more promising suspect, so he decided to focus on him. The names of the officers who had arrested him for petty theft were in the files. Stachel knew the officer from the last arrest and found him in the canteen, on his break before heading back out on patrol.

"He's a shifty guy, all right," Officer Claussen said. "But what do you do with someone like that these days? We should have kept him in the concentration camp, along with the Jews and buggers. But he isn't worth the effort."

"Do you think he could have graduated to more serious stuff, like murder?"

"Munzel? Wouldn't believe it, but no one's acting normal these days. You never know. Why, you got something on him?"

"No, just suspicions."

"It's the Mintert case, isn't it? I heard you were working on it."

Stachel said yes, thanked him and quickly left, before Claussen asked any more questions.

Chapter Twenty-Two

S tachel woke up early the next morning. Too early. He had slept through the British bombing raid, for the first time he thought, but he had only gotten in total about three hours sleep. Every muscle cried out with fatigue, as though he'd just run through the Kripo exercise course as a rookie. But where before he would have a few hours of silence before the Americans came, now the Russian artillery started up. Relentless noise combined with the harsh anxiety of your impending death.

He laid in bed, pulling the covers up to his chin, staring up at the ceiling, noting that there seemed to be more cracks, more spider webs twisting out from the center to the corners. It had dropped down in the low forties last night and he had stupidity left the bedroom window open. Low forties seemed warm after a few days of freezing weather, but it had started raining, putting a bite in the air, a sharpness that cut into his lungs. Wishing he could stay in bed but knew he couldn't, Stachel willed himself up. He pattered across the floor to his shoes near the front door. First order of business was to get some coal.

Out on the street, Stachel walked the two blocks down Luisenstrasse and crossed the Marschalbrucke bridge, where the street name changed to Wilhelmstrasse. It sounded like the Russians had picked a location far to the south to pummel this morning. The Baumarkt was a block south of the bridge and despite the artillery barrage, a sign hanging from the metal shudder said it would open within a few minutes. Life goes on, or tries to, regardless of the circumstances. There were only a few people in line, all silent, all bundled in their greatcoats. He got in line, hoping that he would remain anonymous. Usually, he made a point to be sociable to everyone, given his position in the Kripo, but today he didn't want to talk to anyone. He needed to think. The case was weighing on him. He knew Banze was up to something. That was apparent from last night. Probably the black market, but did that mean he would kill to protect himself? Or was Banze taking revenge on the Nazi party? His history showed he had no love for them. But arresting him could cause all kinds of trouble. Lederer would go on the attack, defending his patrolman. And Gottlieb would want to sweep it under the table, make Banze disappear and then deny his existence. Himmler would let him, but Goebbels would want to turn it to his advantage. Hitler's henchmen spent more time at war with each other than with the enemy.

His gut told him that Banze was not the murderer. Didn't fit his personality. For all Stachel knew, the man standing in front of him, small, rounded shoulders, a crop of grey hair under a dirty brown hat, could be the murderer. He heard noise from the store, then the metal shudder was pulled up and a tall greasy, soot covered man yelled *"Guten Morgen"* to the first person in the queue. The line moved quickly and within a few minutes Stachel was walking back to his apartment, holding a bag with four lumps of coal.

As he neared the building, he saw his neighbor Minna standing in front talking to the woman he had met the other day in the air raid shelter. He couldn't remember her name. He was going to walk by them when Minna turned and lightly touched his arm.

"Please don't rush by without saying hello," she said. "I was just telling Eliana that you were the *kriminalkommissar* in the Kripo and that it made us in the neighborhood feel safer."

Stachel laughed. "Not chief, just a lowly inspector. But thank you for the compliment. Maybe someday, when this war is over, I can look to a promotion."

"Of course you will. You're too important to not be recognized."

"Maybe that's the problem. It's not good to be recognized these days."

"Have you had breakfast? We just heard that one of the bakeries near the Plaza has some morning cakes for sale. Would you like to join us?"

Stachel initially wanted to say no, that he was too busy, but then he thought that talking to anyone who had nothing to do with his case might be a good thing. Let his subconscious work away while he forgot about it. So, he said yes. Holding up his bag of coal, he said he needed to drop it in his apartment but would be right down. When he came back, Minna was looking up at the second floor, to her apartment. One of her daughters was leaning out, asking Minna to come upstairs, that the youngest wasn't feeling well and she didn't know what to do. Minna excused herself, told them to go on without her and she would hopefully follow soon.

"Well, we might as well start," Stachel said to Eliana. "Those cakes won't be there long." They started up Luisenstrasse towards the Robert Koch Platz.

"I do not normally associate with policemen," Eliana said, pulling her black hair back and tucking it behind her right ear. "It must be a strange life. Have you been in the Kripo long? I assume you have a title?"

Stachel looked down the street, not wanting to look at her. She was beautiful, her long black hair, slim shoulders and hips, wearing a colorful pastel dress that made her stand out from the grey that was Berlin these days.

"Hauptsturmführer, though I try to avoid it now. I've been in the Kripo all my life. I joined out of school and have been an inspector for over twenty years." Stachel felt proud that he could say that. It showed that he was dependable and most importantly, that he had been in the force before the Nazis.

She was looking at her feet. She had on short heels and she made a point of striding forward heel first. She noticed that Stachel was glancing at the way she walked. "It's better on the knees," she said. "I had a knee injury a few years ago and the doctor told me walk heel first to put less pressure on the knees. Hauptsturmführer, so you are in the SS?"

He knew she would ask that question and dreaded it every time it was asked.

"Officially, yes, though I try and ignore it."

"And are you good at what you do?"

"I hope so. But you're only as good as the last criminal you arrest." And that meant he wasn't very good right now.

"Married? Children?"

Stachel stopped and turned to her. She walked on a few feet then turned and faced him. "You ask a lot of questions," he said. "This isn't a good time to ask questions. The answers are rarely good."

"That's why you must ask more questions. In hopes that you'll get at least one nice answer." They continued walking in silence, Stachel mulling why he was so defensive about her questions. It was hard to trust anyone these days. But not to respond made him look like he was someone with hidden dark secrets. People with dark secrets, like the SS, tended to be criminals.

"Well, I'm not married. Not anymore. My wife died a few months ago. No children." God, it felt like yesterday. He could still remember coming home and being told by a neighbor that Hilda was dead, buried under the rubble of their apartment building. He had clawed at the debris, but it was all stone and brick and was a futile effort. He gave up after an hour, his hands bloody, knowing his future was lost. For all he knew, she was still buried there. He had never returned to the area after that day.

"I'm sorry. Sorry about your wife. And you're right. There's too much death these days to ask questions. My husband was, or is, a soldier. I haven't heard anything from him since late '43. I don't know if he's still alive, so I don't know if I'm still married or a widow."

They reached the Platz and turned left onto Hannoversche Strasse. The shop was on the left side of the street. The inside of the shop was ruined, covered in debris, tables turned over, a path cleared leading into the back kitchen. Though it was still cold, the sun was shining directly on the shop, so the vendor had setup four tables outside, clearing the sidewalk as best he could. Only one of the tables was vacant and it had only two chairs. They went to it and Stachel asked a nearby table if he could borrow one of their chairs, sitting the empty chair across from him, making Minna's absence more conspicuous.

Hopefully, Minna will join us soon," he said, sitting next to Eliana. A waiter came up and they asked about the cakes. The waiter said they were in luck, there were only two cakes left. And they had coffee, real coffee, an added surprise. While they waited for the cakes, Eliana talked about when she first came to Berlin back in the mid-30s. Her husband and her came from Frankfurt-un-Main. He was already in the military and had just been promoted to a *feldwebel*, a sergeant, in the Wehrmacht.

"He wasn't really a military man," she said. "At least, I didn't want to think so. He joined the military because he felt it was a good way to get ahead in Germany."

"A lot of people did that back then. It was easy to get caught up in Hitler's talk. It was a disease we all suffered from." Stachel glanced at the other patrons in the café. This was starting to veer toward defeatist talk, talk that could get you arrested, talk that could get you an all expenses paid trip to the guillotine. But the patrons all seemed like normal citizens of the Reich, trying to ignore what was happening around them. Of course, any of them could say something to the Gestapo or the SS. The stab in the back reversed. Stachel tried to motion with his eyes to Eliana that they should change the subject. But either she didn't notice or didn't care. There was a lot of that these days. Many people had given up hope and didn't care what happened to them.

Their cakes and coffee came, though neither touched them. "I'll save mine for Minna," Eliana said.

"I'll save mine for her children."

"It was madness," she said. "How else do you explain what we did, electing a monster." She looked down and put her hand to her forehead. "I'm sorry. I shouldn't have said that."

The table next to them emptied and the people left a copy of *Das Reich* on one of the chairs. Eliana reached over and grabbed it, looking at the front page.

"Everyone didn't vote for him." Stachel decided to leave out the fact that he had, a decision that would haunt him for the rest of his life. "But after the Reichstag fire we all, like good Germans, stood in line to save our country from what we thought was the enemy. We never realized that the enemy was right in front of us."

Stachel couldn't decide if he was attracted to her. As soon as he started thinking he was, he'd think of Hilda and guilt would take over. Hilda had been so much a part of his life that he couldn't let her go without also letting go part of himself. But the world was coming to an end. Germans were no longer acting like Germans. He heard of people bedding down together, neighbors who a few years ago said nothing more than hello to each other, were now wrapped in relationships that would embarrass them once the war was over. Everyone acted like animals now, base instincts had taken over: eat, sex, sleep, and at all costs survive. What was the point of anything else? The end of days was near. Maybe he could find love again, maybe he could once again have a normal life. It would give him something else to live for, something other than this damn investigation.

'Yes," Eliana said, "but when we realized what he was, we did nothing. We allowed Hitler to be Hitler. We continued with our jobs, with our normal lives, as though nothing had changed. And we continued to do nothing when the Elser's and the Stauffenberg's and the Scholl's stood up and told us of our folly."

Stachel felt that last remark was directed at him. She was looking at him, staring into his eyes as she said it. Because of his job he was part of the Nazi regime, whether he liked it or not. A member of a country that had destroyed most of Europe. "I'm not like them. I'm just a policeman trying to uphold the law."

"A policeman who is paid by the government. Whether you believe in the Nazis or not, by your actions you keep them in power."

Stachel knew she was right but didn't understand why she was attacking him. She barely knew him; didn't know if he would turn her in, send her to a concentration camp, destroy her life.

"Why are you saying this?" he asked, looking perplexed. "I was forced to join the party, but I have no love for them. But it's true," he said, reluctantly shaking his head, "I too look the other way. I pretend I don't know what the Gestapo is doing in the basement or what goes on in the concentration camps."

"We let others do our dirty work for us. And we'll stand by and let the Allies take care of Hitler and his henchmen." She leaned back in her chair. "This is madness, real madness. We just sit here with a nice meal as though nothing is happening, as though it's just a normal Spring day."

"We take what pleasure we can. It won't last long."

Stachel noticed that a few people were looking askance at them. They could hear the conversation but didn't want to, wanted them to go away. When you sat next to a defeatist, you became a defeatist. Eliana noticed that he was nervous, took a sip of her coffee, and looked at the newspaper.

"Our Hitler," she said, folding the paper and shaking it at Stachel, as though the article was his fault. "Goebbels praising Hitler. Germany should give unconditional loyalty to him. God help us for signing a pact with the devil."

"We should go." Stachel grabbed the two cakes, wrapped them in a napkin, motioned to the waiter and paid him. "Maybe we'll see Minna on our way back home."

Eliana was about to say something, then thought better of it and followed after Stachel, who was already walking down the street. They headed back down Luisenstrasse.

"We can't go on like this," she said. "This waiting for the end. Sometimes I just want it to be over with. Let the Allies come. Let them do what they will and then whoever is left can start to pick up the pieces."

Stachel didn't say anything. He just kept walking, hoping by silence to get Eliana to stop. He also just wanted it over, but part of him didn't see what he would do after the war was over. Germany would probably be in the hands of the Bolsheviks. And they would have no use for him. If he wasn't arrested, he would at least lose his job, and his job was all he had left.

They never saw Minna on the way home. When they reached the apartment, they stopped and looked at each other.

Stachel wanted to escape from her, from her defeatist talk, but he also liked to hear that someone agreed with him, that someone was willing to stare at reality and not blink. And talking to her made him feel that maybe he could have a life outside of the police force.

"Can I see you again?" he asked. "I enjoyed our talk."

"No, I don't think that would be appropriate," she said. "You're a policeman, a man in authority, and I'm one of Hitler's victims."

"How can I make you believe that I'm not the horrid man you think I am?" Stachel held his hands out, pleading with her in a hushed voice, realizing that she was judging him by his job rather than by who he was.

"I don't think you can. Maybe we'll see each other again. After all, we have a good friend in Minna. But thank you for breakfast. I also enjoyed it. You'll give the cakes to Minna?"

"Of course," he said, holding up the cakes, as he suddenly realized his sister-in-law was standing next to him. Eliana noticed the tension between them and quickly left, not bothering to be introduced.

Sommer stared at Stachel, waiting for him to say something. When he didn't, she started in.

"Where were you last night?"

"Working."

"With her?"

"Quit it, Sommer." She could attack him all she wanted, but he wouldn't let her attack anyone else. "I was working, and no, I didn't get any extra ration cards."

"You've forgotten Hilda already. Thrown her memory out like so much discarded trash. And I suppose you've done nothing about the exit papers."

"I haven't forgotten my wife. I think of her every day. And I told you I can't do anything about exit papers."

"Did you talk to your neighbor?"

"No."

Stachel felt helpless. He wanted to just walk away, flee up the stairs to his apartment and lock the door, leave her on the street and let her scream up at his window. But he felt like his feet were nailed to the ground. He couldn't move before her vile stare. Reluctantly, he held up the wrapped napkin.

"For the children."

She quickly grabbed it, opened the napkin and saw the cakes, and broke off a piece and nibbled at it, like a mouse eating a crumbled bit of food.

"This is nice, but hardly what I wanted. But, please, Reinhardt, we need those exit papers. Surely, you don't want us here when the Russians arrive." She had changed her tone, pleading now, hoping sympathy would win where venom had not.

"I will try. Now please, I must get to work. It's already late."

"Not too late for your girlfriend."

"I said quit it. She's just an acquaintance, nothing more."

"When can you get the papers? Later today?"

"I can't answer that. Again, I'll try, for my niece and nephew, but I doubt I'll have any success." He made a point of not mentioning her, and she noticed it. She started to say something, thought better of it, and turned and left, walking briskly down the street, ignoring the suffering around her. It would serve her right if he could get exit papers for the children and not for her.

I'm a fool, Stachel thought, as he slowly climbed up to his apartment. Time to get to work, where I can deal with bigger fools.

Chapter Twenty-Three

S tachel was ready for a fight by the time he got to the office. Sommer and Eliana had upset him and left him filled with guilt; guilt that he couldn't help his niece and nephew; guilt that he was a policeman upholding the laws of madmen. He was complicit by his deeds. Too many times, when an investigation became political, he ran away. Well, not this time. It might be his last case, but he'd do it right, regardless of what the damn Nazis thought. Either way, he was spoiling for a fight and he didn't care with who.

Climbing the stairs to the second floor, he cursed again that the elevator had never been fixed. It only made his mood worse. Breathing like an asthmatic, when he got to the top he ran into Gottlieb, who immediately demanded an update on the Mintert killing. His first thought was to tell Gottlieb to go to hell, he'd get his update when Stachel was good and ready to give it to him, and not before. But he held himself in check, like he always did.

"I have a suspect," Stachel said. "But it's early in the investigation so I can't give you his name," he added, as though poking Gottlieb with a stick.

"Can't or won't! I want to know now." Gottlieb was leaning into him, pointed finger almost touching Stachel's nose, his face flush in anger. "You're supposed to give me daily reports. I've only seen one."

"What's wrong, boss? Someone hike up your underwear when you couldn't provide them with someone to blame the murder on?"

Gottlieb clenched his teeth, looking like he was gnawing at a bone for the marrow. "I won't take that from you. Maybe you need a visit to the Sachsenhausen hotel."

"I've heard the rooms are very comfy. Unfortunately, it's probably under Russian management now. But go ahead. Put me out of my misery. I'm still not giving you a name. Not after what happened to Pantel."

Stachel started walking down the corridor, with Gottlieb following. Since threats weren't working, he now tried to reason with Stachel.

"I only want an update so I can help you. It's in our best interest to catch this killer before the Gestapo gets more involved."

"More involved? I wasn't aware they were involved in the Mintert case. Does that mean you all finally agree that Pantel was innocent?"

"Of course not. Pantel was guilty. If he wasn't Holzer's killer, he was guilty of something else. He got what he deserved. And of course, Plettner's still involved. The Gestapo never go away."

Someone raced by, knocking Stachel in the shoulder. He now noticed a sense of urgency in the office. People were either running back and forth down the corridors, dipping into offices, or huddled in whispering groups.

"What's going on?" Stachel asked one of the secretaries.

She looked at him, then at Gottlieb, and only said that there was news from the front. She then excused herself and headed towards the bathroom.

"We heard that Königsberg just fell," Gottlieb answered. "The news came out last night though it happened two weeks ago. General Lasch has been condemned to death by the Führer. There are reports of mass killings and rapes after the city was taken. People are afraid the same will happen here."

Stachel rubbed his hand through his hair, trying to wipe away the images. As if on cue, he heard an explosion in the distance. Another artillery barrage had begun.

Gottlieb continued. "Goebbels has said that the defense of Berlin must be our top priority. That's why we need this killer caught immediately. We can't let the public think we've lost control of the situation. And Goebbels is still worried that this is the start of an uprising."

"Finally getting scared, are they? When are they going to flee to Bavaria?"

"They're not, at least the Führer isn't. He's staying and leading the defense of the city."

"I'm so relieved." How much longer could this go on? When would people realize that the Führer, the great man of destiny, was a fool? "I'll catch the killer," he continued. "But giving you daily updates won't help. Every minute I waste updating you is a minute where I'm not looking for this killer."

They were in front of Stachel's office now. He started to unlock the door and noticed that it was already unlocked.

"I unlocked it this morning," Gottlieb said. "I needed an update, and you weren't here. I found nothing. You must have some files on the investigation. Some notes. You were always good at keeping documentation up to date. Makes me wonder now if you're lying about your progress, about a suspect."

Stachel turned and faced Gottlieb. "Do you want this killer caught or do you want me to spend my time keeping you happy?"

"Both, of course."

"Well, I can't. When Klein was around, maybe I could. But not now, not with Lakain as a partner. He's only good for running errands." He poked Gottlieb in the chest. "And stay out of my office."

"Give me updates and I will. But you didn't answer my question. Where are your files?"

"At home, I was reviewing them last night." Which was a lie. Stachel hadn't written anything down since the beginning. Gottlieb was right, he always kept detailed documentation when on a case. But not this time. He was turning into a lousy detective. "I'll get them later today," and Stachel went in his office, closed the door, and locked it. He heard Gottlieb raddle the knob, then knock on the door, yelling that their conversation wasn't over. He kept knocking for a few minutes, but eventually walked away. Stachel had had it with Gottlieb and all the toadies at the top. Time to show them who was really in charge.

He waited a few more minutes to make sure Gottlieb was gone, then dialed Lakain's extension and asked him to come to his office. Lakain said that Gottlieb was standing next to him right now, but he'd come as soon as he could. A few minutes later he knocked at the door, calling out his name. Stachel went up to the door and asked him if Gottlieb was with him. When Lakain said no, he unlocked the door, let him in, and then locked it again.

Lakain had a perplexed look on his face, like a bird that couldn't decide between two worms. "What was that all about? I thought Gottlieb was going to arrest me right now. I didn't do anything wrong."

"Not yet, but before I'm done you will," Stachel said. Lakain leaned against the door, looking like a boy who had just found out he had failed a test. "Just kidding. Gottlieb's angry with me and he's trying to take it out on you. Don't let him."

"By doing what?"

"Ignoring him."

"That will get me a nice trip to the concentration camp. You know, I don't think I like working with you. All you have me do is piss people off."

"Ah, my son, I have trained you well. In a few more months, you'll be my spitting image." Stachel let out a belly laugh as Lakain looked down at Stachel's stomach, as though trying to picture himself old and overweight and finding the image disagreeable.

"What I'm about to tell you," Stachel continued, "is not a joke. I have a suspect in the Mintert murder, and maybe for Holzer as well. And here's the part you'll like. The suspect is a policeman. A patrolman named Banze."

Lakain had been standing the whole time, but at Stachel's words he collapsed in the guest chair and looked up at the ceiling. "This is a nightmare. Are you trying to turn the whole department against me? First Gottlieb, now Banze."

"Do you know him?"

"I know who he is, but I don't personally know him. He seems to stick to himself. Doesn't talk much."

"Well, he's mixed up in the black market and has a history…"

"I don't want to know," Lakain said, holding up his hands, palms out. "Just tell me how you're going to continue destroying my career."

"Career? What career? In a few weeks, there won't be any police department."

"Something will happen. I have to believe that."

"Something will happen alright. The city will be occupied, and we'll all become slaves of the Bolsheviks."

"The Fuhrer will figure out something."

"He already has. He's figured out how to kill us all."

"Enough. Just tell me what you want." Lakain was clearly aggravated by the conversation and Stachel could tell was close to either storming out of the office or breaking down in tears.

"OK, enough defeatist talk. Reality is something we should avoid. Here's what I want you to do." Stachel stood up and walked over to the window, pausing for a second since he knew what he would say would further upset Lakain.

"I need you to trail Banze. On his patrol, find out what he's up to."

Lakain shook his head. "I'm no good at that. I've never trailed anyone before. Besides, I can't watch him all the time."

"Good time to learn. You trail him when he's on patrol. I'll get someone else to watch him when he's not working."

"Why don't you also get someone to watch him all the time? Get your pigeons out there to do it."

"I'm working on that. If I can get someone else, I will. I need you to do this. That's an order, not a request."

Lakain stood up as Stachel sat down. He rested on the file cabinet in the corner and stared at the wall, as though he was trying to be the exact opposite of Stachel. "I can't do this."

"You can and you will. You want to catch this killer, right?"

"Yes, oh, I don't know," Lakain said, throwing his hands up in the air. "What does it matter these days."

"It matters."

Lakain thrust his hands in his pockets and looked down at the floor, His eyes were closed, like he was lost in a dream. Shaking his head a few times as though to throw off a bad idea, he sat down and sighed. "Ok. When does he work?"

"Midnight to eight."

"Midnight to eight! When am I going to sleep?"

"In the evening. You still have to work during the day. This is an investigation. Sleep is a luxury. And you'll get paid overtime."

"So what," Lakain said, shaking his head. "The money is worthless. I'll follow him, but only for a few days. If nothing happens, then I think we do something else."

"Fine. Follow him for three days, call me if you see anything, and after three days we'll see where we are."

Lakain stood up and went to the door.

"Someday I want you to tell me what's really going on," he said as he unlocked the door and left.

There was an added benefit to having Lakain watch Banze at night. That kept him out of the office and away from Gottlieb. Now, about this guy Munzel. He called the duty officer and told him to have someone bring Munzel in for questioning. Then he went over and relocked the door. Maybe he was getting paranoid, but a locked door gave him comfort these days.

Stachel was waiting in the interrogation room when they brought in Thomas Munzel. Drumming his fingers on the metal table, he wished he had a cigarette right now. Pictures of Hitler and Himmler faced each other from opposite walls.

Munzel was a thin man, no more than five two. He was wearing a light-colored raincoat and a derby hat that was pulled down low on his forehead. His eyes were red and dried out and his skin looked like the scales of a dead herring. He had the sunken look of a drug addict and was constantly rubbing his eyes, especially, Stachel noted, when he was asked a question, he didn't want to answer.

They had him in handcuffs. Stachel told the policeman to take them off immediately.

"Are you sure, sir?" the policeman said. "He tried to make a run for it when we knocked on his door."

"Well, he can't do that here, can he?"

"I suppose not, but you never know with these people."

"What do you mean, these people," Munzel shrieked. "I'm a law-abiding citizen, unlike some of you."

"Enough of that," the policeman said and cuffed Munzel across the back of the head, knocking his hat to the floor. "You see, he's no good."

Munzel grabbed his hat from the floor and put it back on his head, like it was part of some uniform.

"Take the handcuffs off anyway. I'll be responsible. But lock the door on your way out." Stachel leaned back and waited for the policeman to take off the handcuffs and leave the room. "Now you see, it's just you and me, and the door's locked so you're not going anywhere until you answer a few questions."

"Why am I here?" Munzel said. "I've done nothing wrong."

"Then you have nothing to be afraid of. So, what do you do for a living? You obviously have some money. I've heard that you live quite comfortably, while the rest of us are just trying to get by on a few scraps of food."

Munzel looked down and rubbed his eyes.

"Look at me," Stachel said.

Munzel looked up with concern in his eyes. He looked like he was trying to figure out how much Stachel knew. It was a game they played. Stachel pretended he knew more than he did and Munzel pretended he knew less than he did.

"Living? What living? There's no work these days. I made my money before the war and I'm living off that now. And who told you I lived comfortably? I wouldn't say that."

Stachel waved his index finger in the air in front of Munzel's face. "I'll ask the questions. You provide the answers. If I like your answers, you'll be able to leave. If I don't, you could be here for a while."

"You can't lock me up. I've got friends."

"Of course we can. And friends have a way of turning into enemies. We're searching your apartment now and I'll soon have an inventory of everything you've stolen."

"I didn't steal anything. Why are you saying things that aren't true?"

"Look, we both know that money can't buy anything these days." There was a knock on the door. Stachel said to come, and a policeman entered and handed him some papers.

"Here it is. A list of everything he had in his apartment." Stachel thanked him and the policeman left.

"So let's see what we have," Stachel said. "Forty cartons of cigarettes, four baskets full of potatoes, pork in the refrigerator, a case of Schnapps. If not stolen, this looks like you're hoarding. That's also a crime, you know."

"It's not all mine. Because my building hasn't been hit, I keep stuff for friends who are less fortunate."

"And who are these friends?"

"I'd rather not say. They've done nothing wrong. If I tell you their names, you'll just bring them in and accuse them like you're accusing me." Munzel looked at Stachel with a gleam in his eyes. As though he was confident Stachel couldn't do anything to him.

"You know, just from this," Stachel said, holding up the papers and waving them at Munzel, tapping him on the bridge of his nose, "I can arrest you and put you away for a good long time. The concentration camps are still going strong, still full of people on holiday."

Munzel's face turned pale, and his lips trembled. "You can't do that," he said in a hushed whisper.

"You know I can. Tell me what I want to know."

"Tell me what you want to hear. Isn't that how you play the game these days?"

"Don't play stupid. Where did you get this stuff? And don't tell me again you're holding it for your friends."

"On the black market, of course! Where else are you going to get it. I use my money and buy things. I'm saving stuff so I can go into hiding when the Russians get here."

"I'm not a fool," Stachel yelled. "No one will accept money these days. Try again."

Munzel was squirming in his chair, hands clasped in front of him, then nervously rubbing his eyes. A few tears ran down his face, though Stachel couldn't decide if it was because he was rubbing his eyes or because he was afraid. And this was getting tiresome. Stachel leaned over the table and slapped Munzel on the cheek.

"Look at me." Munzel hesitantly looked up. Stachel reached over and knocked his hat off his head. "There, now I can see you better."

Munzel reached down again to pick up his hat. Stachel yelled at him to leave it.

"Tell me about your partner?"

"Partner? I don't have any partner. I never said anything about a partner."

"It's obvious you have a partner. Just tell me who it is. Who's helping you steal this stuff?"

"I didn't steal anything. You keep saying things that aren't true. Making statements that I've never said."

"Tell me who your partner is and how you got this stuff and I'll let you go."

Munzel looked over at the locked door and then back at Stachel. "No you won't. If I say anything, you'll just lock me up and go after my partner."

"Ah, so you do have a partner! Tell me who he is, or I'll have to bring in people who aren't so nice. A little pain helps loosen the tongue."

"You've already said that I have a partner so that must mean I do." Munzel had a look of fear in his eyes now but was still trying to look like he was in control. He leaned across the table. "I've told you. I have friends. They'll help me. They won't let you torture me."

"You know they won't. It's every man for himself these days. In the end, they'll save their own skin."

"No! You're wrong."

Munzel looked again at the door, as though trying to will one of his so called protectors to come in. Stachel slapped him on the cheek again and told him to look at him.

"It looks like we're done here. I'll send you down to the basement. Let my friends have a little fun."

Munzel started shaking, started to stand up and then thought better of it and remained sitting.

"Look, all we did was break into a few houses and steal ration cards. It was from people who were going to die anyway. The cards were just going to waste."

"So, not only hoarding, but robbery too. That will get you a nice holiday. Who's your partner?"

"I can't tell you. He'll kill me. And as long as I don't tell you, you'll let me live."

"Why would we do that? Criminals don't get a lot of sympathy. How did you pick out your victims? And what happens if they fought back? How many people did you kill?"

"Kill! We never killed anyone. That's the truth. If they fought, we left them alone. There's always an easier mark."

"Right, you just walked away if they said no thank you. And you expect me to believe that. Tell me the truth. You murdered people for their ration cards. As you said, they were going to die anyway."

"You keep putting words in my mouth. We didn't kill anyone. I'm done talking to you." Munzel sat back, crossing his arms on his chest, trying to look confident that he would get out of this in the end.

"Alright, that's enough. Time for a visit to the basement." Stachel got up and waved the inventory papers in front of Munzel's face. "I've got all the evidence I need to convict you and send you to prison for a long time. I don't need anything else." He stood up and knocked on the door, yelling to unlock it. He told the policeman standing outside the door to take Munzel down to one of the rooms in the basement and wait until someone arrived. Then he headed back to his office.

Though he hadn't gotten that he wanted out of Munzel, namely admitting that Banze was his partner, Stachel could tell that it was only a matter of time before Munzel confessed. Right now, Munzel was holding on to the perception that Banze would save him in the end. Once he realized that wasn't going to happen, he'd tell everything.

Stachel sat at his desk, thinking about what to do next. It could take hours if not days for them to get anything out of Munzel. Stachel couldn't just wait around for that to happen. He had to do something, he had to continue pushing, continue putting pressure on Banze.

Maybe it was time to get Banze's boss, Lederer, involved? He knew Lederer and didn't think he was on the take so he thought some indirect pressure from Lederer to Banze letting him know he was being watched might make Banze do something irrational. Banze had to be worried that his little game had been discovered, and if he indeed had murdered Mintert and Holzer, then he'd be looking now for a way out, including cutting Munzel loose to take the fall.

So Stachel went to Lederer and told him about his suspicions about Banze and the black market and got about what he expected. Complete denial.

"How dare you," he sputtered, "accuse one of my men of working with the black market. As though that's a major crime anyway. Haven't you noticed that the city is in turmoil, that there's little food to be had and there are refugees from the East pouring in every day. Buildings destroyed, fires everywhere and little water to extinguish them."

Lederer sat back, smacking his lips and taking a drink from a glass of water. "Accept reality, Stachel. I expect that all my men these days are doing a little business on the side. They must, to stay alive. The people can't exist only on rations. There will be riots in the street and the people could possibly revolt against their leaders. We can't have that."

"And murder," Stachel said, raising his eyes and staring at Lederer.

"What murders?"

"Heinz Mintert, Justice in the People's Court? Sophie Holzer, wife to August Holzer?"

"That's ridiculous. Banze would never do that. Where's your proof?" But Stachel could see that Lederer had doubts and was starting to rethink what Banze might be up too.

"I think he's doing a lot more than just dabbling in the black market. I think he's gotten a little overzealous at protecting his turf."

Lederer exhaled and closed his eyes for a minute. "Shouldn't we all. Hitler's put us in a fine mess. Will any of us survive, do any of us want to survive?"

"That's treason."

"Treason according to who? Treason is plotting to destroy your country and Hitler's done a fine job of that. He's the one who should be hanging by a piano wire."

"He will."

"No, he won't. He'll escape to the south, leave us all to our fates, and continue the war, continue the bloodshed, from the mountains. Well, I've given you enough so that you could put a noose around my neck."

Stachel also stood up, fingers sprayed on the desk to give himself support. "I don't want your neck. I want Banze's. Will you help me? I'll get him with or without your help. It just might take longer. I've already got his partner downstairs sweating through a nice conversation with some of the boys."

Lederer looked concerned for a moment, blinking his eyes rapidly and looking everywhere but at Stachel.

"Who?" he said.

Stachel laughed. "Thomas Munzel, and he's not getting out alive from that room until he tells us what Banze and him are up too."

"I haven't heard of him," Lederer said, though unconvincingly. Stachel could tell that he knew exactly who Munzel was. Maybe he was wrong and Lederer was also somehow involved in their little scheme.

"Alright, I'll say something to Banze, but only if you keep me in the loop about what happens. If Banze is involved, of course I want him arrested."

"I'll let you know what I can."

What did Stachel have that linked Banze to the murders? Nothing really. It was barely circumstantial evidence. Banze was a patrolman, he walked the streets, he was involved in the black market. A lot of people fit two of the three. Banze potentially fit all three because he might know the details of the Holzer murder scene. It was all he had right now. Stachel wanted more, he needed more, but he doubted in the time left that he'd get it. So, he had to go with Banze and try and bring him out. The best way to catch a rat is to make him panic, close off his escape route, and watch him try to claw his way out. And Stachel would be watching, knowing that enviably he'd incriminate himself.

And today, luck was with Stachel, for it didn't take long for Banze to panic. He was talking to Lakain in the coffee room when Banze came in as though the dogs of fury had been unleashed.

Stachel had just poured himself a cup of coffee and was explaining to Lakain the finer points of trailing someone, not that Stachel knew much himself. Banze came up to him and demanded that he talk to Stachel immediately, in private.

"About what?" Stachel said, playing the innocent.

"You know what it's about," he shouted. "I'll be waiting in your office." Banze left as quickly as he had come. Stachel pretended that Banze's outburst was no big deal and continued talking to Lakain, who was looking at the ground, shaking his head to acknowledge that he understood what Stachel was saying. Stachel could tell though that he was really thinking that Banze was angry, knew what was going on, and would be harder to tail.

"Remember, he's got a route that he follows. So you don't need to be close to him. Stay far back. You only have to watch what he does and where he deviates from his route."

Stachel set his cup of coffee on the counter, though it was still half full, and headed back to his office. Banze was there, standing in the corner, behind the desk, arms crossed over his chest, looking as angry as he had in the coffee room.

"We talk again," Stachel said as he closed the door. "And how may I help you?"

"Don't play coy with me. You know what this is about." His voice was a low growl, a whisper ready to lash out and find new victims.

"About our discussion before?" Now Stachel was in the opposite corner, leaning back against the wall. "You told me you didn't know anything about the Mintert murder."

"It's not that. It's about a friend of mine."

"I didn't know you had friends. Who might that be?"

"Munzel. You have him downstairs, probably being worked over now by some of the goons in this department."

"Well, at the very least he's guilty of hording food. We searched his apartment. And we think he was murdering people for their ration cards."

Banze pushed off from the wall and stood in the middle of the room. "That's a lie. Munzel wouldn't do that."

"Well, I'm sure we'll have an answer soon enough. Besides, he doesn't seem the kind of person a policeman would befriend."

Banze paced the room, fists clenched. Then he stopped, let out a sigh, his shoulders drooping like a building about to collapse.

"Look, I shouldn't tell you this." Banze tried to look like he was reluctantly giving away a terrible secret. "Munzel keeps me informed about the black market. He's my little pigeon."

"You mean so you can arrest someone?"

"Of course," Banze said, irritated at the tone of Stachel's questions.

Now Stachel pushed away from the wall and stood next to Banze, looking him in the eye. "But I've looked at your files. You've never arrested anyone for black market activities. Munzel must not be a very good spy."

Banze started pacing back and forth again. Stachel stepped around him and sat down at his desk, motioning to Banze to also sit down. Banze ignored him and continued pacing.

"Why do you care?" he asked. "The Nazis are filth, and you know it. All they care about is their precious Aryan bloodlines. If you can't prove you're a pure Aryan, you don't get anywhere. I've asked for a promotion and I always get the excuse that I'm not the right kind of person. Them and their talk about creating a new man to rule the world. Yet look at Himmler and Goebbels and Goring. One's a fat pig, one's a cripple, and one should have been an accountant. Maybe I'll get a promotion after the war, they say. Well, the war's ending and they'll soon be gone. Maybe then I can rise to the top, where I belong."

"You sound like Hitler twenty years ago."

"Hitler," Banze spat in the waste basket. "A charlatan. He wasn't the leader we needed. We all thought he was strong, another Bismarck or Frederick the Great. Instead, he turned into a whimpering fool, blaming everyone else for his faults. We need a new leader, one who will rid us of Hitler and the Bolsheviks." Banze was ranting, still pacing back and forth, drumming his left fist up and down.

The man is mad, Stachel thought. This petty little man thinks he's the next Hitler, the next Great Leader that's going to save Germany. It seems like everyone is mad these days. And he must be mad himself to sit here talking to a madman. Stachel decided it was time to throw a punch and see how Banze reacted.

"You know, Munzel has confessed to killing Mintert, and I think he also killed Holzer."

Banze stopped pacing and looked at Stachel. "Quit lying. He wouldn't confess to something he didn't do. Yes, Munzel's a small time crook. He's taken a few ration cards here or there. I look the other way as long as he's giving me information."

"Look the other way? Or do you hold out your hand? Or are you the one telling Munzel what apartments to hit. It must be dangerous and, of course, you can't let anyone find out."

"Prove it. You're just throwing stuff out. You don't know anything."

"I don't need to these days. A visit to the basement works wonders."

Banze leaned over the desk, shaking in anger. "Munzel didn't kill anyone. He's harmless."

"He might be. It's you I'm worried about."

"What? You think I killed Mintert? Holzer? Don't make me laugh. I was on my patrol the night they were killed."

"Patrolmen have a way of wandering off."

"Not that far."

"And what do you do when your little scheme is threatened? Do you lash out, like you're doing now?"

"You're mad."

"What do you think we'll find if we search your apartment?"

"Go ahead, there's nothing there." But Stachel could see the worried look on his face. The look of someone trying to figure out a way to get home quick.

"I've had enough of you and your lies," Banze said. "I'm out of here and I'm not talking to you again. And I'll get Munzel away from you. You're just another Nazi stooge refusing to see reality."

"You're entitled to your opinion. But I'd give up Munzel. He's not worth it."

Banze ignored him and stormed out the door. Later Stachel heard, as he expected, that Banze never tried to free Munzel.

Chapter Twenty-Four

Stachel had followed Banze for most of that night, but got nowhere. Banze was obviously on his guard. He walked his route, never deviated, barely talked to anyone. Just before three, Stachel gave up and headed home, hoping he could get a few hours' sleep. But the Russians were up early, so he ended up in the bomb shelter, next to Minna and her kids. He didn't get to his apartment until five, knew he'd never get to sleep, so he boiled some water and made a cup of ersatz coffee from a bag of grounds Minna had given him in the shelter earlier.

He was at the office by seven, sitting at his desk, door closed, thinking that he had royally screwed up the investigation. If Banze was the killer, Stachel had stupidly put him on alert, so that now he'd never get anything out of him. Either Munzel would talk, or he'd have to find other evidence.

Then, without a knock, his world finally fell apart. The door burst open, and Gottlieb walked in, dressed in a SS uniform that didn't fit. Stachel immediately knew things had gotten worse.

"Get your coat," Gottlieb said, "you're coming with me."

"I'm in the middle of something."

"Middle of what? Pissing off patrolmen? Whatever you're doing, this is more important. Goebbels and Holzer want to meet."

"Can't you go alone? Besides, I don't have anything new to report."

"Well, I think that's why they want to meet. If you had given me daily updates like I asked, maybe you wouldn't need to go, but since you haven't, you're coming. Blame yourself."

Begrudgingly, Stachel grabbed his coat, muttering under his breath that this would come to no good, and followed Gottlieb out of the Alex.

There was a motor car waiting outside. Within twenty minutes they were walking down into the bunker behind the Chancellery. The place was crawling with activity, soldiers everywhere, either headfirst on a mission or mingling in small groups. Again, they were in the Vorbunker, at the same conference table. Stachel sat down at the far end of the table and crossed his legs, trying to look calm, though his mind was racing. He kept thinking that at that very moment the beast himself could be right below him. It made his lower back hum in pain. Gottlieb stood against the wall, arms crossed, below a leering Hitler.

After a few minutes, Goebbels and Holzer came out from a side entrance, followed by a SS soldier. Goebbels sat down at the head of the table and Holzer sat to his right. Gottlieb bounced off the wall and started to sit down to Goebbels left. Holzer motioned for him to sit next to Stachel. The SS soldier remained to the side, standing at attention, acting as though he was deaf.

Goebbels ignored them and started talking to Holzer in a whisper. Then he looked up, his chiseled nose pointing directly at Stachel, like a gnome who had just crawled out of a cave. Then he looked over at Gottlieb and spoke as though Stachel wasn't there. He talked in a loud voice, almost yelling, clearly upset.

Well, I'd be upset to, Stachel thought, if I knew I was going to die within a few days.

"The Mintert investigation is not progressing as I had hoped."

Gottlieb nervously looked at Goebbels and said that was not correct, that they were chasing down leads, but that he needed to understand that with the current state of the city, it was difficult. The artillery barrage had everyone hiding in shelters. Except for the *Volkssturm,* he added quickly.

"We are preparing to defend the Fatherland. The fate of Europe hangs in the balance. This is a fight against Communism. The Ally coalition will fall apart, and the Capitalists will join Germany to ensure that Europe remains free. And everyone must do their part, including you. This killer must be caught before he breeds insurrection in the public. And once again, like with Sophie Holzer," and he nodded his head toward Holzer, "you have failed to catch the killer. Your incompetence aids the enemy."

Gottlieb looked over at Stachel and asked him to give a detailed update. Stachel started to speak but was cut off by Holzer.

"We don't want to hear from you. You were asked here so we could tell you ourselves what a buffoon you are. A disgrace to everything Germany stands for."

All Stachel could think about was how much be loathed these two men. If he was a real policeman, if he really cared about justice, these were the men he should arrest. He wanted to tell Holzer that he was the disgrace, but he knew it would only lead to his arrest.

"Why do you keep this man on the force?" Holzer asked Gottlieb. "He should be fired."

Gottlieb squirmed in his chair, leaning back as though Holzer was a snake about to strike. "He used to be our best investigator. I say use to because I admit that recently he has been less than successful."

Stachel hated the fact that they were talking about him as though he wasn't in the room, as though he was no longer important enough to be recognized. They're now treating me like they've treated the Jews for the last ten years. Too late, I've always been too late to realize how despicable these people are. And he finally couldn't take it anymore. He stood up.

"It has only been two days. And we have no witnesses…"

"Shut up," Goebbels yelled. "Excuses are meaningless. Two days is an eternity right now. Have you no idea what is going on?"

Stachel sat back down but continued talking. "You realize that the two murders, Mintert and Holzer, are connected? And that the murderer could be anyone, someone who blends into the shadows. Like Paul Ogorzow, the S-Bahn killer."

"We know that, of course," Goebbels said, motioning to Holzer to keep quiet.

"So you admit that Pantel was not a murderer? That the Gestapo arrested the wrong man."

"They never arrest the wrong man. He was guilty of something. You mention Ogorzow. Are you saying we have a serial killer loose in the city?"

"I don't think so. The method for both killings was the same. And Mintert and Holzer were both connected in some way to the black market. The answer must be there."

"My wife was not connected to the black market," Holzer said. Again, Goebbels motioned for him to be quiet.

"Why was this not mentioned before?" Goebbels asked.

"We've discussed this," Gottlieb quickly lied, since Stachel had never mentioned the black market connection to him before. "But at the time we though it more likely that Mintert was a copycat killing."

"I never thought that," Stachel said.

Gottlieb looked as though he was going to lean across the table and strangle him. "Hauptsturmführer Stachel loves to be the renegade. Sometimes it's better to be quiet."

"Whether it's a serial killer or not," Goebbels said, "he must be caught. And you are not any closer to doing that."

"And I won't if I waste my time here," Stachel said, standing up, grabbing his hat, and starting to leave.

"Sit down." Goebbels motioned to the SS soldier to stop Stachel. He was young, muscular, well over six feet. Stachel knew he didn't have a chance against him. He stood there, staring at the soldier, then at Goebbels and Holzer. Their eyes were digging into him like they could already see the shots of the firing squad. He sat back down.

Holzer spoke to Gottlieb. "You are through with this investigation. We are turning it over to the Gestapo, where it should have been from the beginning. I want all files immediately given to Sturmbannführer Plettner. We don't care what you do with him," and he pointed at Stachel. "We want him out of our sight. Permanently."

"I will talk to Reichsführer Himmler," Goebbels said. "I think we're done here. Get this man out of my sight."

Goebbels stood up, again smoothed the wrinkles out of his suit and left, the SS soldier following him.

Gottlieb leaned over and tried to get Holzer's attention. Stachel quickly got up and left, hoping he could get out of the bunker before Gottlieb followed him. He didn't know what he was going to do, but the word "permanently" gave him the chills. And he'd be damned if he'd drop the case and hand over his files, not that he had any. They'd have to find him first.

Stachel refused to go back to the office with Gottlieb. He needed to think, needed to decide whether to continue with the case. Despite the threat from Holzer, he knew he couldn't drop the case, knew he had to see it to the end. What else was he going to do? Go to a shelter, hide, like everyone else, and wait for end of the war. That would be walking away and admitting defeat. And he'd done enough of that for the last twelve years. If only to show to the Allies that all Germans weren't bad, he needed to bring this murderer to justice.

Holzer, much to his regret, was no longer a suspect. That left only Banze, and he didn't see much hope of finding any evidence connecting him to either murder in the time he had left. The rumors were that the Russians were now on the outskirts of the city. It was only a matter of days before they got to the Mitte district, to central Berlin, to the Chancellery and the Reichstag.

Other than the *Volkssturm* and a scattering of military, mostly SS, there were very few people on the street anymore. Small fires pocketed the Mitte district now, the smoke like lost souls blanketing the city, most streets reduced to rubble. A cold drizzle cast reflection of the city's destruction, like there was another city beneath. Berlin before the war, before the Nazis, before the undercurrents of hate surfaced. If only you could jump back to that other Berlin and forget everything that had happened.

And his mind was like those two cities, torn between defending his country or hiding in the dark and coming out when the war was over. The whole walk back to the office, he bounced back and forth between the two alternatives. His world was coming to an end and this murder case was the only thing he could cling to that told him otherwise. But wouldn't it be nicer to chuck it all?

He had no sooner sat down at his chair in his office, thinking now that it was time to give it all up and try to flee west, when there was a knock on the door. A secretary popped her head in and said that Sturmbannführer Gottlieb wanted him in his office immediately. She looked scared, as though she was the one wanted. He thanked her and told her to close the door. After waiting a minute to make sure she was gone, he went over and locked it. He was damned if he was going to talk to Gottlieb. Gottlieb only wanted the files, of which there were none except for whatever Lakain had written up, and to berate him for his actions at the meeting. Gottlieb and the Nazis would go to hell, but hopefully without him.

He started to leave his office, but as soon as he opened the door, he saw a determined Gottlieb coming down the corridor like a wild animal about to pounce. He closed his door and locked it. He knew he had to get out without being seen. Gottlieb was now at the door, twisting the knob and then banging against the door, demanding that it be opened. He heard Gottlieb yell out for someone to bring the office key.

The only way out was the window and a drop of twenty-five feet. Opening it, he braced himself for the cold, rainy air laced with smoke. But surprisingly the air was fresh and cool, probably the first fresh air he had breathed in weeks. It cleared his head. He looked down. There was a small hedge of bushes against the wall and a concrete sidewalk beyond that. If he hit the concrete, he might break an ankle, but the bushes didn't give much of a cushion and would undoubtedly tear his clothes or worse skewer him on a branch.

He could now hear Gottlieb scratching against the doorknob with the office key. It was now or never. He sucked in his breath, hoisted his right foot onto the windowsill, grabbed the sides with his hands, and lifted himself out the window and out into space. It seemed like he hovered there for a moment, looking at a panorama of a burning city, then he dropped like an exploding artillery shell and hit the sidewalk, miscalculating his roll on impact, his shoulder taking most of the impact. He lay there for a minute, groaning, groping at his body to make sure he hadn't injured a leg or arm. His shoulder hurt, but he felt it was only a painful bruise, not broken. He willed himself up and around the corner to a dark doorway. As he waited for the pain in his shoulder to subside, he could hear Gottlieb yelling that he was outside and to quickly search the area.

Stachel started for home. Then he stopped. His apartment would be the first place they'd check. He needed somewhere else, and the only person he knew in Berlin that would not turn him in was Hugo Baer. He turned to the left and started the long and painful walk to Baer's apartment.

Chapter Twenty-Five

Stachel rang the buzzer to Baer's apartment. Though the windows were all blacked out, light leaked through from the foyer, making him feel naked and vulnerable. A million eyes watching him right now, ready to ambush and haul him away to his death. If Baer was home, he'd be the one answering. Baer's wife never answered the buzzer or the phone. And she wouldn't allow the children to either. Technology scared her and she would have none of it.

Just as Stachel thought that Baer wasn't home and he would have to start thinking of another alternative, he heard Baer's scratchy voice through the speaker. Stachel said he needed to speak to him, that he needed help, could he come downstairs. Baer responded that he would be right down and to wait around the corner, in the alley.

Baer entered the alley, his overcoat pulled up to cover his neck, a hat pulled down, looking around the neighborhood to ensure they weren't being watched.

"I need a place to hide," Stachel said.

Baer wouldn't look at him. He kept looking over his shoulder, across the street, to another apartment.

"There's a crazed Nazi living on the third floor," he said. "He's always watching the street, watching his neighbors, and reports everything to the party."

Stachel looked across at the apartment. "There's no one there right now. I'll watch the windows. Keep your back to them. I don't really care if he sees me."

"Probably too late. If he was watching, he would have seen me come out the door. He always has the lights off and hides behind a curtain." Baer was silent for a moment, struggling with himself.

"You should care who sees you. I can't have you here. The word is out to arrest you immediately. Treason."

Stachel immediately thought that Gottlieb must have issued the warrant. But that didn't make sense. Gottlieb didn't have the spine to make that kind of decision. Besides, having someone who reported to him wanted for treason made him a suspect too.

"It's not true," he said. "They're upset that I haven't solved the Mintert case yet."

"The word is that you refused to follow orders, that you're a lone wolf and an enemy of the state."

"Well, the first part's right." Stachel shrugged his shoulders. "And we have different opinions on who the enemy is."

"This isn't funny. You know if they catch you, they'll execute you immediately. The order was that if you resisted arrest, take all necessary means to detain you. In other words, they're hoping someone will just shoot you and make the whole thing go away."

Baer patted Stachel on the shoulder and walked deeper into the alley, until they were in complete darkness. Baer was just a disembodied voice, like a subterranean god talking from the depths of the ocean.

"I can't help you. You can't be here, and you can't go back to your apartment. There are probably a few Gestapo agents sitting there right now, waiting for you to return. And I must think of my wife and children. If they found you here, I'd also be arrested, and my family would be sent to a concentration camp. You know, it's crazy. They keep sending people to the concentration camps, even though the Red Army is on our doorstep and most of the camps have already been overrun."

Stachel thought of asking if he could stay for a few hours, until he figured out what he'd do next, but knew Baer would refuse. The Gestapo knew they were friends. When Stachel didn't come home, the first place they'd go is to Baer's place.

"The world went mad years ago," Stachel said, "and like fools we joined the herd."

"I'm sorry but I must be going. They could arrive here any minute and I must be in my apartment when they do." Baer shook Stachel's hand, told him good luck, and started for the front door.

"Can I call you in a few days?" Stachel asked.

"You shouldn't. They're sure to bug my phone. There's a public phone at the end of the block that's still working. Call me at that number at six in the morning in two days. OK?"

"No, but what else is there." Stachel started down the street and didn't look back. He got to the phone booth and memorized the number, then headed for the Tiergarten. He needed to figure out what to do next. There was no reason to be in the Tiergarten, especially at night, so it was a good place to hide. Though before the war a park dense with foliage, what trees hadn't been destroyed by bombs or the artillery had been chopped down for firewood.

Sitting on a bench, overcoat pulled up and hands thrust in his pockets, he could see the dark shape of the Reichstag off to his left. It was after the Reichstag fire that Hitler had shown his true colors, when the whole country started crashing down.

Baer had been his only hope. Everyone else he knew was in the Kripo or Gestapo, and he didn't trust any of them. He had never gotten to know anyone in his apartment building except Minna, and he couldn't talk to her anyway since they would be watching the building. And if he stayed outside, on the run, he knew eventually he'd be caught. Hiding in an abandoned building was possible, there were plenty of those around Berlin. Or he could hide in the U-Bahn tunnels among the other refugees but hiding underground scared him. It was like he was already fitting himself out for his burial.

He thought of Eliana. Other than Minna, no one knew of her. He barely knew her, but at least he knew that she had no love for the Nazis. But why would she take him in? It would only endanger her. But what other choice did he have? Besides, the worst thing that could happen was that she'd say no and tell him to leave. If that happened, he'd be no worse off than now.

First problem solved. He would ask Eliana for help. But he didn't know where she lived, and the only person that he knew who did know was Minna. So, he'd have to risk going back to his apartment.

When he needed the noise of the artillery to hide his steps, there was nothing but silence. A silence that seemed more oppressive than the constant barrage. He guessed even the Russians must sleep sometime.

At the end of the block, he searched the neighborhood for any men huddled in doorways, shadowed by light leaking onto the street from half covered windows. His apartment windows on the third floor were dark, but he knew Baer was right. The Gestapo was there, waiting patiently for him to return home. The back of his apartment had a small yard where some of the women kept gardens. Trying to grow vegetables in this hell was crazy, but it was the only way sometimes to get any fresh food. The gardens backed onto an alley, and that's how Stachel approached the building. Stachel saw a man huddled on the other side of the alley, smoking a cigarette. Without the glow from the cigarette, he probably wouldn't have seen him. Stachel couldn't tell if the man was a neighbor or an agent guarding the back entrance. There was no way to get to the building without being seen by the man, which meant that Stachel would have to take him out. Knocking someone unconscious was something he hadn't done in years. There had always been someone younger and stronger to do that.

Stachel circled around so he was behind the man, crouched and fumbled on the ground until he found a good sized rock. If it didn't work and there was a fight, he had no doubt that he would lose. Stachel crept up behind the man, feeling that every step echoed. The man was busy with his cigarette and trying to keep himself warm. He hit him on the head as hard as he could, feeling the spray of warm blood on his hand. The man dropped to the ground like a bird shot out of the air. Bending over, he checked the man, hoping he hadn't killed him. The man was bleeding from the head wound but still breathing. Stachel had no idea how long the man would be unconscious, so he needed to act quickly.

Minna's bedroom faced the back of the building. Grabbing a few small pebbles, he threw them at the window. When nothing happened, he tried again, and again, until he saw the ruffling of the blackout curtains and Minna's face peering out from the corner. Stachel waved and whispered his name, hoping she would hear him. Apparently, she did because she opened the window and called down to him in a whisper.

"The Gestapo. They are here, in your apartment. They made a lot of noise earlier and asked all of us if we knew where you were."

"I figured that. I'm in trouble and I need a place to hide. Can you give me Eliana's address?"

"Eliana? Why do you want her address?"

"I don't know where else to go. I need someplace that they can't connect to me and she's the only one I can think of."

"I don't know. I shouldn't do it without asking Eliana first."

"I know, but I don't have much time."

"Wait one minute." Minna disappeared from the window and came back a few minutes later. "I've called her. She'll take you in, but only for tonight. Twenty-Seven Linienstrasse, just off Friedrichstrasse."

"Thank you. And of course, I wasn't here."

Stachel waved and then disappeared down the alley. Eliana lived close by, near the Oranienburger Tor. As he neared her building, he searched the windows and saw her looking out from the third floor. She came down immediately and opened the front door. The foyer was dark, and she told him in a whisper to follow her. Stachel stood there for a minute, watching her slim figure walking up the stairs, wondering if he was doing the right thing, if Hilda would approve. She stopped at the top of the stairs and looked down, wondering why he was still on the ground floor. I'm acting like a schoolboy, Stachel thought, shaking his head and starting up the stairs.

"Did you enjoy the view?" she asked.

"I'm sorry," Stachel said, embarrassed that he was so obvious. "It's a crazy night. I don't know what I'm doing."

She looked at him for a second than continued up to the third floor and her apartment. "It's late. You can sleep on the sofa. We'll talk in the morning." She said good night and then went back to her bedroom and closed the door. There were already some sheets and a pillow on the sofa. He didn't bother making the bed. He laid down, fully dressed, put the pillow under his head, and stared at the ceiling. More cracks he thought. When am I ever going to stop seeing things falling apart? It was a few hours before he fell asleep.

He woke up at six and for a second wondered where he was, until the memories of last night came back.

God, what had he done? He was in deep trouble and had no way to get himself out. And now he had put someone he barely knew at extreme risk. He knew he couldn't stay here. He sat up and rubbed his hands through his hair. He hadn't had a bath in two days and was smelling ripe now. Probably no worse than any other Berliner, but it made him feel like a common street bum. Which in a sense is what he had become. A man with no home and no family. Then he realized that he was warm for the first time in days. He looked at the fireplace and the cooling embers of coal that were still generating some heat. Where had she gotten so much coal? Stachel thought it was impossible these days to get anything other than a few small lumps. She had enough coal to heat an apartment twice this size. He needed to go to the bathroom, which was near her bedroom door. He didn't want to wake her, because he knew once awake, she would throw him out. So instead, he slipped down the stairs and outside and relieved himself in an alleyway.

When he got back to the apartment, he heard stirring from the bedroom. A few minutes later she came out fully dressed and was startled to see him standing at the front door. Stachel said good morning and then went back to the sofa and sat down.

"Did you sleep alright?" Eliana asked, coming into the room and sitting at a desk chair in the corner. "You didn't make the bed." She pointed to the sheets that had fallen to the floor.

"I was too tired. I slept fine."

There were a few minutes of silence. Stachel knew he had to make the offer to leave but wanted to figure out first where he would go. Eliana continued sitting at the desk, looking very tired and worn out. She kept pushing her hair back behind her left ear, which made Stachel look at it. It was a beautiful, small ear and brought stirrings of lust. He shook his head to wipe the thoughts away. He couldn't think of that now.

"Since you're here, I guess I should ask," Eliana said, "what happened? Why do you need to hide?"

"I shouldn't tell you. I've already put you at risk by coming here."

"Gestapo?"

Stachel shook his head yes. "I'll leave shortly. Can I have some water?"

Eliana didn't respond. She walked into the kitchen and turned the faucet. "No, it's still not running. The water main was hit the day before and it's been out ever since. I can go down to the pump at the end of the street."

"No, don't do it for me. I can go down there."

"And be seen immediately. Better if I go. I should go anyway, while it's still early. You stay here and figure out what you're going to do. I'll be back quickly." She threw on a coat, grabbed two buckets that were in the kitchen, and left. His stomach was reminding him that he hadn't eaten in over a day. Feeling guilty, but needing something, he went over and opened the icebox. It was bare except for a worn grey onion. He couldn't take her last bit of food, no matter what it was. He went over to the window and peaked out of the blackout curtains, watching Eliana walk down the street to the pump. There were already several people there, waiting in line.

What should he do next? Where could he go? He had no answers. Should he continue looking for this killer? It seemed stupid to bother. How could he get anywhere with the investigation when he also was considered a criminal? He couldn't he knew but hiding out until the Red Army took the city was more than he could stand. He had to do something.

Eliana came back a half hour later. He rushed to the door and took the heavy pails of water from her and carried them into the kitchen. "Throw one pail in the sink. Glasses are in the cupboard to the right of the sink."

The water tasted stale and had small pieces of grit in it. Building debris was getting into everything.

"I should leave," he said, standing up.

"Where will you go?" Eliana asked.

"I don't know. Everyone I know is in the Kripo. You were my last resort."

"I seem to be a lot of people's last resort these days. Yesterday, the widow upstairs wanted to move in with me. Said there would be less of a chance of rape when the Russians get here if we're together. I don't know why it matters. They can rape two women just as easy as one."

Stachel grimaced, not wanting to hear but knowing she was correct, and sat back down on the sofa. "We're dead, aren't we? They'll never let any of us live after what we did to their country."

"Do you blame them?"

"No, but what do you mean that you're a lot of people's last resort?"

"I shouldn't tell you. It's better to keep some things private."

Stachel wanted to press her. Her tone of voice, the glancing look on her face, told him that what she wanted to say was serious and something he should know about, given that he was hiding in her apartment. But why should she trust him? He was a policeman. He wanted to leave, but at the same time he wanted to stay. He was afraid to ask because when she told him he had to leave, he'd be lost.

She sat down at the desk, hands on knees, staring at him, waiting for him to say something. He looked her in the eye and that feeling of lust came back that he thought he had chased away. She was beautiful, so similar and yet so different from Hilda. Would Hilda ever forgive him for these thoughts? When he met her after death, he hoped she'd understand.

"Can I stay for a few days?" he asked meekly, staring down at the floor, ashamed of himself for looking so weak. "Just for a few days."

Eliana clapped her hands together, which startled him, and laughed. "Of course you can stay. You know what I think of the Nazis. It's my way of helping the war effort, having them waste their time looking for you instead of killing Russians."

"Thank you," Stachel said, relieved that that question was answered. "I'll sleep here," and he padded the sofa.

"Yes, you will."

"I have some ration cards, for food, though I won't be getting any more."

"Give them to me." Eliana held out her hand. He gave her the crumbled cards, being careful not to touch her hand. "You must stay here, inside. You can't go out. I don't trust the neighbors and they'll all start gossiping if they see you."

He shook his head no. "I have to go out, but I'll leave only at night. I still must catch this killer. I can't let that go."

"Why? Give it up. Let the Russians deal with him. You don't owe anything to the Nazis."

"It's not the Nazis. It's me. I owe it to me to catch him. This is what I've always done, and I can't stop doing it now. If Germany is to survive the war, it will be because of our belief in law and order, despite what has happened the last twelve years."

"Law and order. You think the Russians care about that. Revenge is all they care about."

"Yes, but they will leave some day. I have to believe that."

"Yes, well, I doubt any of us will be alive on that day." Eliana put the ration cards in her coat and started for the door. "I'm going to try and find some food. Promise me you'll stay here and not leave before I get back."

Stachel shook his head yes and asked if he could use the phone.

"Yes, if it's working," she said, pointing to the bedroom. "It comes and goes like everything else."

Stachel waited for her to leave, then called Stehen's number and left a message, saying to call back immediately at Eliana's number. He sat down on her bed and waited for the phone call.

Stehen called back a few hours later but refused to meet Stachel that night. He would give an update over the phone.

"Despite what I said earlier," Stehen said, "I did start asking around and watching Banze now and then." Stehen paused for a minute until Stachel asked if he was still there. "I don't think he's murdered anyone. He's definitely involved in the black market, but everyone is these days. His game is robbing houses and selling what he finds on the market. He's been caught twice by the occupants that I know of, and he beat the people who found him, but he didn't kill anyone. Everyone considers him relatively harmless, at least compared to the alternative."

"Does he have a partner?"

"Yes, but I don't know the man's name."

"Thomas Munzel?"

"I don't know."

"So you don't think he killed Mintert or Holzer?"

"Yes, I'm pretty confident. I could be wrong, but he seems too small time to be involved with murder."

"That doesn't leave me with much. I still need to catch this killer."

"One more thing. This shadow man I mentioned before. Something's not right. I've tried three times now to track him down, but with no success. I still don't know where he lives, and I still don't have a description of him. Once I caught a glimpse of someone who I think was him. I tried to trail him, but he gave me the slip almost immediately. He knows what he's doing. Everyone in the neighborhood fears him, though I think it's because they don't know who he is, rather than that he's harmed anybody. I think he's a loner, but I can't prove it. And he only comes out at night."

"He's probably just a refugee from the east who's paranoid. I wouldn't spend much time on it. Keep working the black market angle. That's all we have right now."

Stehen hung up and Stachel went back to the sofa and waited for Eliana to return.

Chapter Twenty-Six

By the end of the day, Stachel was ready to put a gun to his head. Eliana was gone much of the day, so he had no one to talk to except the bare walls.

Though he had told Stehen to continue pursuing the black market angle, that that connection was looking more and more dubious. If Stehen was right, then Banze was no longer a suspect. That left him with no one. August Holzer was out. Stachel couldn't think of any motive for him to have killed Mintert. If the Gestapo were involved in the killings, there was nothing he could do. They'd arrest him long before he could arrest anyone else.

He needed someone to talk to, someone to bounce ideas off of, someone like Klein, his old partner. It depressed him to think that if Klein was still around, they might have solved both murders by now. Somehow Klein would have figured it out, would have seen something, a dangling thread that connected the two murders, something that Stachel in his stubbornness wasn't seeing.

Maybe it had nothing to do with the black market. Maybe someone just wanted to kill Nazis. He didn't want to consider that because it made the murderer more of a savior than a criminal.

It seemed hopeless. He didn't see any way he was going to solve the murders in what time he had left. The fuse that had been there from the beginning had finally been lit and was growing shorter every minute. The artillery barrage was constant now, which could only mean that the Russians were softening up central Berlin before the troops moved in.

That there would be another killing he had no doubt. Could he predict where the killer would strike next? Or who? Probably not who. Too many were connected to the black market, too many fervent panicked Nazis out on the street. Location was all he had. Each victim had been killed at night and in a public place. Mintert's death at the Victory Column, celebrating German victories over France and Belgium in the nineteenth century. Holzer's death at the Gendarmenmarket, where the statue of Schiller, German's greatest poet, had stood before being moved into storage by the Nazis in 1939. Holzer, an attack on German culture. Mintert, an attack on Nazi justice. Where next?

He went over to Eliana's desk, looked in the top drawer, and found a few pages of loose paper he could use to write down his thoughts. The Reichstag or the Chancellery, attacking the government? A museum, another attack on German culture? One of the many Schloss' around the city, attacking German royalty? There were so many places that could be used as a symbol. Though many of the buildings were in ruin because of the bombings, there were statues, museums and palaces all over the city that were still relatively intact. But, since the killer had already made a statement about culture and justice, Stachel reasoned that would eliminate a museum or statue. So, it made sense for the next killing to be at one of the Schloss' or a symbol of the Nazi government. The killer could do both by picking

Frederick the Great. It was widely known that Frederick the Great was one of Hitler's heroes. Stachel had heard that Hitler had been mentioning his great victory in the eighteenth century, his victory against overwhelming odds when he thought he would lose, as hope that the Reich would also pull off a victory now. So, without much else to go on, Stachel decided to focus his attention on Frederick the Great. That meant the Sanssouci Schloss or Neues Palais, palaces built during his reign, or his statue on Unter den Linden.

The Schloss and Palais were in Potsdam, in the Park Sanssouci. Southwest of Berlin. He didn't know if the Allies had overrun the area. The rumors said the Russians were in the South, North and East. The Americans and British had stopped about forty miles to the West. So, Potsdam could be under Allied control, or it could be a pocket that they ignored. He didn't know. Regardless, it would be difficult, if not impossible to get there.

Besides, his gut told him that the killer would stay in Berlin. All the killings had been in Berlin and in the Mitte district. That meant that the Frederick the Great statue on Unter den Linden would be the likely place for the next murder. So, he would watch the statue at night and sleep during the day at Eliana's place.

It was April twenty-third. It wouldn't be long before the Russians got to the center of the city.

Eliana came back later that day, holding a small bag that had a few turnips and a piece of pork wrapped in greasy paper. She put the package in the icebox, telling Stachel not to peak, checked that the water was still not running, grabbed the bucket next to the icebox, and headed for the water pump.

When she returned, she poured the water into the sink, then started out again to fill another bucket.

"Wait," Stachel said, "I have something to say."

"Can't it wait? There's no one at the pump right now."

When she got back, she put the bucket on the floor in the kitchen, then sat down in the chair across from Stachel. Part of him wanted to ask her to sit on the sofa, next to him, but the thought of Hilda's disapproval kept him from saying anything. He wanted to be close to her, to have someone to hold, to protect, someone he could trust, but he knew he couldn't trust anyone anymore. He was on the run from the people he had worked with his whole adult life. He had no one to run to now.

"I need to leave this evening. I have an idea where the killer might strike next."

"That's foolish. Why risk yourself now? The Gestapo doesn't punch a time clock. They'll be out there, looking for you."

"Perhaps. But I'm not giving up."

"I'm not saying you should give up. Risking your life is giving up."

"Doing nothing is giving up. I must find this killer and I don't have much time. It's already the twenty-third. It can't be long before the Russians finish us off."

"Which is why you should stay here. Within a few days, this killer won't mean anything anymore."

"He will still mean something to me. I'll stay here during the day, as we agreed, but I will continue to work this case at night."

"And if someone sees you leaving the apartment? There are still lunatics everywhere who believe Hitler will pull a weapon out of a hat."

"I know. I'll be careful. If you'd rather I leave, I will. But I can't just stay here. I'll go mad if I do nothing."

"No, stay. Out there, on the street, during the day, you'll be dead within hours."

Stachel tucked himself into a dark doorway, fighting the cold and watching the equestrian statue of Frederick the Great, residing in the center between the roads. From the doorway, he had a clear view through the rubble to the statue. Because of Hitler's fondness for the Emperor, the Nazis had encased the statue in concrete to protect it from bombs, but everyone still knew who was hidden inside. There were even rumors by some that Frederick would bust out of his concrete prison at the last moment and save Germany.

Unter den Linden was barely a street anymore. The basswood, or linden, trees that lined the pedestrian mall in the middle of the boulevard were mostly gone. A few stunted trunks remained as ghosts of what once was.

It was a long night and Stachel fought to keep himself awake. Nothing happened. Just before the sun came up, and the artillery onslaught started again, he headed back to Eliana's apartment.

When he got to the apartment, Eliana was sitting on the couch. A young woman was sitting next to her, dressed in a gray woolen skirt and pleated blouse, her hair tied back with a kerchief, trying to look older than she was. When Stachel walked in, they stopped talking. Eliana led her to the door and said they would talk later.

"She's a Jew, isn't she?" Stachel asked.

"Yes," she answered without hesitation. "She and her family are hiding in the basement."

"If the Gestapo find them, they'll shoot everyone in the building. You know that."

"It's a risk everyone in the building is willing to take. The Allies must see that all Germans do not hate the Jews."

"I doubt it will make any difference. There's already too much blood on our hands. But don't worry. I won't tell anyone."

"I'm not concerned. You're with us now, whether you like it or not."

"Who's us?"

She ignored his question, walked over to the desk, and handed him two letters.

"Someone slipped them under the door last night, while I was asleep. I thought no one knew you were here?"

"No one but Minna," Stachel said, turning the letters over. Standard white envelopes that could be purchased anywhere. His name was scratched across each envelope, and on one was also written, "you're a hard man to find these days."

"At least I thought so. It's not the Gestapo. They don't send letters."

"Open them."

"I'm afraid to," but Stachel grabbed a letter opener from the desk and sliced open the letter that only had his name on it, pulling out a piece of paper folded into three parts. He expected it to be typewritten but was surprised to find that it was in cursive. It was real paper, like before the war, not the coarse newsprint that existed today.

I sometimes think that the Dolchstoblegende, the stab in the back, is the dominant myth of the Nazi Party. Without it, they would never have come to power.

There was a poster published a few years back that showed Siegfried, you know who Siegfried is don't you? Dressed as a German soldier with a Jewish banker as Hagen about to stab him in the back. We all know now that the real stab in the back was from Hitler, our twentieth century Hagen. But am I then Siegfried or Kriemhild? I suppose I am Kriemhild, come to revenge the murder of Siegfried. I was always taught that women were slow to burn but when in rage to fear them above all.

And what happened with this man, Pantel? That angered me. Whether he was guilty of other misdoings or not, I don't know, but the idiots think he killed Holzer. And I heard this morning that they've arrested someone for Mintert's death. I don't know who it is, but I'm sure they'll execute the man and say the case is closed. The only closure will be when Germany is destroyed, when Germany is brought so low that there is nowhere to go but up. The country is on fire, the city is on fire. We have created our own hell and there can be no escape for those accountable.

But what they have done! The genocide, the murder of innocents, the destruction of Europe. Germany was one of the great cultures of the world. Bach, Beethoven, Goethe, Schiller, Kleist, Brahms. There are so many. The list goes on forever.

We lost our way after the Great War, lost our reason, blamed others for our shortcomings. We were afraid to admit what we had become. A second rate country controlled by a foreigner, the Austrian clown. A rogue state with criminals as leaders.

I have heard that Hitler and his clowns are looking to retreat south into the mountains. To abandon the people of Berlin and continue the fight from Bavaria, from where it all began. Their Alpine Fortress, where the fools expect to wait it out until the Allies fall apart and the Americans start fighting the Russians. That's a fool's hope. We have done such horrible deeds that our enemies are completely dedicated to our destruction. Maybe the Alliance will fall apart and a real war between communism and capitalism will be fought, but it will be when we're gone. But I don't worry about what will happen after my death.

If only I could get to Hitler, I would feel I had done some good in the world. But I know I can't get to the monster, he's hiding in his underground tomb, so I will have to make do with his underlings. And I think I have my next victim. One civilian who tried to murder our children, a judge who sent many innocents to death, and now it must be someone from the Kripo or Gestapo, someone whose job it is to uphold the law but has willingly created lawlessness.

Oh, if I only had Siegfried's invisible cloak, what I could do.

Why haven't you picked a name for me? If you don't do it, I'll have to.

At last what Stachel had been hoping for had happened. The killer was reaching out, was trying to justify what he did. He wasn't mad. Maybe everyone else was mad. Well, these days he might be correct. But at least Stachel now had something to work with. A voice, a personality that he could try and understand.

Stachel turned the paper over, looking for something that would help him. He was holding the letter in his bare hands. He had no one to dust for fingerprints anyway. The writing was very neat, as though the killer had been calm when writing it. No words were misspelled, nothing was scratched out, which meant he had probably written it out beforehand and then copied it to this page. And he seemed to know more about the case than Stachel, since Stachel had not heard anything about someone being arrested for Mintert's murder.

He grabbed the second letter and sliced it open. As before, it was one page, written out in the same neat, orderly script.

By now you are probably hopelessly confused. You don't know who I am, and you don't have any way to find out. So much for your beloved investigation. All it's done is delayed your evitable death sentence. You could have just waited for the end like everyone in Berlin these days. So, what are you going to do now? How are you going to find a rat in a city of rats? I don't even need to watch you anymore. Your every step is so predictable. Watching the Frederick statue only means that I will strike somewhere else.

Oh, and don't worry about your stooge, Stehen. I have taken care of him. I don't have time to watch both of you, so I've removed Stehen from the picture. I hope that's alright. Don't worry about Lakain. I'll leave him alone. He's just a boy who doesn't understand what he's doing.

You've been working alone for so long, you've probably gotten used to it.

I've heard that the Gestapo is looking for you. Seems you've not been following the orders of your criminal leaders. The Nazis don't like that. That's very un-German. As a favor to you, I'll watch them and if I think they're getting too close, I'll let you know. I can't have you shepherded off to one of their nice playpens, can I? The game is only just beginning. Though the end is near.

We need to talk. I am putting together the pieces for what might be my final triumph. Hopefully, before end of today I will have everything in place, and then I'll know what I need from you.

But relax, don't get your hopes up. If others cooperate like they should, then I will have no use for you. But you know how it is these days. No one does what you want.

We will meet before the end.

Stachel read the last sentence again. *"We will meet before the end."* Before what end? Before he stops killing or before the end of the war? Or does he plan to kill me at the end? And if he was threatened, was Eliana also at risk? Stachel felt like a trap was closing around him and not only did he not know what to do but he didn't even understand what the trap was. Was the killer someone he had put in jail years ago and was now free and seeking vengeance? And what about Stehen? Apparently, Stehen was dead, though the letter did not directly state that; only that Stehen has been removed. Kidnapped? Held as a prisoner somewhere in the city? Stachel was predictable, the killer had said. He seemed confident that Stachel would never find him.

Be patient, Stachel thought, wait. The killer might contact him before end of day. But Stachel was never very good at waiting.

Eliana spoke, pulling Stachel out of his thoughts.

"What?" he said.

"What's in the letters? Who's it from? How do they know you're here?" Eliana had her arms folded across her chest and was leaning against the wall. She didn't sound afraid. Her voice was firm and direct, as though she dealt with something like this all the time.

Stachel didn't know what to say so he handed the letters to her and waited while she read them.

"It looks like he wrote the first one. Then found out I was on the run and only found me here after he wrote the second letter."

"But how did he know you were here?"

"Undoubtedly by trailing me, though he must be very good since I watched carefully and never saw anyone. Unless he got to Minna. We need to call her and make sure she's alright. And this is putting you at more risk. Not only from the Gestapo but also from this killer. I should leave now."

"I'll call Minna later. I'm sure she's alright. She can take care of herself." Eliana went over to the window, pushed open the blackout curtain and looked down to the street. "And no, you'll stay here. You're no good to us dead."

Stachel looked at her and grabbed the letters out of her hand. "Again, who's us?"

She hesitated for a minute, tracing her right foot across the floor as though drawing a line between her and Stachel. "Us is a small resistance group. Those who have decided to do something about the Nazis."

"A little late, isn't it? What, are you killing Nazis?" Stachel started pacing around the room. The resistance. How could he get himself caught up in the resistance? Even though he hated the Nazis, taking the law into your own hands went against everything he believed.

"No, definitely not, not killing. We're no better than them if we do that. We're organizing people to not defend the city, to let us lose the war."

"And when were you planning on telling me this?"

"I hoped never, but these letters change things." Eliana walked over and put her hand on Stachel's left cheek, gently pulling his gaze so he would look at her. "Let me help you. We're a small group but we know a lot of people who have no love for the Nazis. They can be our ears. We can cast a wider net and hopefully find this guy."

He pulled away from her and walked over to the window. He wanted to go back in time, to before Hitler. The country was a mess then, everyone believed that Germany needed a strong leader who would lead them out of the shame of defeat. And now, as their world collapsed, that time seemed like heaven. He looked out the window, saw the debris from the bombing, saw the light from a fire a few blocks away, the smoke rising up and scattering in the wind. Like Germany, he thought, we will be blown away like smoke in the wind. Our country destroyed, our culture gone, slaves and parasites to the world. But he had to go on, he had to see this investigation through, and he needed all the help he could get. He turned back to Eliana.

"I need to stay ahead of this killer. Not let him control me. I can't wait, hoping he will contact me later today." He shook his head, looked down at the floor, like a small boy ashamed to admit that he had done something wrong. "But if I can't go out, what can I do? I need help but I have no one to turn to."

Eliana walked over to the desk and picked up a small porcelain pottery of a boy sitting on a pig. She turned it around in her hand, as though examining it for the first time, then placed it back gently on the desk. "You know what must be done," she said, looking down at the pottery. "Quickly, before he kills again, before the Gestapo realize they still don't have their killer. And If they're out looking for a killer, they could find us. We can't risk that. We can be your eyes and ears during the day."

"And who's we?"

"My group of course. There's eight of us."

"But that's foolish. His letter says he might show himself to me later today. What can we possibly do before then? Besides, what's to stop him from killing us all?"

"He can't kill eight people. We have safety in numbers."

"Of course, we could do nothing. Berlin will be occupied soon and we all could very likely be dead or in prison. We'll have new killers to worry about then."

"That was my point earlier. If you believe that, then why are you still trying to catch the killer? No, you want this man. He sticks in your craw, he's making you look like a fool, and you can't have that."

She seemed to know him better than he knew himself. Of course, that was it. This wasn't about law and order now. He admired the man for killing Nazis. But he was making Stachel look like a fool and that he could not allow. "Yes, you're right. I want to catch this man, if only to prove to myself that I'm better than him. If he doesn't contact me before nightfall, I'll go out again."

He walked into the kitchen and tried the faucet. Only small drips of brown water came out.

"Stehen mentioned a shadow man that people in the area had seen. They seemed frightened by him. It's not much, but it's all I've got right now."

"Like the man in those posters the Nazis put up? A man with a hat lurking in the background, listening, looking for defeatists and spies and saboteurs."

"Maybe. I want to tear down those posters every time I see them."

"We'll ask around. We'll watch for him and if he shows himself, we'll capture him…"

"And then what? Turn him over to the Gestapo? Give the killer to the killers."

"I don't know. Lock him up somewhere. Stop him from killing anyone else. We'll figure that out once we have him. One step at a time. I will talk to my group today."

Chapter Twenty-Seven

The boys were playing in the ruins of a bombed out building. Where Stachel saw the ruins as a stark reminder of Germany's destruction, to the boys the debris was merely part of their playground. There were eight boys, all whooping and screaming as they ran back and forth, playing soccer, using a rock as the ball. They used parts of the building that were still standing as the goal posts. They gingerly moved the ball up and down the field, a game of finesse rather than power, since you couldn't deliver a power kick within risking breaking a toe. There was already one boy sitting on the side, nursing his right foot. One team scored a goal, and the four boys raised their arms in triumph, jumping and hugging each other, their cries of joy like a primal scream echoing through the ruins.

Stachel could see three *panzerfaus* and bicycles lying to the side. They were part of the *Volkssturm,* good little soldiers, ready to die for a monster.

It was dusk and Stachel was taking a chance being out, but he couldn't stand sitting in Eliana's apartment anymore. He needed to be doing something, anything, and just walking around the city made him feel like he was making progress. He had his hat low on his forehead, hoping it would prevent any prying eyes from recognizing him. Any eyes but the killer's. The second letter had said he might contact him by end of day. But would it be for the help he mentioned, or to kill him? And what help? Stachel couldn't image what the man would need from him.

He started walking and saw a piece of paper blowing in the cold wind from the east. He grabbed it, recognizing Goebbels's daily newspaper, now no more than one page of cheap newsprint. It talked about the glory of the military fighting spirit, that Germany had turned the corner, that Germany would now be victorious. If you ignored the propaganda and noted the locations where fighting was taking place, you could tell that the army was in retreat: The Seelow Heights were lost. Rumors said that there was fighting at Tempelhof. Of course, the rag wouldn't mention that.

Stachel crushed the newspaper into a ball, looked for a trash bin, laughed at the stupidity of not littering with the state of the city, and threw the paper on the ground. Staying off the main streets as much as possible, he headed into an alley, and started towards the Frederick the Great statue. Though the killer had said he would strike somewhere else, Stachel felt close to him there, as though Frederick would come alive, raise his arm, and point to the killer. He couldn't help thinking that the killer was nearby, following him, the heat from his staring eyes boring a hole in Stachel's back.

By the time he got to the statue it was dark. He stationed himself in the same doorway as before, sitting down and pulling his coat around him so he looked like one of the many refugees that had fled the Red Army. It had been drizzling off and on all day and the street was wet. The blackout kept the streetlights off so Stachel only had the moonlight, a full moon, that bathed the statue like it was an actor on stage. A few people out walking looked like the chorus of a Greek tragedy.

He waited about an hour and then told himself it was a waste of time. The letter said that the killer would contact him again today. He should head back to the apartment, thinking that another letter might be there. So, he started back, walking down Mohrenstrasse. As he crossed the street, he noticed a commotion on Charlottenstrasse. People were mingling in a circle, muttering to themselves, looking at something in the center. Stachel couldn't see what they were looking at. At first, he thought it was a haphazard attempt at forming a queue, so he continued walking, but curiosity got the better of him and he turned onto Charlottenstrasse to see what was going on.

Staying at the back of the group, he stood up on his toes and peered over people's shoulders. He recognized two Kripo officers and quickly ducked down before they saw him. But the policemen's attention was on the ground. Stachel bent down and tried to look through people's legs. He saw a body covered with an overcoat, a black circle of blood reflecting off the moonlight. He stood up and looked again at the policemen. He didn't know either of them. Feeling stupid but needing to know more, Stachel pushed his way to the front of the group. At that moment Uhl, the coroner, showed up. Stachel blended back into the crowd as one of the policemen pulled the coat off the body.

"Who is it?" Uhl asked the policemen.

"Man named Bernhardt. Gestapo. We've made a call, and someone is on the way."

"Not on his way. Here," said a man sharply, who was pushing his way through the crowd. "Get these people out of here."

He leaned over, pushed Uhl aside, and examined the body. Stachel knew the man, Grasel, one of the real horrors in the Gestapo. And Grasel definitely knew Stachel and would know he was wanted. Stachel started to back further into the crowd, slowly, trying not to draw attention to himself. The two policemen were making no attempt to disperse the crowd.

"How did he die?" Grasel said, bending over the body.

"Don't definitely know. Probably strangled, knife wounds. Either one could have killed him."

"Doesn't look like much of a struggle. Either he was surprised or knew the killer."

"Yes, it looks that way. I believe the murder is recent, within the last few hours."

Grasel stood up and looked at the policemen. "Get rid of this crowd now." The policemen jumped, as though waking up, and started pushing the crowd back, yelling that they should leave immediately.

Stachel quickly left. He had heard and seen all he needed too. Was this the murder the killer had mentioned in the first letter? Or had Bernhardt seen Stachel, and the killer dealt with him before he could arrest him? The killer had said he would let him know if the Gestapo was getting close. This certainly was one way of doing that. He felt more hopeless than ever, more out of control.

He headed west on Mohrenstrasse and turned up Friedrichstrasse. He had walked a few blocks and was nearly to Unter Den Linden when a man walked by him, thrusting a piece of paper into his hand as he passed. Stachel turned around and ran up to him, grabbing him by the shoulder and spinning him around. He was an old man, probably in his seventies, unshaven, a small dirty wool cap on his head. Despite the cold he was not wearing a coat.

"What's this?" Stachel asked, holding the piece of paper out and shaking it under the man's nose.

"I don't know." The man was clearly afraid. He was shaking and looking to his left and right, for a way to escape. "A man gave it to me just a minute ago, along with a tin of beef, and asked me to hand it to you." He pulled the tin of beef out of his pocket as proof that he wasn't lying.

"Where is this man? Can you point him out?"

"Back that way," and he pointed behind Stachel. "He gave me the letter and then took off down Jagerstrasse. Let me go, please. I'll give you the tin of beef if you let me go."

"Don't bother," Stachel said and turned away from the man, who scurried south. He looked around, but there was no one else on the street. He walked up to the corner and looked both ways down Jagerstrasse. There were only two women, holding buckets and heading for the public water pump. Leaning against the wall of a building Stachel unfolded the letter.

Meet a friend of mine at the Reichstag tonight, one in the morning. He'll be waiting for you in the back of the building. Bring no one.

The letter was scrawled in the same handwriting as the previous letters. Balling up the letter he threw it on the ground. So, he wasn't going to meet the killer, but a friend. The other letters had made it sound like he was acting alone. How many people were involved in this? Was the killer part of a resistance group? Or the beginning of a public uprising? And was he meeting this friend so they could ask for his help, or was he going to his execution?

Chapter Twenty-Eight

When Stachel got back to the apartment, Eliana was waiting for him. She stared at him through eyes that couldn't decide if he was a misbehaving boy or had gone insane.

"You look so guilty," she said.

"That's because I am. At least, according to the Gestapo."

Eliana sat down on the sofa, clutching at a handkerchief, twisting it into knots. Stachel came over and sat down next to her. He couldn't help thinking that this was probably the closest he'd ever physically been to her. The faint stirrings of lust came back. Thinking of Hilda, feeling guilty, he slid to the other side of the sofa.

Germans were acting strange these days. He had seen women yelling at each order, fighting over a pail of water, pulling at each other's hair. He had seen old men, there were no young men left, trading food for a bottle of liquor. People weeping, clawing at rubble, trying to find a loved one who was already dead.

Even those in denial now knew that the end was near. There was no secret weapon, the Alliance will not collapse. Many wouldn't say it openly, for fear it was true, but they knew that the Führer was not Frederick the Great, was not a military genius, but nothing more than a criminal.

Eliana looked at him strangely, noticed him moving away from her, noticed that he was lost in his thoughts, noticed that he was staring at the desk.

"No letter from your killer, but I've talked to the group. They're intrigued by the idea of this shadow man. One person had heard of him, but they all think it's probably nothing. There are a lot of people acting odd these days. But they agree to help. It gives them a purpose, which they need right now."

"Good. Yes, people are acting odd. But that's good that they can help. Let's have them canvas the area, looking for this shadow man. The more people with their eyes to the ground the better."

Stachel decided he would not tell Eliana about the meeting tonight. He knew he should, he knew he should trust her, but he couldn't think of any good it would do. She'd either want to go along or have the group secretly follow him. And Stachel had no doubts that this friend would see these amateurs immediately and disappear. If things went well tonight, if indeed he was getting close to eventually meeting the killer, then he would tell her.

"I hope you didn't give them my name?" he asked.

"No, I didn't. I just mentioned the shadow man. Do you want to meet them?"

"God no!" Stachel said, startled that she had even asked. "Let all communication go through you. I don't want them near me."

"You don't trust them."

Eliana stood up and walked into the kitchen. The water main was fixed, though the brown water that came out looked like mud. She filled a glass, thought better of taking a drink, and set the glass down on the counter. "And you don't trust me either, do you?"

"It's stupid to trust anyone these days." He looked over at her. God, she was beautiful. Maybe he could get close to someone again, get married again, have a normal life, dream of the future. "Yes, I trust you. I have no one else. But it's better for your group if they don't know about me."

"That's not much of a vote of confidence. But I suppose that's all we have these days. They'll start tonight, asking around the district, keeping their eyes open for anything, and report to me in the morning."

"OK. At the very least, maybe they'll stir up some trouble and get this guy to show himself." He hated lying to her. He thought again of telling her about the meeting and then chastised himself for his indecision. Be decisive, take control, he said to himself, and do it alone.

"What will you do?" Eliana asked.

"Go out, continue watching the statue," Stachel lied.

"I'm going to try and get some sleep. You should do the same. It will be a long night."

"Like every other night."

She closed the door to the bedroom as he went through the act of making his bed on the sofa. It was ten o'clock. Once she was asleep, he'd slip out and head over to the Reichstag. He wanted to get there early and survey the area. Be ready for anything, have an escape route. Since nothing had gone his way the last week, he couldn't help thinking that this was a trap. The words "…delayed your evitable death sentence" from the second letter burned like the fires that were engulfing the city.

Chapter Twenty-Nine

It had been raining off and on for four days now. At night, the temperature hovered near freezing. Without anything to heat their apartments, it was as though Berlin had moved North, to the Artic. The only good that came of it was that the smell of death was now locked in a freezer. The rain washed away the debris of dust that blanketed the city, but it couldn't stop the constant fires. Once a fire was close to burning out, an artillery shell would hit the area and start a new fire. The smoke that never left now plodded out the sun, leaving the city in near darkness, like a partial eclipse that never ended.

As he walked to the Reichstag, Stachel could hear the rasping of people struggling to breath. If the Allies didn't end the war soon, everyone would die from the smoke.

Every day the Russians increased the intensity of their shelling and everyone knew it meant they were getting closer to central Berlin.

Stachel ignored the artillery as much as he could. It was God's will whether he died today or tomorrow or sometime in the future. Only when he heard the piercing whistle of an incoming shell did he look for cover.

He was standing outside the Reichstag now, looking up at the inscription on the façade. *Dem Deutschen Volke,* "To the German People." The public had been kept out of the building since the fire in 1933. The building had never been fully repaired. The roof and rotunda had been boarded over and the main meeting hall had been cleaned up, but the rest of the building had been left a burned out shell. As though Hitler had wanted to remind people of the ruthlessness of Germany's enemies. He had used the fire to seize dictatorial power, blaming the communists. Though riddled with pockmarks from shrapnel and covered in the soot from burning fires, the building still stood, dark and silence. Ironic that the Reichstag, the symbol of Germany democracy, would still be standing after Hitler was long gone, despite his attempts to destroy it.

Last change, he thought, to back out, head back to the apartment, let the Allies deal with the killer. But he knew he couldn't do that. Though he knew he couldn't bring the killer to justice, he had to know who he was. He had been delayed getting there by the artillery fire. His plan to get there early and canvas the area was lost. He would be meeting the killer's friend on his terms, with no backup plan, no retreat, if they intended him harm.

Once inside the main hall, he looked around at the statues of former German kings that decorated the walls. An attempt to show that Germany had always been a country, like France or England. Another charade. Before Bismarck, Germany had been nothing more than a patchwork of separate states ruled by petty princes out for themselves.

It was so quiet that Stachel could hear his rasping breath. And there was a wet chill that made the place feel more isolated. *"Meet a friend of mine. In the back of the building,"* the letter had said. A friend. So, killers had friends these days. Stachel had to step gingerly around the rubble, hearing his steps echo through the hall. He headed for the anterooms, behind the main conference room.

Once in the back of the building, he headed to the right. All the offices were on his left. The right side of the hallway was a stone wall, perfect as the backdrop for a firing squad. Strangely, the stone floor had been cleaned recently. The sides and corners were still covered in dirt, but the center was like a path guiding Stachel. As he slowly walked down the hallway, he listened for any sound, the crack of a footstep, the rasp of a life struggling to exist. But it was as quiet as a church during silent prayer. If the friend was here, he came by a different entrance.

As he passed by one office, he thought he heard breathing. He stood at the doorway, peering into the office, trying to will his eyes to see through the darkness. He thought he smelled tobacco, good tobacco too, though he couldn't tell if it was coming from the office or somewhere else.

"Ah, good, you came. I knew you would find your way," a voice in a deep baritone came from the back of the room, echoing like a cannon shot. "Please, come into my office and have a seat," he continued with a laugh.

Though Stachel still couldn't see the man, he could make out the outlines of a few desks in four rows, two desks to each row. And at the back there was a desk in the center. Like a secretarial pool had once been here, and the supervisor in the back cracking the whip. He walked slowly down the center aisle, looking straight ahead, waiting for the man to appear out of the darkness. But even when he got to the desk, all he could see was an outline, like a shadow cast on the chair. The smell of cigarette smoke and hair oil waffled out from the shadow.

"Did you know that Stehen was a homosexual?"

"No" Stachel said, sitting in the one chair in front of the desk. "Does it matter?"

"Of course not. Unlike the Nazis, we don't care about that. I only brought it up to show you how informed we are and that we will share information with you."

"So you killed him?"

"Well, not me exactly. And we prefer the word assassinate. We don't murder people. We are carrying out a just punishment for what they've done."

"It's still murder. And what did Stehen do to justify his death?"

"I told you we were informed. We believe that after he heard the Gestapo wanted you, he was planning on turning you in."

"He would never have done that."

The dark shape of the man's head shrugged. "We disagree."

"Well, in the spirit of sharing, why don't you show yourself."

"Ah, you don't like the voice in the dark. It's a nice special effect, don't you think? But for now, I think I'll stay in the shadows."

The man was no more than six feet away. It would be easy to lunge across the desk and grab him and pull him close.

"Yes, I know, you could reach across and grab me. But you see, I have a gun, and I will use it if you make any sudden moves. Until we know we can trust you, we'll stay anonymous."

"Who's we?"

"Me and my partner, of course, as it said in the letter."

"And who's writing the letters, you or your partner."

"He is. Let's say I'm his research assistant."

"Researching his next victim?"

"You could say that."

The man was toying with him, talking but not giving him anything useful.

"So, will you admit that you and your partner killed Holzer and Mintert?"

"Yes."

"Why? Why were they killed?"

"Because they were Nazis," the man said, laughing like he had just heard the end of a good joke. "Come on, we assumed you'd already figured that out. Ask me something difficult."

Stachel wanted to get up and walk out of the room. The man was playing games. Stachel was no closer to finding out who the killer was then when he walked into the Reichstag.

"Convince me that you did what you claim. Give me a detail from each crime scene. Something no one else would know."

He could see the man shake his head. "I didn't kill them. I only do the research, my partner does the dirty work. So, I can't give you any real details. But I'm sure you noticed that my partner stabbed his victims twelve times after killing them. Twelve times, for the twelve years of Hitler's perverted years. Does that convince you?"

"Maybe. Give me something else."

"The paperclip. Surely you noticed the paperclip we added to their collars."

"I noticed, but it didn't mean anything to me."

"It's a sign of the Norwegian resistance. We thought it would throw you off our scent, send you in another direction. Obviously, it didn't work."

It was strange. This disembodied voice was so calm, so matter of fact, as though killing was somehow normal. No remorse, no sympathy. Were they really any better than the Nazis? But many killers usually believed that what they did was good. "So, why am I here?"

"Isn't it obvious?" The man said, throwing his arms out to the sides, like a dark angel raising his arms to heaven. "The end is near. The Red Army is already at the airport and will be here, in the heart of the city, within the week. We're running out of time. And we need help with what will probably be the final step in our little escapade."

"Escapade? You call killing two people an escapade?"

"I call killing Nazis just punishment for what they've done to this country and to Europe. And we believe that their punishment, their execution, should be done by Germans. The Allies will do their fair share when the war is over, but it's important that we show them that we Germans recognize our sins and are doing something to atone for them."

"Taking the law into your own hands makes you no better than the Nazis."

"Oh stop it. This isn't some kind of morality play. The Nazis are evil, and they must pay. The rest is just excuses to do nothing. Now, will you help us?"

"Help you with what? You haven't told me anything."

The man shuffled in his chair and then lit another cigarette, turning away so the light from the match didn't show his face. Stachel could see the bare outline of his head. He had dark hair, combed back and greased with hair oil, and judging by the collar wearing a dark woolen coat.

"Before I forget," the man said. "You forgot one victim. But he wasn't part of the plan. Bernhardt, the Gestapo agent. He was getting close to you, too close, so we had to get rid of him. For your safety, you understand."

"Thanks. I'll bring it up at your trial."

"There won't be any trial. We'll be dead or slaves to the Bolsheviks before the week is over. Or maybe they'll give us metals. After all, we're killing their enemies. Anyway, everyone we've eliminated so far is small potatoes. Even Mintert was small compared to what we want to do now. We need to get to someone higher up. Someone that will be our final statement on our precious government and their guilt. Hitler is untouchable, but maybe we can get to one of his goons."

Stachel blinked his eyes in disbelief. This man was mad. There was no way to get to these people. Even if you could, they were surrounded by guards. This was lunacy. And how could he help them? He was on the run, trying to avoid them, not meet with them.

"Who? Goring, Himmler or Goebbels? Right? Just walk up and shoot one of them. Do you know how many bodyguards they have? Besides, I've heard that Goring and Himmler aren't in Berlin. Probably trying to save themselves by surrendering to the Americans."

"Well, Goebbels is the one we're thinking of. And you have access to him, through Holzer."

Stachel laughed. "Holzer is more likely to turn me in. We didn't exactly get along."

"He's had a change of heart. He knows Germany will lose the war. You see, Sophie Holzer was not planning to escape to the west alone. Her husband was coming along. Her murder ruined those plans. We didn't know that when we killed her, but once we found out, we reached out to him for help. And he's agreed. Of course, he's just looking for a way to save his own skin, a way to gain favor with the Allies, and what better way than to help get rid of his boss. Now, will you help us?"

"By doing what? I still don't see what I can do."

"By meeting with Holzer. We've already arranged the meeting, but we need a go-between."

"What do I get out of this?"

"Why, knowing that you've helped eliminate one of the worse criminals in history."

"As you've said, within weeks he'll be dead anyway. What else?"

"You'll meet my partner. The man you've been chasing."

That made Stachel think. He had been ready to say no deal and walk out. But the chance to meet the killer, the chance to look him in the eye and tell him what he thought of his deeds, was too great an opportunity. Even though he still couldn't decide what he would say when he met him.

"I need time to think about this," Stachel said.

"There is no time. We need to act now. If you don't agree, we move on and find someone else. Regardless, we're going to do it. With you or without you."

"And me? Do you kill me if I don't agree?"

"No. My partner does not want you harmed. I disagree, but he's in charge."

"Nice to know someone is looking out for me. I still need to think about this."

"Fine, you have one hour. Avail yourself of the splendid facilities around you. Go wherever you want but don't leave the Reichstag without giving us an answer. I will wait here."

It seemed like a simple decision. What else was he going to do? The man said he would meet his partner, but he didn't particularly trust him. For all he knew, this man, this shadow man was the real killer. But eliminating Goebbels would make a statement to the Allies. And if there was true evil in this world, the Nazis were it. But being a part of murder went against everything Stachel had believed in, everything his life had stood for. Maybe Goebbels should die, but wouldn't it be better to let the course of events play out? The Allies would surely capture, sentence and execute him. That was the rule of law played to its conclusion. Trying to short step the law wasn't right. Yet where was the rule of law if he gave up a chance to catch this killer?

Stachel had become so lost in his thoughts that he kept tripping over debris in the building. Twice he had to brace himself against a wall to stop from tumbling over.

Though not where it had all begun, the Reichstag fire was when the true nature of the Nazis had shown itself. And Germany had remained quiet. The mass arrest of communists, the trumped up trials, the beginning of the anti-Jewish laws. Hitler took a little at a time until all of a sudden, he had absolute power. The communists, the opposition party, the social democrats, the unions, the Jews and the Gypsies, the handicapped. Was there no one left to protest?

Without noticing it, Stachel had somehow wandered to the front of the building and was standing at the entrance to the huge conference room where the parliament use to meet. Other than for speeches by Goebbels, the hall had been unused since the fire. Stachel walked down the aisle and stood at the podium and looked out at the seats, thinking that this is where the poison dwarf had stood, this was where he had spit out his venom of hate, his toxic intolerance. How could Stachel live with himself if he allowed such evil to exist. By doing nothing, he had allowed the Nazis to destroy the country, and he couldn't let it continue.

So that was it. Move forward, do something, and deal with the consequences later. He started back to the office in the anteroom, his mind racing back and forth, still looking for a third option. Kill Goebbels, catch the murderer, kill Goebbels, catch the murderer. God, give me another option, Stachel thought, raising his eyes to the dark heavens.

When he got back to the office, he realized that he would have to play their game. There was no other option. He would have to go along with them and hope that he would meet the killer in the end. How could he face God knowing that he had done nothing to stop a murderer? Should he stop them from murdering Goebbels? He didn't know. Right now, all he wanted to do was face the killer. He would decide then what to do next.

The man was still sitting in the back, at the desk, calmly waiting for Stachel's return. Stachel sat back down in the chair and stared across at the man, wishing he could get a better look at him.

"And…" the man said.

"I will help you. On one condition…"

"No conditions. You help us, you join our cause, or you don't. It's simple."

Stachel silently shook his head in agreement. "Ok, when do I meet Holzer?"

"I will talk to him and arrange a time and place. Let's meet again this evening."

"Here?"

"No, this place depresses me. It's a symbol of Nazi hatred. In the Bebelplatz. There's a café called the Razendoff."

"I know it."

"Nine tonight. I'll be at a table in the back."

Chapter Thirty

When Stachel got back to the apartment, Eliana was gone, and when he woke in the morning, she still was not there. Was she with her group, looking for this shadow man? Or was she doing something else? He was growing paranoid, looking for the worse in everything. He could imagine her right now meeting with the Gestapo. The only thing that kept him from fleeing was that she had to know that it would also incriminate her if she told them he was sleeping at her apartment. The more he tried to focus on the meeting this evening, the more he thought of Eliana. He was putting his life into the hands of someone who he barely knew. He was so close now to finding the killer, and yet it could all be snatched away because he trusted someone.

He sat down at the desk, head cradled in his hands, trying to sort everything out. Though he had committed to the meeting with Holzer, he still couldn't decide if he was doing the right thing. He would be breaking the law, something he prided himself that he had never done before. No matter how hard the case, he had never planted evidence, never forced someone to sign a false confession.

Killing Goebbels. Assassination. He was no better than the Nazis.

When he met the killer, what would he say? What would he do? Arresting him was stupid. If he took him back to the Alex, had him locked up, would Gottlieb call Plettner and the Gestapo and tell them not to arrest Stachel? He doubted that. He had been labeled an enemy of the state, and that was a death sentence these days.

The whole justice system, or the mockery of it that the Nazis had created, would be wiped out soon. Though he doubted the Russians would replace it with something better.

Besides, who was the real criminal here? Goebbels had committed crimes well beyond anything the killer had done. Goebbels needed to be punished, but it was a perverse logic to say that he was doing good by assassinating him.

And it graded on him that he had become a pawn to everyone else's game. What was he? Master or slave? Should he be a master and weight his actions by their consequences? Or a slave and weight actions by their intentions? Consequences or intentions, did it really matter? Either way Goebbels had to pay for his crimes, and eventually so did the killer.

But killing Goebbels seemed like a fools errant. Everything Stachel had heard put Goebbels safely hiding away in Hitler's bunker beneath the Chancellery. No one could get to him there. But if they succeeded, what then would happen to Stachel? Would he be next? Eliminate all witnesses?

All he had was questions and worries and no way to get answers other than to go along with the killer.

Stachel's intentions were good, and the consequences were acceptable. He had to believe that. He had to go along, meet the killer face-to-face, help him get to Goebbels, and then afterwards decide what to do. One step at a time.

He heard footsteps and knew immediately that it was Eliana by the short, quick shuffle of her shoes on each step. She came in, pulling a scarf from her neck and flinging it at the desk, where it landed on Stachel's shoulders.

"Oh, I didn't know you were here," she said, holding her hand to her mouth, and quickly grabbing the scarf.

"Where else would I be during the day?"

She looked at him mournfully, wanting to say something reassuring. "This can't last for much longer. Either the Gestapo will find us or the Russians will."

"Nice thoughts. Of course, with my luck I'll be the last man killed."

"Don't be pessimistic. Besides, I have some news."

"Good?"

"Well, not bad," she shrugged. "This shadow man is definitely not a refugee. He knows his way around Berlin too well to be someone from the east. Some say that he's an ex-soldier, others that he's a Russian agent."

"Do you think he's our killer?"

"Don't know. Nothing says he is, but nothing says he isn't."

Stachel lightly hit his fist on the table and twisted it, like he was trying to tighten a screw. "We don't have time. I need information and all I get is maybes."

Eliana came over and put her hands on his shoulders. He tensed immediately, realizing this was the first time she had touched him. Confused, he tried to will himself to relax.

"Where were you yesterday?" she asked. "You left during the day."

He stood up and walked into the kitchen, grabbing a glass and turning on the faucet. Again, brown water with small particles of grit came out.

"Don't drink it? You'll get sick."

He walked back into the living room, holding the glass up and turning it around, as though it was filled with a fine wine. "Better sick than dead," and he took a slow drink, draining the glass. "Tastes disgusting, like the city."

There was no sense hiding the meeting from her. He rolled the empty glass between his hands as he spoke. He explained his meeting at the Reichstag, about the offer to help assassinate Goebbels, and about the next meeting tonight with the killer's partner to arrange a meeting with August Holzer.

At first, she was startled by the news, asking why he hadn't said anything earlier, perturbed at his secret. But he told her he had said nothing to protect her, and she accepted that, though she knew it wasn't true.

"It could be a trap," she said. "From either side. From them or from Holzer."

Stachel shrugged. "I thought of that. But it's worth the risk. I'm trying to look at the good side. We get rid of that horror Goebbels and I finally catch my killer."

"I don't like it. If you succeed in killing Goebbels, the Nazis will go crazy. Like with Heydrich, they'll kill everyone. It will be a blood bath."

"It's already a blood bath. And no different than what we'll get from the Russians. It will just come a little earlier. Besides, we deserve it."

"Not we, them, the Nazis. They deserve the Russian's revenge. We haven't killed anyone. We didn't invade Russia."

"But we let them. We didn't say anything." Stachel looked down at the floor. "It's a collective guilt. The only moral act left is to punish those who have done so much evil. So I will play along. I don't have anything else."

"They'll kill Goebbels and then they'll kill you."

Stachel waved his hand in the air, as though swatting at a fly. "Them or the Russians. What do I care who does the deed. I'm dead either way."

"Stop talking like that. You will survive, we all will, we all must if there's going to be anything left of Germany after the war."

"Do you really want to see what's left after the war? It will be ugly."

"When has it ever been anything else? We take it one day at a time. We're Germans, not Nazis. We will survive. I can't think any other way. You're talking like a nihilist."

Eliana stood and started pacing around the room, her arms crossed at her shoulders, her shoes clicking on the bare wood floor. Stachel remained quiet. Finally, she stopped and leaned against the wall on the other side of the room. "This meeting, can I come?"

Stachel looked at her in surprise. He hadn't thought of that and for a minute considered saying yes. It would be good to have someone else there, someone that maybe he could trust. But it was foolish. They'd never agree. "Of course not. They won't meet if they see you there. You stick to your plan, use your people to try and find this shadow man, and I'll stick to mine. Hopefully, one of us will be successful."

"And what happens then? What happens after you've caught your killer? There's no courts anymore. You can't take him to jail. The Gestapo will kill you both."

"I don't know. I'll worry about that when the time comes. One day at a time. Let's not try and get too far ahead of ourselves. We don't know what we'll be facing tomorrow, let alone in a week, so why worry about it."

They hung around together for the next few hours, barely talking to each other. It was still raining outside, and the clouds lay thick over the city, over the building, wrapping both of them in feelings of hopelessness. The end was near and neither of them knew how to face it.

In the afternoon, Eliana said she must go out. They needed food, and she wanted to check in with a few of her people and see if they'd found anything. She left, leaving Stachel alone again, sitting on the sofa, lost in his thoughts, wishing he could just get this over with now. Maybe he'd find peace at the end, though he wasn't sure anymore what that would look like.

Chapter Thirty-One

L eft to himself again, Stachel felt the apartment walls were talking to him. He wondered if this was what someone in solitary confinement felt. The silence enclosed you like you were lost in a catacomb. The artillery fire was constant now. Stachel blotted it out, like it was the noise of a busy city street.

He looked at the clock. Five in the afternoon; three hours until his meeting with the killer's partner. Did prisoners have clocks in their cells? It seemed a cruel punishment to give them a clock so they could watch their lives slowly waste away.

Thirty minutes later, Eliana came in all in a rush, not pausing to take off her scarf or coat.

"Have you heard?" she said, and then laughed. "Of course you haven't. You've been stuck here all day. The Nazis are deserting the city, fleeing south to Bavaria, to the mountains. They've leaving us to the Russians."

Stachel shook his head. "That's just a rumor. It's been making the rounds for the last few weeks. I've been told that Hitler refuses to leave Berlin."

"Well, maybe the rest of the rats are deserting. They're all cowards. They talk about defending the city, saving the

Fatherland, when all they really care about is saving their own skins. I've heard Himmler and Goering aren't even in the city. There's another rumor that Himmler is up north trying to negotiate our surrender with the Allies."

"Wouldn't that be nice if Himmler turns out to be our savior. Saved from a monster by another monster." Stachel chuckled lightly, but he couldn't decide if he was laughing or crying. Maybe the Allies will pin a metal on the bastard. Serve us right to have that weak chinned bureaucrat as our new Führer. "There's also a rumor that the twelfth army is coming to defend Berlin. Another rumor says the twelfth army surrendered to the Americans. Which rumor do you want to believe?"

Stachel looked over at Eliana and noticed that the door was still wide open. "Close the door. If someone hears us…" He left the rest unsaid. It was too horrible to say.

Eliana hurriedly closed the door. "No one would turn us in. Everyone hates the Nazis now."

"Regardless, it's better not to trust anyone. These rumors don't change anything. I still must meet Holzer. I still have to catch this killer."

"Does it matter?"

"It matters, and I don't want to get into that conversation again. That rumor about Himmler. Was there any mention of Goebbels?"

"No. Only Himmler was mentioned. Maybe Holzer will also leave, and you won't have to meet him."

"I don't think so. He always struck me as spineless. He'll either follow Goebbels to his grave or want to save himself."

They both stood at opposite ends of the room, both lost in the shadows of the setting sun. Then the phone rang, breaking the silence.

Eliana hurried into the bedroom where the phone was and picked it up. "Yes," and then after a few seconds gently put the phone back in its cradle.

"Who as it?" Stachel asked.

She stood in the bedroom doorway, arms folded across her chest, suddenly looking very cold. "A voice, in Russian, laughing. I know a little Russian. He said the Red Army was here, that they were coming for us. That Hitler was *kaput*." She came into the living room and sat down on the sofa. "Are they already here? All around us? I thought we still had a few days."

"They were at the airport yesterday. If they've taken that now, then they'll be heading here, for the city center. You know that phone call is a prank to scare us. That soldier could be anywhere, dialing a random number."

"Give up this killer, don't go to your meeting. Let's get out of the city, head west, now, before it's too late."

"You should do that. Get your friends and try and get out. But I can't. I have to stay and see this through." Stachel knew she was right. But he would not repeat Memel. Maybe he had a death wish. He certainly had no wish to see what would happen to Germany after the war was over.

"See what through, capturing your killer? That's over now. It doesn't matter anymore. There's a new group of killers coming."

Stachel walked over to her and started to put his hands on her shoulders, then dropped them to his side and looked at the floor. "I'm sorry, I have to stay. If I flee, I'll never have any respect for myself, and I can't live like that."

"Yes you can. We all can. All that matters now is to stay alive, to still be here when the war is over, to begin the rebuilding of our country."

"You rebuild it. I just want it over. I can't think of what will happen afterwards. I don't care anymore about anything other than catching this killer, this guy who's mocking me. I can't be spending the rest of my life wondering if the person next to me is the killer I never caught."

Eliana turned and walked back into the bedroom. "Fine, I'm going to try and leave. At least I have hope."

Stachel looked again at the clock. Six in the evening; two hours. He might as well start walking to his meeting. There was no reason to be here.

Chapter Thirty-Two

It took Stachel fifteen minutes to walk over to the Bebelplatz. Pockets of light dotted the street, giving him enough light to wend his way around the debris. As he neared the café, he heard the sound of an incoming artillery shell. Before he had time to think, the shell exploded down the street, the blast throwing him to the ground like a broken doll. The ringing in his ears made him think of the earlier phone call by the taunting Russian, "Hitler *kaput!*" He rolled over onto his side and looked directly at an unexploded shell. He jumped up and danced away, expecting it to go off at any moment. Written on the shell in German were the words *für Waisen und Witwen*, "for orphans and widows." He leaned against a wall for a minute, gathering himself. Though he had been thinking of death for the last few weeks, getting this close to the actual unnerved him.

The Café Razendoff was around the corner from the platz. It was in ruins. Chairs and table were upturned, the windows shattered. The café looked like a miniature version of the city. He walked up to the front door and looked in. In the back, one table with two chairs stood upright. A candle burned in the middle of the table, a pulsing light that bathed the solitary figure at the table, who looked like an angel from hell.

The man nodded slightly and Stachel worked his way past the tables and sat down opposite him.

The man was about thirty, with long brown hair swept back with the same smelly hair oil. He was thin and wore a ragged black sport jacket that had a few spots of smeared dirt. A man who cared about his appearance no matter what the situation. A dandy, maybe homosexual, though Stachel knew that homosexuals were either in concentration camps or dead. Another present from the Führer. The man had a nervous twitch on the side of his mouth, and he looked at Stachel with glaring and distrustful eyes.

Stachel sat down and immediately started talking. He always thought that whoever started a conversation controlled the conversation.

"What's your name? And before we go further, I want some background."

"Call me Siegfried," he said, his head tilted down, looking at Stachel through thin eyebrows. "Full many a wonder is told us in stories old, of heroes worthy of praise, or hardships dire, of joy and feasting, of weeping and of wailing, of the fighting of bold warriors…"

"So you were the one writing the letters. Siegfried was mentioned in the first one. Maybe you are the killer, and this is all a charade. Besides, Siegfried dies, but I guess it's appropriate. The *Nibelungenlied* is about revenge."

"A heroic poem from medieval times that we have embraced. No, my partner wrote the letters. Over my objections I might add. His name is my name. We are both Siegfried."

"But no feasting."

"Granted, but as you mentioned, a poem of revenge, and we are taking out our revenge on the monsters."

This man unnerved him. He had met so many distasteful characters in his life, worked with the scum of society, had become desensitized to the horrors that people did to each other, yet now, looking at Siegfried, he felt as though he was talking to the devil, or rather to the devil's disciple. He felt that this was a man who had witnessed worse things than Stachel.

"Where are you from?" Stachel asked. "Who are you?"

Siegfried leaned forward with a leering smile. "I guess we can start with questions. I suppose you deserve that. I grew up here in Berlin, joined the military in '42, fought in Russia, deserted in '44, came back to Berlin and have been working against the Nazis since then."

"And how did you get caught up with your partner?"

Siegfried shrugged. "It happened. You don't need to know the details. Let's just say we had a common cause. But enough of that. I assume you still plan to help us?"

Stachel nodded yes. "I'll help."

"Good," Siegfried said and sprayed his hands across the table, as though wiping dirt to the floor. "I talked to Holzer earlier today. He'll meet you here, at this café, tomorrow at eight in the morning. He's very nervous. He knows the Russians are almost here and he's trying to save his own neck. He'll give us information about Goebbels and in exchange wants help getting out of Berlin. He will ask you about that and you should say that once Goebbels is dead, he should meet me in the Bebelplatz three hours later."

"And what if he wants out immediately? Doesn't want to wait 'til afterwards?"

"He'll do what we want. He has no other choice."

"What about the rumor that the government is retreating south, into the mountains? Surely he'll be included in that group."

"Rumors are nice, aren't they, but it's only a rumor. There's no organized retreat. Some people are leaving, but you need papers. Holzer's already tried that route and was denied. Goebbels wants him close, and Goebbels is going nowhere without the Führer."

"What do you want from him?"

"Goebbels's schedule for tomorrow. We know he's moved into Hitler's bunker, that he's living there with his wife and children, but he still leaves for various reasons. We need to know when he's planning to leave the bunker and where he'll go."

"Do you really think that at this point Goebbels has a schedule, has appointments?"

"Goebbels still believes that we will win the war and that he will make a difference. We know he goes to one of the Reich radio stations periodically to spread his lies about our eventual victory. He usually goes once a week, on Wednesday's, tomorrow. That's what we want from Holzer. If Goebbels is going tomorrow, what time. If not, then Holzer is to call us once he knows when Goebbels is leaving for the station."

"But isn't the radio station in the eastern part of the city? I've heard there's already fighting in the eastern suburbs."

"That's one station and, yes, it's probably too risky for him to go there. There's another on the west side of the city."

"But why doesn't he just do the radio broadcast from the bunker? They undoubtedly have the equipment there."

Siegfried shook his head in agreement. "I'm sure they do. Maybe he just wants to get out of that tomb. Will he leave tomorrow with the Russians so close? We don't know. That's why we need Holzer."

Now was the time for Stachel to make his demand, to make sure he got want he wanted, rather than what they wanted. "First, I want to meet your partner."

"No way."

"Then I walk."

Siegfried sat back and stared off to the left, to the other side of the restaurant, as though looking for someone. Stachel followed his gaze but didn't see anyone.

"He's here, isn't he?" Stachel said.

Siegfried continued looking to his left. "Of course not. It would be stupid for him to be here. He refuses to show his face in public. I can't answer you. I'll have to talk to him. It's his decision, though I doubt he'll agree. But you want Goebbels dead, don't you? He must be punished, and it must be done by Germans, not by the Allies."

"I don't care. I meet your partner or there's no deal. That's my terms. Take it or leave it."

"How about we compromise. You meet Holzer, get the information we want, and you can be there when we kill Goebbels. You'll meet him then."

Stachel thought for a few minutes. Apparently, he was not going to get what he wanted, a meeting with Siegfried's partner now, before meeting Holzer. The compromise was dangerous. He hadn't thought of being there when they tried to kill Goebbels. Even if they succeeded, escaping afterwards would be difficult.

"No. I want a meeting with him. I'll meet with Holzer, but then I will only give what Holzer tells me to your partner."

"I'll talk to him, but I can't promise anything."

"I want an answer, a simple yes or no, before I meet with Holzer."

Siegfried stood up, clearly unhappy. "I'm disappointed. We thought you cared about your country, we thought you wanted to help us ensure there's a Germany after the war."

"Sorry to disappoint. He shows or no deal. If he cares about Germany, he'll agree."

"Ok, I'll try and get a message to you later tonight. But you're not giving me much time."

"How?"

"Don't worry, we know where you are."

Chapter Thirty-Three

For the first time in weeks, Stachel had slept well. The artillery barrage was constant now, but he had slept as though the noise and threat of death meant nothing. He knew what he was going to do, and he would accept the consequences. He was a master, not a slave.

He padded his way into the kitchen and started to boil water for coffee. He didn't want to know how she did it, but Eliana always seemed to have something to eat or drink that hadn't been available in Berlin for months, if not years. He knew she had to be involved in the black market, but hopefully for the last time, he would choose to look the other way.

Yesterday, she had come home with a half pound of real coffee. Staring at the package in disbelief, Stachel asked her where she had gotten it.

"It has to be the black market, but I didn't think they even had real coffee."

"It's better if a policeman doesn't know some things," she said. "Just pretend that I'm a witch and conjured the coffee out of thin air."

"Well, can you please conjure up this killer for me?"

"I wish I could. It would put your mind at rest."

"It's at rest. I know what I'm going to do, though I can't help thinking that I'm being setup. That this Siegfried fellow really works for the Nazis and I'm going to be arrested once I get to the café. Which is stupid, I know, because if he was with the Gestapo, he wouldn't go through all this subterfuge."

"If you're worried, don't go."

"I'm not worried. Besides, what do I do then? I can't just sit here waiting for the Russians to arrest me."

"Throw away your badge, throw away everything that might identify you as a policeman. Become another man who was too old to fight in the military."

"You make me sound like something that should be discarded, thrown in the rubbish. Besides, it won't work. They'll still figure out that I'm not just another old man, as you say. My eyes will give me away."

"You're just a pawn. The killer is in control and you're just going along."

Stachel knew she was right but was still irritated by having it out in the open. "Yes, I'm a pawn, but I have made some demands. I refused to go along, as you say, unless I get to meet the killer."

"And they agreed?"

"Well, no. He needed to get back to me."

"And how do you know that this Siegfried isn't the killer?"

"I don't, but I don't think so."

"And what if they don't agree to your demand?"

"I go anyway. I'll be getting closer to this killer. That's all that matters."

Now, the next morning, while the water boiled, Stachel walked into the living room and immediately saw a piece of paper on the floor near the front door. It was from Siegfried.

Eliana was still asleep, so he went into the kitchen to read the letter. His partner had agreed to meet with Stachel assuming he was successful in getting the information from Holzer. If he wasn't, then there was no point in another meeting.

Immediately after the meeting with Holzer, Stachel was to go to the Brandenburg Gate and wait.

Eliana was still asleep when he grabbed his coat and slipped out the door. He felt anxious walking on the street in daylight. He kept looking around, checking everyone to make sure he wasn't recognized, looking behind to make sure he wasn't being followed.

As Stachel walked over the Ebertbrucke bridge, he heard gunfire echoing down the river. He looked to his left and saw fighting on the Monbijoubrücke bridge. A detachment of Russians had appeared on the north end of the bridge. The south end was barricaded and there were soldiers behind it. The soldiers didn't look like *Volkssturm*, which meant the army had already been pushed back to Berlin. The fighting for the heart of the city had begun.

The shots fired across the bridge from either side sounded like small firecrackers. Grenades were thrown from both sides, landing on the bridge and blowing up before reaching their targets, spits of fire and smoke jumping into the air. There was screaming, in German, *kein Rückzug, kein Rückzug*, "no retreat, no retreat" and in Russian, *ubejte zverej*, "kill the beasts!"

It's almost over, Stachel thought. One way or another, it will end soon. If he was to catch this murderer, it must happen now. There would be no tomorrow. A newfound sense of urgency drove him across the bridge. Goebbels would die. Either we will do it, or the Russians will. Better the Germans, and then Stachel would have his killer.

As he got to the end of the bridge, he looked again at the skirmish. The Russians were winning. Already, the German soldiers were looking behind them, thinking of retreat. Two men laid sprawled on the street, apparently dead. Since there was no more screaming from the German side, Stachel assumed one of them must be an officer.

Stachel quickened his pace. He scampered across Am Weidendamm to the safety of Geschwister-Scholl Strasse. Once walking down that street, he was protected by the buildings from stray bullets.

As he neared Georgenstrasse, he noticed a man on the other side of the street who looked familiar. Wasn't that the same man who had been right behind him when he walked over the bridge? Why was he on the other side of the street now? A tall man with a pointed nose and squinting eyes, like someone who wasn't used to sunlight. Not wanting to talk chances, Stachel turned into the university grounds, walking briskly until he reached Planckstrasse, where he turned right and then another right onto Dorothenstrasse.

He ducked into an abandoned retail shop, its windows broken, merchandize strewed on the floor, obviously looted. He headed into the back and crouched down behind the counter, the cash register above him. Peeking out he saw the man pass by the shop's windows and then come back and peer inside. He heard the front door open, the sharp crunch of glass against shoe. There was an open doorway behind the counter leading into a storeroom. On his hands and knees, Stachel slipped through the door and around the corner. It sounded like the steps came up to the counter. In a minute he would come into the storeroom. Stachel stood up and readied himself for a fight. Muscle tense, barely breathing, he looked around the storeroom for a weapon. Nothing. But the man never came into the back. He heard the footsteps retreat, the front door open and then close. He waited a few minutes, then looked out into the shop. No one was there.

Stachel went to the window and peered out, looking down both sides of the street. No one. If he didn't hurry, he would be late meeting Holzer, so he pulled his hat down over his eyes and rushed out the door, retracing his route down Planckstrasse. And now on the other side of the street he saw another man, younger and shorter, but with the same squinting eyes. *Vater und Sohn*, Father and Son, they looked like they had just jumped out of the comic strip. And coming towards him, on the same side of the street, from the other direction, was a third man. So much for the comic. He was pinned. If he tried to run down either side of the street, they'd have him in a minute. He looked around for any means of escape. There was an apartment building to his left, still occupied. A woman was unlocking the front door. Stachel quickly ran up to her as she opened the door and pushed her inside, following behind and then locking the door.

"What are you doing?" she said, trying to get away from Stachel.

"Police," and he pulled out his badge. "Get into your apartment and stay there." The woman immediately opened a door on the first floor and closed it behind her. Good Germans did what they were told, Stachel thought. That was the problem.

Two of the men were now at the door trying to open it. Realizing it was locked, they started hurling themselves at the door with their shoulders. Stachel looked them both in the eye and smiled, then quickly started up the stairs, two steps at a time. The building was three stores high. By the time he got near the top, he was winded. He stopped for a second on the stairs to catch his breath. The crack of the door breaking gave him renewed energy. He sprinted to the roof top, closed the door and braced it with a piece of wood that had been lying next to the door. The roof was empty except for two chairs, a small, weathered table and some discarded pieces of wood over in a corner. Evidently people came up here in better days to get some sun, before it had disappeared in the smoke from burning fires.

He could hear the men racing up the stairs and knew he only had seconds to react. There was nowhere to hide. The only option was to get off the roof. And there were only two ways to do that; down the fire escape or jump to another building. He went over to the fire escape that was in the back of the building, but as he suspected, one of the men was waiting at the bottom. The distance from the building to his left was probably too much. Stachel estimated it was about ten feet. But the building to his right looked closer, maybe only six feet or so. Rather than a stone parapet, it had an iron railing running around the top of the building. The men were now at the top of the stairs and pushing against the door. He ran over to the wood pile and grabbed a piece that was about four feet long and one foot wide. He braced it against the parapet of the building, creating a ramp that he hoped would give him enough extra lift to clear the six foot canyon. Taking a running leap, Stachel jumped to the next building. It was farther than he had thought. Thinking only of the three story drop, he flailed wildly with his hands at the railing, just catching it with his left hand. He banged against the side of the brick building, feeling a jolt of pain in his shoulder and his left ankle. Cursing himself for not being in shape, he struggled to pull himself over the railing, his arms feeling like they were going to break, bracing himself on the railing with his armpit and rolling over onto the roof. When he tried to stand up, he collapsed, his left ankle giving him pains like a hot poker had been shoved up his leg. He didn't know if it was broken or just a strain, but he didn't have time to find out. Struggling to his feet, he limped over to a door leading down. Fortunately, it was unlocked, and he stepped inside just as he heard the men breaking through the other door. He looked through a crack in the door and saw the two men searching the roof. He figured he had a few minutes lead until they saw his ramp and realized he must have jumped to the other building. He worked his way downstairs, clutching the handrail to keep his weight off his left leg. At one point, he slipped and fell four steps to a landing, hitting his left ankle against the wall. His ankle burned. If he hadn't broken it before, he probably had now. He picked himself up and continued limping down the stairs and out the front door. Walking as fast as he could with his limp, he continued down Planckstrasse, past Unter Den Linden and turned left onto Behrenstrasse, heading for the café. He was determined to still meet Holzer and hoped he wasn't being setup. If the men had been sent by Holzer, they'd know about the café and he'd be screwed.

He arrived at the café well after eight and collapsed into the same chair Siegfried had sat in the day before. He was covered in sweat and his ankle was pulsing with waves of pain. Holzer wasn't there yet. Maybe he'd been spooked when Stachel didn't arrive on time and had left? But he needed to stay off his ankle, so he sat there, hoping that Holzer would eventually arrive.

Sunlight peeped over the roof of a building, giving some light in the café. Stachel thought of moving into the light, where there would be warmth, but feared that he would be seen. Better cold than dead.

When Holzer finally arrived ten minutes later, he looked out of sorts, hesitant, his shoulders slumped forward like he was a beaten dog. He sat across from Stachel, at first on the edge of his seat, then sliding back, stiff and upright, holding his hands on his crossed knees. He mentioned that he was late because he'd been across the street, watching, making sure Stachel came alone.

"I see you're working for the criminals now," Holzer said.

"We're all criminals these days. I've just picked the ones that are less guilty."

"And have you solved my wife's murder?"

"I thought Pantel was the murderer?"

Holzer snorted and let out a short bark of a laugh. "I never believed that and neither did you. Pantel was a convenience."

Stachel looked out to the street, worried that he'd see the Gestapo staring in.

"I need to ask. Why did your wife meet with the black market? Why was she buying food? Surely you had enough?"

Holzer smiled, rubbing his right hand across the table. He saw a crumb of bread, picked it up and popped it in his mouth.

"That was a decoy. In case she was stopped by someone. She was really picking up the five thousand dollars from a contact of mine."

"And you were going to use that money to bribe your way West, to surrender to the Americans?"

"Or the British. Whoever we ran into. We weren't picky. Your murderer ruined everything."

"My murderer?" Stachel laughed. "You act as though it was my fault."

Holzer shrugged. "I have to blame someone. So, do you know who killed my wife?"

"Yes, I know, but I haven't caught him yet." Apparently Holzer didn't know that the people he was helping had killed his wife. Stachel wasn't about to tell him.

"Why did you have me followed?"

"What are you talking about?" Holzer looked genuinely confused, gazing at Stachel with his head tilted to the side.

"Three men, I assume Gestapo, were following me. But don't worry, I gave them the slip."

"Believe me, I had nothing to do with it. Since an arrest warrant is out for you, I expect they are only doing their duty. You are a wanted man."

"It seems I'm wanted by everyone now. Anyway, I believe you have something for me."

"Maybe. First, I want papers that will get me out of Berlin. And I want them before I give you any information."

"No. You give us the information first."

"How do I know…"

"You don't. You can't trust us, but what other choice do you have? You play it our way, or you can welcome the Red Army to Berlin. I'm sure they'll be very respectful guests."

"I don't know if I can get you what you want. Goebbels has moved his family into the bunker and is living there now. So far, he's kept to his schedule, but that will probably change."

"And will you know if it changes?"

"Maybe. As you know, there's not much left of the government these days. You're either going down in flames with our beloved Führer or you're trying to flee to the west, away from the Russians. Or shooting yourself. There's a lot of that now."

Holzer kept looking around the café. Stachel wanted to tell him that there were no one else there, that he was safe, at least for now. But then thought better of it. Let him squirm, let him feel fear, let him get a taste of what he'd done to millions of people.

"I don't like this," Holzer said. "Everything tells me to walk away, to put my trust in the Führer. He will save us, he always has, but I know that's the fool in me talking. Time to think of myself." Holzer was now picking at his fingernails, nervously looking at Stachel and then at the wall over his head.

"You know," Holzer continued, "there used to be a picture of the Führer on that wall. The owner could be arrested for removing it."

"And he could be killed for keeping it. What did you just say about every man for himself." Stachel was getting inpatient. He couldn't sit here forever waiting for Holzer to make a decision. Those guys were still out there, looking for him. Eventually, they'd look in the café.

"Time to meet your maker," Stachel said. "What's Goebbels schedule today?"

Once again, Holzer looked around the restaurant, alternating between picking at his fingernails and rubbing his hands for warmth. "He's supposed to give a radio speech at two this afternoon. In Charlottenburg, at a station on Neufertstrasse. I wrote part of the speech. More hype about our glorious soldiers and the great German victory. I doubt he will show but he's always been a very punctual man. Either way, he'll be heavily guarded."

"And you'll be there?"

"God no. I'll be as far away as I can. Whether you succeed or not, Hitler won't take kindly to his death. You've heard what they did to that village in Czechoslovakia after Heydrich was killed?"

"Only rumors. And what does it matter. Haven't you heard the latest? The Russians have taken the military hospital complex at Beelitz-Heilstaffen. They raped the women and randomly shot the men. There's going to be a bloodbath in Berlin. If Goebbels changes his schedule and goes to the station earlier or later, you will contact us, correct?"

"If I know, but how do I contact you?"

"Someone will be around here every hour, watching the cafe. If you show, someone will meet you." And Stachel hoped that would be true. He had never discussed that contingency with Siegfried.

"And afterwards?"

"Someone will meet you in the Bebelplatz at five. That person will give you exit papers."

Holzer stood up. Clearly the meeting was over. "Two," he said and quickly left. Stachel waited a few minutes and then started limping his way to the Brandenburg Gate. It was half past nine, plenty of time even with his ankle, which had started to swell up. He never saw any of the agents, though part of him wanted them to find him and put him out of his misery.

Chapter Thirty-Four

There was something in his walk that looked familiar. A forward thrust, back straight, shoulders in front, like a solider leading a hopeless charge.

Stachel was standing near the Brandenburg Gate. Like all of Berlin, it was pitted and scarred and littered with debris. Because it was easily recognized from the air, it had been a favorite target of Allied bombing. Built as a symbol of peace more than one hundred fifty years ago, it had become one of the most recognized symbols of the German love of war. At least that's how the Allies saw it.

Stachel's foot was starting to swell up. He should be back at the apartment, the foot up and wrapped, with an ice pack. Of course, like everything else that made life livable, ice was a luxury these days. He was sitting on a bench, facing the gate, wishing that he could walk around to help stay warm. All he could do was huddle deeper into his overcoat, arms hugging his sides, looking like a Russian bear.

The man was walking up Ebertstrasse, staying on the side of the road across from the Tiergarten. Wise of him, Stachel thought. If the man thought anything was amiss, he could easily dart into the building ruins where he would have many places to hide. Though it was cold, and a brisk wind was coming out of the west, the man wore no overcoat. He looked as though he was out for a casual stroll on a bright and sunny summer day, without a care in the world. Stachel put his hand in his right pocket, grasping for the gun that wasn't there.

As the man came closer, his outline coming into focus, Stachel suddenly realized who he was. A ghost from the past, a corpse, Stachel saw death walking towards him. The man walked up to him, keeping his eyes locked on Stachel's eyes, showing no emotion until he was standing in front of him.

Gaunt, skin as pale as ice, wearing shoes with holes in them, clothes threadbare, Stachel could see he had lost at least thirty pounds in the last few years.

"Inspector Stachel, I presume?" he said, smiling at his joke. His voice hadn't changed. It was still the deep baritone that made people immediately notice him at any crime scene.

"You were always one for Sherlock Holmes," Stachel said. "You've been hard to fine."

"It's funny. They call me the shadow man, after that ridiculous poster. As though I was working for Goebbels."

"Maybe you were. You certainly scared enough people. But how are you? Killed anyone recently?"

"Nice, coming from someone who was part of the Nazi terror."

Stachel tried to stand up, the pain shooting up his leg sending him back to the bench. "I was never part of it, you know that. I did my job."

"What all Germans are saying now to try and absolve themselves of our collective guilt. It doesn't work. Doing one's job meant working for the devil."

"And you're innocent?"

"Of course not. I'm as guilty as everyone else. We are all guilty. Except I decided to do something about it."

"By killing people…"

"By killing Nazis," Franz Klein spitted out. "By punishing those in authority who have destroyed this country."

Germany was truly a mad house, Stachel thought. My old partner, upholding law and order by murder. Vigilante justice. It's like we've become characters in a Karl May novel. Maybe that was the beginning of Germany's decline. An infatuation with the American West, with cowboy justice. Hitler had always said that he loved Karl May and read all his novels as a boy. He had even ordered that the novels be given to soldiers fighting in Russia.

"Germans killing Germans. You know the bloodbath won't end with the war. The killing will go on."

"The killing will stop when those responsible, when those in authority, are dead, not before."

"Sophie Holzer was hardly someone in authority."

"By her radio broadcasts, she advocated killing our children. She had to be stopped." Klein was still standing, looking down at Stachel. During their conversation, Stachel could see that he was getting more and more upset, more impatient, more like the old Klein, who always hated talk. He wanted action, "do something," he always said, trusting instinct over reason. "Enough of this, I don't need to justify myself…"

"But you want to, you need to. You were once a policeman, a good one. But you joined the military. I've heard they slaughtered Jews, killed women and children, wiped out whole towns. You must have been involved."

"Yes, I was. But remember, by the time I joined we were in full retreat, willing to do anything to stop the Russians." Klein shook his head and looked down at his hands, holding them away from his body as though they were covered in blood. "But with these hands I'm now trying to do something to atone for the stupid decisions I made."

"By murdering more people? Aren't your hands dirty enough?"

"I think my actions speak for my intentions. Besides, you voted for Hitler. You're hardly innocent."

"I did," Stachel said, wishing he could change the past, "and I find it hard to look in the mirror at the man who did that. If I knew then that the madman would invade Poland, France, Russia, I would never have voted for him. But I didn't, and I'll accept the consequences of that action."

"And let others do the dirty work."

"No. I'm here, aren't I?"

Klein laughed, throwing his head back and looking up at the sky as though pleading to God. He looked back down at Stachel with the void less stare of a madman. "You're here because you wanted to catch your killer. I know you. And now your killer is standing in front of you. What next? Do you continue the charade that you're working for law and order? Do you arrest me now? Or do you wait, see if I can get to Goebbels, do the dirty work you refuse to do, and then bring me in?"

Stachel couldn't answer that question. Klein's actions were wrong, yet which was the greater evil? He didn't know anymore what was morally right. Maybe he was the psychopath now, not knowing right from wrong, devoid of empathy? Should he let Klein go free, should he help him with his dirty deeds? The world would be a better place without a dwarf like Goebbels. But if they didn't kill him and he escaped from the Allies, fled south to Bavaria, the war would continue. How many more innocents would die then?

"Well," Klein said. "You look like you're still struggling with your decision. It's actually pretty easy. You tell me what Holzer said and then you walk away. Do you still think that any other decision would be morally right?"

Stachel knew Klein was right and silently berated himself for his continued indecision. He had no choice but to go forward with the plan. Time to act, to make a stand, deal with the damage later. "Two in the afternoon. Goebbels is scheduled to make a radio announcement at two at the radio station in Charlottenburg. He'll be heavily guarded you know."

"That doesn't matter. One thing the army taught me is how to shoot. I was a sniper in Russia before I deserted and came back here. You can join us, if you still want to. My partner, what do you call him, Siegfried? Not a very original name. He'll meet you one block north of the radio station."

"And where will you be?"

"I'll be there, though you won't know where. You see, I don't trust you. I wouldn't put it past you to try and shoot me afterwards."

"I'm not a killer…"

"Yes you are. We all are. You just don't want to admit it. Just keep reminding yourself that Germany will have a better future because of what we do today."

"Germany has no future. You know it. It doesn't matter what we do anymore. Germany is a dead country."

"Such nihilism. Think positive, by two-thirty today there will be one less villain in the world." And with that Klein started walking back down Ebertstrasse.

Like it or not, Stachel was now a partner in their hatred.

Chapter Thirty-Five

Getting to the district of Charlottenburg was a nightmare. The constant artillery shelling had finished what destruction the bombings had missed. People had disappeared into their cellars, barricades of ripped up railroad ties and turned over tramcars were everywhere. Children riding bicycles, holding haphazardly to their *panzerfausts,* were the only ones left who believed that Germany would win the war. Everyone else knew it was hopeless.

Stachel started the long walk through the Tiergarten soon after meeting with Klein. With his swollen ankle, he didn't know how long it would take him. He had to constantly stop to rest his ankle. As he neared the Victory Column, an open bed truck came down Strasse Des 17. Juni, its occupants fleeing to the west. Stachel limped out into the middle of the road and stopped the truck. There were two soldiers inside. When they saw his badge, they allowed him to ride in back. They took him through the rest of the Tiergarten and down Bismarckstrasse. At the Sophie-Charlotte Platz he got off and continued limping up Schlossstrasse towards Schloss Charlottenburg, the castle built in the seventeenth century for Friedrich the First. The radio station was off Schlossstrasse, on a side street called Neufertstrasse. Stachel was glad of that. He didn't want to see the castle, which had been heavily damaged by the bombing raids. It only reminded him that Germany's past had been destroyed. As always, he had to wend his way through the debris. And his ankle stabbed at him, a constant reminder that he shouldn't be doing this. If things went wrong, how was he going to escape, limping along like a lame bear?

Once he turned onto Neuferstrasse, he heard his name called out and saw the shadow of a man at the door motioning him inside a building.

"Siegfried?"

"Yes, of course. Quick, up to the third floor, we have an apartment where we can wait for Goebbels."

As Stachel started towards him, Siegfried looked at his foot.

"You're limping?"

"Took a fall running from some former friends."

"Can you run? You get caught, we all get caught."

"No, I can't, but I'll deal with it. It's not your problem."

"It is our problem. If you get captured, you can give us away."

"And what would I tell them? I don't know where you're holed up. I don't know your real name. Klein, yes, but he's shown he's good at hiding. Besides, do you really expect to live through this?"

Siegfried smiled and shrugged. "One can always hope. No one wants to die."

Stachel followed Siegfried to the third floor, thinking about what he had said. No one wants to die is true in normal times, but in the disaster that Germany has become, maybe the only legitimate response is death. By who's hand didn't matter.

Siegfried went into an empty apartment that faced the street. One half of the wall was caved in, giving a clear view down both sides of the street. The wall had not completely collapsed, so there was plenty of room for concealment. There were two Karabiner 98k rifles leaning against the wall. It was quarter to two and the street was quiet.

"Not many people around this area anymore," Siegfried said. "The castle was a target of the Americans and British bombing raids. Pretty much everyone has left for safer parts of the city or the countryside. Now the bombings have ceased, they moved a radio station here. Farther away from the Russian artillery. Good for us. Won't be many people to get in the way."

Stachel leaned out and looked down both sides of the street. An eighteenth-century neighborhood with two or three story buildings and a one lane road. Most of the buildings were in ruins, hollow shells pointing to the sky. The front façades of at least half the buildings had fallen to the street, leaving open views of people's former apartments. Some washing still hung from one apartment. A grand piano was hanging out of another apartment, one leg hovering in the air. All it needed was another explosion to send it crashing down to the street. Stachel wondered how many of these people were still alive and how many were still in Berlin. So much waste. Charlottenburg had always been a prosperous borough of the city. Now these people, who could have helped rebuild Germany, were dead or had left, never to return. He walked over and picked up one of the rifles. "Looks clean, though I can see it's had a lot of use."

"I killed a lot of Russians with that one," said Siegfried. "That one is mine. The other rifle is for you. Klein will focus on Goebbels. We'll take out the guards."

"And where is Klein?"

"Don't know. He's here, in another hiding place. What's wrong? Getting lonely? Want your old partner back?" Siegfried laughed. "We'd all like to return to better times, times when people could trust each other."

Stachel grabbed the other rifle, walked over and stooped down next to Siegfried, handing him his rifle. "There's never a better time when you're a policeman. You're always dealing with the scum. There's just more scum now."

"Well, I doubt you'll see Klein again. He'll take his shots and then disappear." Siegfried reached into his pocket and pulled out a handful of bullets, dropping some on the ground and giving some to Stachel. He loaded five bullets in his rifle's magazine, then took the rifle from Stachel and loaded it to.

"I hate to screw up your plan, but I won't shoot." Stachel leaned his rifle against the wall. "Which building is the radio station in?"

"That one, directly across the street." Siegfried pointed to a three story building that had little damage. Siegfried grabbed Stachel's rifle and held it out to him. "Hold it anyway. Once the shooting starts, you might change your mind."

Stachel took the rifle and laid it on the ground. "What's our escape route?"

Siegfried pointed at the ceiling. "Up one story to the roof, across to the other building, and then down the fire escape in the back. At least for me." He looked down at Stachel's foot. "Can you jump? It doesn't look like your foot can support much weight."

"That's how I got injured. But I'll jump. What other choice do I have?"

"None."

Stachel could hear the sound of motor cars off in the distance. A sound you rarely heard in Berlin anymore. "You hear it?" he said.

"Yes, they're coming. It must be Goebbels. There should be four guards." Siegfried looked over at Stachel, biting his lip, looking worried. "It would be better if you helped. The plan was for each of us to take out two guards. I can't shoot all four myself."

Stachel shook his head. "No, I meant it. I won't shoot."

"You still want to arrest us, don't you? That won't happen if you don't pick up the rifle."

True enough, so Stachel picked up the rifle and slide a bullet into the chamber. He still had no intention of shooting anyone, but he'd use the rifle to protect himself if he had to.

"And if there's more than four guards?"

"Then we hope we can shoot two guards with one bullet."

A car turned down Neufertstrasse and slowed down. A black Mercedes Benz 540k, followed by two other cars. There were Nazi flags on either side of the front of the Mercedes. The motorcade came to a stop in front of the radio station. But no one immediately got out. The cars just sat there, motors idling. Siegfried had his gun trained on the back two cars. Then the doors opened, and four soldiers piled out, two from each car, guns drawn. They quickly stationed themselves at their positions, one guard at each end of the street and two at the door to the radio station. All four were carrying MP 40's, standard issue for the SS. And they were all SS, right down to the SS symbol on their lapels. Once they were at their stations, one guard at the door nodded. The door to the Mercedes opened and a colonel stepped out, followed immediately by Goebbels.

The front door to the building was only about ten feet away. Goebbels, hunched over, his hands in his coat pockets, started for the door. The muffled sound of a rifle cracked the air and splinters of concrete burst off the side of the building, missing Goebbels's head by no more than an inch. Goebbels quickly continued into the building, acting as though he hadn't seen or heard anything. The Colonel stopped and turned, pointing at one building, waving to the guard at the end of the street.

Siegfried got off a shot, hitting the Colonel in the head, who collapsed back against one of the guards, blood spraying the building and the guard's face. He turned to the guard to his right. The guard at the end of the street, to Stachel's right, was running towards them, rifle pointing up at their building. Stachel hesitated, then raised his rifle and took a shot at the man but missed. Siegfried had shot the guard at the door, hitting him in the shoulder, dropping him to the ground. He then turned to the other guard, who had thrown the colonel to the ground and was aiming up at them. He missed with his first shot, but his second was a clean head shot, adding more blood to the wall behind him. Stachel was aiming again at the running guard, trying to hit him in the chest. He missed but hit the guard in the leg. The guard leaned against the wall on the other side of the street and started spraying their position with bullets. Both Siegfried and Stachel ducked down until the shooting ended, then Stachel stood up, aimed, and shot the soldier in the chest. Three guards down, one left. Siegfried focused on the guard to the left, who had been running towards the building where Klein was. But he was too late. He took one quick shot, missed, and then the guard was in the building.

"We're busted. Let's get out of here," Siegfried yelled as he ran out of the room and up the stairs to the roof. Soldiers were pouring out of the radio station, heading for their building. Stachel followed him as quickly as he could. He could hear the soldiers entering the building from below and running up the stairs as he stumbled up to the roof. Siegfried was already running across the roof, getting ready to jump to the other building. He made it easily and then turned back to Stachel. "Now, jump, we don't have much time." Ignoring the pain in his ankle, Stachel ran across and jumped, barely reaching the other side. He crumpled to the ground, which saved his life, since he was hidden by the parapet. He lost his grip on his rifle, which slid across the roof. Siegfried was standing, looking down at him as a soldier came up to the roof and quickly sprayed the other building, hitting Siegfried multiple times in the chest. Siegfried collapsed next to Stachel. Stachel reached for Siegfried's rifle, grabbed a bullet from his pocket and pushed it into the magazine. The soldier came up to the side of the building, searching for Stachel. Sucking in his breath, Stachel stood up and shot the soldier in the head. No one else was on the roof. The other soldiers must be searching the apartments. Then he ran to the back of the building and started down the fire escape, sliding his good foot down one rung at a time, keeping his sore foot dangling.

When he got to the bottom, he was in an alleyway. He started to his left and then thought of Klein. He couldn't let Klein get away. Turning around, he started towards where Klein had been, hugging the sides of the buildings. Towards the end of the alleyway, maybe one hundred feet away, he saw Klein come running out of a building, holding a rifle. Klein turned, a frantic look on his face, and saw Stachel. He had a questioning look on his face as he gazed at Stachel, as though he couldn't believe he was still alive. Klein was about to say something when shots rang out. Blood spurted from his chest as he fell to the ground. A guard was on the roof top, leaning over the side of the building.

Stachel dropped the rifle and quickly made his way down the alley, where he crossed over to Schlossstrasse, constantly looking back to see if he was being pursued. He worked his way back to Bismarckstrasse. He longed for a truck to hitch a ride, but only a fool would travel East. What seemed like an eternity, he limped through the Tiergarten to Eliana's apartment, collapsing on the sofa, wishing he could be rid of his ankle. Still shaking from the close call, his clothes covered in dirt, he tried to sort out what had happened. Klein and Siegfried were dead. Goebbels had gotten away. The whole thing was a complete disaster. The dwarf was alive, and history would probably never know what had happened that day.

Taking off his overcoat, he went to the kitchen for a drink of water, but the water main was broken again. He sat on the sofa and leaned back, looking up at the ceiling, following the cracks once again. This building was also about to collapse, along with Germany. He waited for Eliana to return. She would know what to do.

Chapter Thirty-Six

Stachel and Eliana were lying in bed, covers pulled up to their chins, not touching, both staring across at the wall.

April twenty-sixth and both knew that the Third Reich was finally coming to an end.

"You're safe now," Eliana said, leaning over and putting her hand on his chest. For once, he didn't automatically think of Hilda.

"Safe from what? From the Nazis? Safe from our country? Safe from those who would turn us in: our families, our friends, our neighbors? Safe from the Russians? We'll never be safe again. Germany is lost. We'll be nothing but the pariahs of Europe now, the slaves of the Russians."

"So gloomy. One must have hope." She pulled at one of the buttons on his shirt.

They were both fully clothed, expecting to see Russian soldiers walking down the street. Or worse, the Gestapo, on a feeding frenzy after the botched attempt on Goebbels. Eliana had prepared a hiding place, a false panel in the bedroom closet, a small room that would barely fit both of them.

"Hope is for the young. The old have no hope, only memories, which for us have been destroyed." He wondered if Holzer had gone to the café last night, waiting patiently and then in fear when no one showed. Maybe the Gestapo had suspected him, and he had already been shot? Another Stauffenberg for Hitler's trophy room.

They had both decided they would not escape to the shelter tonight. Let the barrage fall. They would trust fate to decide whether they would survive. They knew God didn't care. They could hear artillery shells exploding to the south, near the Chancellery. Eliana got up and shivered as she walked to the window, her dress waving in the breeze as she peeled back the blackout curtains and opened it. She could see the glow of fire lightening up the clouds off to the left.

"It looks like the whole area around the Chancellery is on fire. Let's hope they finally killed the bastards."

"Doesn't matter. None of them will survive for long."

"That might be the only good thing to say about the Red Army," Eliana said as she got back under the bed covers.

"Do you think we'll survive?" she asked.

"Do you want to survive is the real question?" Stachel put his arm around Eliana's shoulders, as though he was going to protect her from what was to come. Yet he knew that he could do nothing. He was powerless. And maybe that was a good thing. Maybe that should have been his dream all along. Not the dream of retiring to the countryside, of opening a pastry shop. That was a fool's dream. He should have dreamt for subservience, for some routine job without responsibility. In the Germany of the last twelve years, responsibility turned you into a criminal.

"Of course," Eliana said. "We both must live through this. Germany will need us."

"I don't expect too." Stachel said, looking up into the darkness of the ceiling, visualizing the cracks that got bigger every day. "The Red Army's retribution will be swift and brutal. As a policeman, I'll be viewed as a collaborator. I doubt they'll have much sympathy for me. But you can survive. They'll have nothing against you, no reason to want to hurt you. At least you can live through this. And maybe Germany will also come out as a better place, as a country where people will want to raise their children, where people will once again be proud of their country and their heritage. But I don't think that will happen soon. It will take time to heal the wounds we have created. If only we had taken another path twelve years ago, if only we had seen then what we see now. Maybe this would never have happened. Maybe we'd be talking about the future, about retiring to the countryside. But that didn't happen, and now we'll have to face what we have sowed. It's time for revenge. And we have earned it."

Afterword

The following books were used in researching the fall of Berlin.

I looked all over the web for photos of Berlin in April 1945 to help visualize the city, but I could find nothing. All the photos I found on the web were of Berlin after it fell. In other words, after the street fighting that took place between Germans and Russians in late April. Therefore, I had to assume that, though Berlin was in ruins because of Allied bombing, it was not as leveled as it became once the Russian army started artillery fire and the final invasion of central Berlin in the last week of April.

As a side note, what I found most interesting from my research was that daily life in Berlin until the last week of the war was not people huddled in shelters waiting for the end. Though there was an increase in suicides, and people certainly fled to shelters when the British and American bombers came, the city continued to function. As Kershaw noted in his book "The End," life continued. European football (soccer) matches were still player, the Philharmonic continued playing concerts until the 12th, and restaurants were open when they could get food. People carried on, even though most knew that the end was near.

As always, any mistakes are entirely my own.

Books about the fall of Berlin 1945

The Fall of Berlin 1945 by Antony Beevor (Viking, 2002)

A Woman in Berlin by Anonymous (Picador, 2006)
The End by Ian Kershaw (Penguin, 2011)
Berlin At War by Roger Moorhouse (Basic Books, 2010)
Inside Hitler's Bunker by Joachim Fest (Picador, 2004)
The Last Battle by Cornelius Ryan (Simon and Schuster, 1966)
Endgame, 1945 by David Stafford (Little, Brown and Company, 2007)
Berlin 1945: From War to Peace by Richard Bessel (Harper, 2009)

General WW2 Books

Inferno by Max Hastings (Knopf, 2011)
Armageddon By Max Hastings (Viking, 2004)
The Third Reich at War by Richard J. Evans (Penguin Books, 2010)
The Second World War by John Keegan (Penguin Books, 2016)
The Second World War by Antony Beevor (Little, Brown and Company, 2012)
Final Entries 1945: The Diaries of Joseph Goebbels (G. P. Putnam's Sons, 1978)
Life in the Third Reich edited by Richard Bessel (Oxford, 1987)
The Longman Companion to Nazi Germany by Tim Kirk (Longman Group Limited, 1995)

Fiction

The Kindly Ones by Jonathan Littell (Harper, 2009)
Potsdam Station by David Downing (Soho Crime, 2011)

Visit me at http:www.ronaldjensen.com